TWILIGHT'S LAST GLEAMING

TWILIGHT'S LAST GLEAMING

LEON ARDEN

... this blindness of ... advisers, who would not see that rebel-
lion was not war: indeed, was more of the nature of peace ...
—T. E. Lawrence
SEVEN PILLARS OF WISDOM

for Flip Schaffer and Berni Benstock

Once upon an air-polluted evening in Brooklyn Heights an attractive blonde was sitting alone in her small apartment reading a fashion magazine when a strange voice ordered her to confront the Dauphin, borrow his army, and go forth to drive the English out of France.

Startled, she looked around and thought, Go forth and do what? Her instructions were repeated by the mysterious voice who, on second hearing, sounded like a master of ceremonies: jolly, energetic, and tinged with desperation. All she could think of, in her fear and confusion, was to take down the message in shorthand and wait to see what happened next. When nothing happened next, she picked up her cigarette, went into the bedroom, and phoned her boyfriend.

"This is Lorraine. I think I'm in trouble."

He promised to hurry right over. She hung up feeling rather foolish. She quickly unlocked the door but found only emptiness in the hallway. Nor was anyone lurking on the fire escape: a mad ventriloquist, perhaps, or a grinning friend turned practical joker.

She sat down and gathered her courage. Then she said, "Hi there."

The faucet dripped once.

"Is there anyone here? ... Beside me, I mean."

Evidently not. At least not any longer. She became frightened now as only a girl living alone in New York could be. Added to fears of murder, rape, loneliness, and the dark, there was now something new. Was it possible for a pretty girl, not yet twenty, with a straight B average and a boring family history, was it actually possible, she wondered, for such a nice young person as that to be losing her mind?

The faucet let fall a tiny splat of doom.

Hurrying to her side, Assistant Professor Justin Warm-flash, age thirty, was busily correcting freshmen history papers in the subway.

1

He had given his students one of his infamous "idiot tests" designed to disabuse them of the belief that after a full year of higher education they had actually acquired any knowledge. For example, no one in his class was able to name a single novel by Emile Zola. Only 2 percent of them had ever heard of Norman Thomas. Nearly 8 percent could identify the man who said that this generation of Americans had a rendezvous with destiny. No one knew the exact number of Beethoven's symphonies. Of course no one could name their representatives in Congress. But 87 percent of the class correctly isolated France as the birthplace of Brigitte Bardot. Sixty-one percent suspected that Ho Chi Minh was a Chinese philosopher.

Professor Warmflash closed his eyes and shook his head over the agonizing task of attempting to teach anyone anything. When he opened them again he had missed his stop and was hell-bent for Flatbush. He jumped up and all the blue-lined strips of yellow test papers splashed to the floor.

Justin Warmflash was born in South Ozone Park and his first memory was of getting hit in the head with a snowball. His mother was a professional singer who was giving her polished rendition of "Down by the Old Mill Stream" on the stage of the Jamaica Theatre on Jamaica Avenue when she first felt labor pains. She had dressed herself up like a fat peasant to hide her pregnancy, and luckily she was able to finish her number without showing signs of distress.

While still in his crib, Justin learned that he had an older brother whom his father called Howie and his mother addressed as Sir Howard. His father worked from door to door selling what Justin understood to be a kind of guarantee against death while their mother earned money singing the songs everyone loves and which Justin grew to hate. She "belted them out" for hospitalized war veterans or at church bazaars and occasionally on the faraway and dying vaudeville circuit. There wasn't a great demand to hear his mother perform but luckily there was always a demand to hear the songs she sang.

He and his brother frequently wrestled, Justin usually losing, often getting bruised. He discovered he could avoid all this by burrowing into books. Soon he read continually, even when other people were in the room and talking. One of the stories was about a heroic horseback rider named Revere. Also a glorious thief named Robin Hood.

When Justin graduated public school, his brother was unable to attend the ceremony because the government had put him in a fine-looking form-fitting brownish uniform and shipped him off to get gloriously shot at in a small thumb-like-looking country on the other side of the Pacific. His mother couldn't attend the ceremony either for she had gotten a wonderful opportunity to sing her songs for an entire weekend in a large hotel in Alabama. But Justin's father came and sat and smiled.

Then summer freed him to read the backlog of books he had saved up all winter. One was about a middle-aged slave who couldn't read but who almost overthrew the Roman Empire. Another concerned a young girl who couldn't read but who almost drove the English out of France. Still another told of some brave Indians who could only read smoke signals but who almost stopped an invasion of their land.

But soon he had trouble concentrating on stories for suddenly in high school he discovered girls. There were times, now, when it seemed as if his entire mind was an erogenous zone. Then he became obsessed by a sunburned goddess named Camilla Epps who jumped and flashed precocious legs as she led the cheering at the basketball games. Depressed by the impossible task of struggling through a phallic forest of male students to win a place at her side, Justin knew in his furiously pumping, helpless heart that he would never be one of the fortunate elect to escort Miss Epps in her fashion parade through life. Yet that summer the father of this goddess, with obvious godlike qualities of his own, arranged through the recommendation of the Humanities Department to hire a highly regarded history student named Justin Warmflash to come to his house and tutor his C-minus daughter.

So on Saturday afternoons the young boy, sitting stiff as a priest in the very bedroom of the semigoddess herself, tried to engage

Camilla's attention in the distant Articles of Confederation and the minicomedy known as the War of 1812. She kept busy in her own way. She chewed gum and nodded often. But she slipped occasionally into a comatose state which required his hurried resuscitation of her public school mind while at the same repressing feverish thoughts of her collegiate legs.

On Saturday afternoon while they were deep in the complexities of President Polk's theft of Mexico's California territory, inattentive Camilla Epps took Justin's right hand and cupped it over her cashmere-covered soft left breast. He stared at her terrifying, semi-innocent face and watched as she popped bubble gum and drew it back into her busy mouth. The room filled with oven heat. She giggled: not like a girl; like Attila the Hun. They sat as if they were part of a Dutch painting. *Boy with Hand on Young Girl's Breast.* Camilla's mother entered. His paralysis cured, he sprang up like a prisoner in the dock.

"And how's my little girl doing, Mr. Warmflash?"

"Finejustfine."

"Is she improving?"

"Yes, ahuh, yes."

"I'm so pleased."

"Soon she'll be teaching me things, ma'am."

"How wonderful."

And Camilla's pink gum went pop.

As he walked away he reenacted the scene in the shambles of his mind. So this was the way it was done. He had always wondered how one traversed that chasm between polite talk and touching. Would it always be this easy? Would there soon be a sharp increase of young women on crosstown buses, or experienced divorcees on the IRT, or somber girls in the silent library, all clasping his hand to their breasts in a kind of sexual civilian salute? Was it impolite not to remove his glove? If he had a Coke in one hand and his books in the other, how would contact be made? And another thing: Once there with all five fingers, what then? The boring lessons with Miss

Epps suddenly took on a new dimension. He could hardly wait for the next installment. And he was getting paid two bucks an hour.

When he arrived home his mother was crying. So was a neighbor from next door. His father had returned early from work and was sitting on the couch without reading his paper. Also it was the first time Justin could remember that the TV wasn't on. Soon, for no reason, he too was crying. An uncle arrived from New Jersey and patted everyone on the shoulder. When the boy asked what was wrong, his father just shook his head. When he asked his mother, she hugged him silently. Finally the boy guessed what was wrong. His brother, Howie, would not grow up anymore. This was the only way he could fully grasp it. Howie had always been five years older. Now, with every passing hour, the difference would shrink until one day they would both be the same age. Then, ever afterward, Justin would be older than his older brother.

He didn't tell them that it was because he had touched his high-school cheerleader that his brother had died, that he had allowed his hand to be put in a naughty place and, worse still, that he had given a little squeeze. Yes, he would have to repay his family for what he had done. He would have to repay them by going off to war and dying there himself or by tutoring full-breasted students for the rest of his life with his hands in his pockets.

But right now he wished he could command the revolutionary fervor of a Samuel Adams and the striding eloquence of a Thomas Jefferson. Oh, then would he dash off such a towering document of protest as is rarely heard in these United States.

Dear Mrs. Epps:

When in the course of human events it becomes necessary for tutors in the Honors Department to dissolve the bands that have connected them with cheerleaders in the Athletics Department in order to establish justice, insure domestic tranquillity and to form a more perfect tutor-student relationship so that we may avoid the injuries and usurpations of your dim, precocious daughter, we in the Honors Department demand that henceforth you employ solely female tutors so that we can safely go forth pledging our knowledge, our fortune, and our sacred honor.

Yours truly.

Justin Warmflash

He longed to write something much like this. Yet he was barely fifteen and depressed by a grieving family, so he buried himself in another book and wondered what would happen when he went back next Saturday afternoon.

At first nothing happened. She simply sat and stared at him as if he were a multilegged greenish thing one keeps on a shelf under glass. He ignored this by launching into a review of the early years of U.S. history ("the olden days," as she called them), summarizing their country's heritage with a voice that was jolly, energetic, and tinged with desperation.

"That's not true," she piped. He stopped. Something had brought her to life.

"What's not true?" he asked, hoping his lecturing skills had scored a triumph at last over her elusive mind.

"Um, it's not true we lost the War of 1812, I mean. America never lost a war."

"We lost that one. No kidding."

"Oh, come on. We've never lost a single war. That's a known fact."

She looked hurt as if John Wayne and Shirley Temple had defected. Once again Justin tried to explain the high farce that resulted from America's invasion of Canada, but Camilla had no intention of listening to such scandalous interpretations of her country's beloved past. She changed the subject.

"Would you like to touch me again?"

"Not at the present time, thank you."

"If you want to, you can. I really mean it."

"I think we should move right along now with our studies."

"You were teasing me about losing that war, weren't you?"

"No, honestly. You can ask anybody. You can ask Mr. Reingold."

"Who's he?"

"Head of the History Department."

"Show me in the book where it says we lost that war."

"Well, our textbook doesn't really say it right out but I've done some extra reading on the subject which conclusively proves..."

"Um, can I ask a question?"

"Sure."

"Do you like my legs?"

"Well, why do you ask?"

"'Cause you look at them an awful lot, that's why."

"I really think we should move right along now."

"If you're nice I'll let you touch them." A coy curator unveiling a private collection, she pinched her skirt and exposed her thighs. The room became an oven again.

"It was," he said, "during the War of 1812 that the capitol was captured and burned to the ground. The President and his wife had to flee...."

"I said you could touch my legs. Why don't you?"

"A death in the family."

"What's that got to do with the price of beans?"

"It's kind of complicated."

"You know what? You read books too much."

With that she ended the lesson and told him to leave. He suggested her mother would prefer they continue.

"Mommie isn't here today and if you ever tell I sent you home early I'll say you tried to touch my legs. And you don't get paid either. Goodbye, Mr. War of 1812."

He began to suspect that much more than just a war had been lost.

Three days later he received a letter from her father informing him that his services were no longer needed. Mr. Epps said he was deeply shocked to learn that Justin was teaching dangerous pinko untruths designed to undermine Camilla's faith in America, especially at a time, as Senator Joseph McCarthy said, when we were being threatened from within as never before. He had intended to write Mr. Rein-gold and inform him of the type of boy they were allowing into their Honors Department. But, he added, Mrs. Epps had restrained him.

Some months later Justin stopped Mr. Reingold in the lunchroom to ask him why their history text didn't admit to losing the War of 1812.

"Because it upsets people," he answered, sourly.

When he arrived at her apartment, Lorraine handed him a yellow slip of blue-lined paper and said: "Read that."

He did or tried to. It looked like one of his idiot tests taken in Sanskrit.

"That's shorthand," she said. "Turn it over. I wrote it out on the other side."

The note instructed him to confront the Dauphin, borrow his army, and go forth to drive the English out of France.

"What is this nonsense?" he asked.

With what she knew to be charming theatrics, Lorraine mimicked the mysterious voice, described her feelings with ecstatic exaggeration, and with her right hand held aloft swore that nothing like this had ever happened to her before. Justin was touched by the way she hid her fear behind a trumped-up cheerfulness. The faucet let fall a tiny splat into the sink.

"I'm not overworked," she said. "I'm not hysterical. I'm not having my period. So what am I? Sounds like one of those dumb riddles about things that have four wheels and flies."

He said nothing and this worried her.

"Or am I insane?"

"Don't be silly," he said. "That's crazy."

"I heard a voice. I swear it."

"I believe you, Lorrie."

"You! What do you know?" She smiled.

"O.K. Tell me everything you did just before it happened."

"Let me see. Did my hair. Sent a nasty letter to the President. Waited for you to call. You didn't. Waited for the President to call. He didn't. Felt ugly. And ignored. Had myself a joint and looked at pictures of pretty dresses I can't afford."

"You were smoking pot? Hell, woman, that's what caused it."

"I've been smoking pot since I met you and I never heard voices before. Except through the damn walls."

"But you never smoked alone before, you ding-a-ling."

"OK. Never alone before. So what?"

He explained that marijuana affected people in different ways. "All you heard was the sound of grass," he said. "It was all hallucination." And he kissed her as fate whispered to him from the sink. Lorraine kissed him back and walked rather seductively, she thought, into the bedroom hoping he'd follow. When she came back out again, she found him locked in a hand-wrestling contest with the hot water faucet.

Lorraine Benglesdorf grew up in Salemville, New York, a picturebook town one-and-a-half-hour's drive from Manhattan. Her father was a lawyer. Her mother collected plants. As long as Lorrie could remember, Salemville had a one-armed sheriff and a mayor who was also the town's barber. They had one newspaper, one movie house, one bowling alley. Lorraine was well liked because she was considered cute and polite and because she made a point of remembering everyone's name just as her father had taught her to. Among the girls of Salemville she was indeed a rarity, for she was the only one interested in politics. At fourteen she rang doorbells for Lyndon Johnson in a town that was 46 percent Republican and 46 percent Democrat and 8 percent undecided. Her interest in public affairs dated back to her ninth year when she wrote a letter to *The Home Bugle* commending Mayor Kinch for having the courage to turn Lindbergh Boulevard into a one-way street although public sentiment was against it.

Dear Editor,

I wish to praise Mayor Kinch for turning Lindbergh Boulevard into one direction because this makes Lindbergh Boulevard safer for everybody including school children like myself who don't have to look both ways now. My Daddy says Mayor Kinch showed courage doing this since some say this would hurt business which I don't believe.

Sincerely,
Lorrie Benglesdorf

That day her name appeared twice in the paper. It was a local record for a nine-year-old and, in school, it temporarily elevated her to the level of folk heroine. She was so happy she held hands and danced in the kitchen with her mother. Mr. Benglesdorf returned the next evening from a business trip and rewarded his daughter with a gift of fifty cents as a reward for her notoriety.

The second published mention of her name read this way:

Another coffee with Mrs. Sally Ranslick will be held on Saturday at 10 A.M. in the Sanctuary of The Mission to be followed by a Bake Sale in Fellowship Hall. A free nursery will be provided. Free coffee and donuts will be served. Lorraine Benglesdorf is contributing Girl Scout Cookies which she bought with her own allowance. Donations of $1.50 go to the repairing of old high-school textbooks and the purchasing of new ones. Would all tutors please bring any dictionaries (not *real* good ones) Saturday for the Sixth grade to use. We only need them for one day. Thanks.

When Lorrie was fifteen she was caught by her mother one Friday night necking in the living room with Nick Columbo. He had completed the delicate task of unbuttoning her blouse and had just wounded his hand on her wire bra when Mrs. Benglesdorf, standing in the doorway, said, "Oh, I beg your pardon," in a voice that always took on an English accent whenever she was trying to be impeccably polite. She backed out immediately and closed the door without a sound. Lorraine jumped up as if doused with cold water. The boy seemed to be searching his palm for signs of stigmata.

"Your old man will kick my ass," he said.

"My father is a lawyer and a civilized man. He doesn't kick people in the ass. The very most he does is sue."

"Shit, that's worse. Then my old man will kick my ass."

Next morning, amid sunlight and fruit juice, Mrs. Benglesdorf, who had seen all, astoundingly said nothing. Lorrie's father paused in his reading of the paper to oleomargarine his toast. The angle of the sun prevented Lorrie from seeing the expression on her mother's face. Mr. Benglesdorf grumbled about Castro and high taxes. Then the sipping and scraping of breakfast ended.

But when her father had left to play golf, her mother ceremoniously sat Lorraine-Louise down on the couch and perched beside her. Boy, here it comes, the girl thought. I bet I get all snippy and defensive and end up crying. Lofty as a judge, her impeccable mother folded her hands in her lap and said: "I'm disappointed in you, Lorraine-Louise. Today is your father's birthday and evidently you completely forgot."

When Lorrie was sixteen, several disturbing events took place in her life. Girl friends became hostile. The crude sketch of a penis appeared on the inside of her history text. During a rush-hour subway ride in New York City a hand was placed on her rump. She heard astringent sucking sounds as she walked in the street. One evening, in Salemville, she received an obscene phone call. She finally mentioned these things to her father. "I got news for you," was all he said. "You're becoming a woman." She had always imagined this event somewhat differently. It was all very sobering.

That year she had her first heavy date. He was Alan Banks not yet seventeen, the school poet, lean, cute, and good-looking even in glasses. His father owned a hardware store on the north end of Lindbergh Boulevard. She and Alan were assigned to do a joint science-lab project, the purpose of which was to demonstrate the evaporation and condensation of water. It proved to be a success, as did her other project, which she worked on alone and which was designed to demonstrate that a young girl could be devious as hell while still appearing pure and innocent in the eyes of the world. This project took more time than did the other, but it was a success as well. Proof was when he asked her out.

Nothing could ruin things now. She had a date with the yummiest boy in school, who even Viola Testi tried for and couldn't get. Romantic fantasies obsessed her normally scholastic mind. Then, on the afternoon of the big day, a girl came into the science lab and said that someone had just assassinated President Kennedy.

For Lorrie Benglesdorf a great crack had just appeared in the twentieth century. School was dismissed and she walked home with a Filipino girl who cried all the way. When Lorrie was alone and watching television she too began to cry. Then she went to her bottom desk drawer which contained carbons of all the letters she had written to public officials over the last six years. It started with one praising Mayor Kinch and included letters to President Eisenhower and Vice President Nixon, President Kennedy, and Vice President Johnson. A few were in praise. The rest not. She selected at random a letter she had sent to the now-dead President complaining about the money he was spending on the new moon project. It insisted that the poor needed the money much more than the moon did.

She felt guilty for having sent it. What right had she to add her two cents to the poor man's problems? How egotistical of her. How arrogant. Then on top of everything else she noticed a spelling error. Shame and a wave of self-disgust. What on earth did a stupid thirteen-year-old hope to gain by sending an illiterate letter to the President of the United States?

She had forgotten all about Alan Banks when he phoned lighthearted and all a-tumble with jokes. Do you think Johnson did it? ha, ha, and who will they get to shoot Johnson, ha ha? Lorrie shut her eyes. The Salemville Movie Palace, he said, was closing for the evening out of respect for the recently departed. He suggested they go to his friend Jimmy's house instead and play Ping-Pong in his basement. She couldn't get herself to say no, for her father had taught her that it was impolite to break a date. In fact, her father preferred that she go out that evening as he saw how disturbed she was by the events in Dallas. Her mother preferred she stay home but was somehow outvoted.

Her date arrived at 8:15 and walked her toward the bus stop. Suddenly, he swung open the door of a blue Chevrolet and told her to get in. He had taken his family car without permission and Lorraine was shocked by the boy's criminal audacity which involved not only stealing from his own father but the dangerous offense of driving without a license. She would rather they walked, she said, realizing how silly that sounded. But when he called her a sissy and a spoilsport, she closed her eyes and entered the car. To make matters worse, he drove with the radio on to catch the latest details of the assassination.

Lorraine was taken to a wood-paneled cellar where she and Alan on one side of the table played raucous Ping-Pong with their two opponents on the other: a girl named Mary who said "shit" whenever she hit the ball into the net and Jimmy himself who responded to Lorraine's bulging sweater as if he had sighted the promised land. A TV set with the sound turned off kept them in touch with the nation's grief. Lorraine was finally the only one who watched, glancing at the screen after each change of score. She grew increasingly isolated from the others as they joked and cursed at the flight of the ball while ignoring film clips showing a young man, slim and well dressed, hurrying through a triumphant career to an early death.

Lorraine said she wasn't feeling well and wanted to be taken home. Alan stalled for half an hour and finally suggested she go up to a bedroom and rest. She stared at him, nodded, went upstairs and out the front door. Walking alone through a silent town beneath frozen stars she felt an immense sadness and relief. But

Alan Banks appeared with his father's car to apologize and drive her home. Near the bus stop, in the same parking spot they started from, he stopped the car, turned and jumped her. She said, "No, stop," loudly and forcefully as though trying to command a disobedient dog. As with most disobedient dogs, it had no effect. What ensued was a sexual sleight of hand. Where his went, hers followed, what he seized, she freed. She twisted and wriggled until to her surprise as well as his she popped free of the car and found herself on Mrs. Meyer's front lawn, missing one shoe and with her sweater half out of her skirt. In a wailing screech of rubber the Chevrolet shot away from the curb and out of her life. She was furious enough to kick a tree or pull his hair or curse loudly, which in fact she did. She hobbled like a war veteran until she removed her shoe and walked on again free and barefoot on the chilled concrete. The Chevrolet returned with a roar and her missing shoe was tossed out like so much trash into the gutter where it bounced to a stop at her feet. She reared back with its matching mate and flung it at him with all her might as the car took off in another wail of injured pride. The brown strapless pump sailed through the rear window into the back seat and vanished as did the car. Again with only one shoe, which she lifted out of the gutter and blew at with puffed cheeks, she walked home grumbling and stumbling and somehow feeling better.

When Mr. Benglesdorf found out what had happened he announced he would sue for attempted rape. Lorraine and her mother said no. The lawyer ignored his wife and concentrated on his daughter. But Lorrie said she didn't want a fuss. He offered as an alternative any number of serious charges: assault and battery, driving without a license, exceeding the speed limit, disturbing the peace, throwing a dangerous weapon with intent to harm. Lorrie said no and her mother agreed. At least let me sue for the return of the other shoe, he said. While her mother was thinking this over, Lorrie laughed outright and said the idea was silly.

"I got news for you," Benglesdorf answered in a burst of pique, "you've got no respect for the law."

Justin Warmflash graduated CCNY, completed his doctorate courses at Columbia University, passed his orals with honors, wrote his dissertation in six months, and won a teaching job in American History at NYU. It was only then that he decided that he really wanted to be a film director. Actually, he had always carried the bug in his system. It flared up each time he saw a film by Bergman or Antonioni. But always the infection subsided and he went on with his study of history. Then one day he took a girl to see a movie called *La Guerre est finie*. This time he had a serious relapse and the disease became chronic. What excited him about this film was the unlikely mixture of cinematic artistry and political complexity as seen through the life of a three-dimensional man as he fails in his attempt to create a revolution. The girl he was with liked the sex scenes very much.

Even before he took her home he stopped to buy some paperbacks on films and filmmaking. Eventually he read forty volumes on the subject in his spare time and, with a teaching workload of only nine credits, spare time was something he had plenty of. He rented a movie camera and shot a number of unchallenging subjects to test his skill: a neighbor's kitten wobbling about like a furry drunk, faces frowning their way through an idiot test, his mother singing "Wait Till the Sun Shines, Nellie" at a downtown beerhall on Seventh Avenue. Soon he was ready to join cinematic artistry with political complexity. But what the subject would be he had no idea, nor where the money would come from either.

On an afternoon heavily laden with carbon monoxide, late in the summer term, Justin Warmflash stood lecturing to a class on what, in the catalogue, was listed as *The United States*, Jefferson vs. Hamilton. 3 points. He had drifted from the subject somewhat, for he found himself saying that Americans have always been a hypocritical people, that they escaped persecution in Europe only to come here and keep slaves, that they allotted areas of worthless land to the American Indian and then killed him for it when the land proved valuable, that they opened their gates to the downtrodden but tormented each group of them when they came to settle.

"What we Americans seem unable to do," he said glancing out the window at the thin veil of smog over Washington Square Park, "is ... is chew our history and swallow."

Their impassive faces were like a wall that needed paint.

"What we in America seem unable to do," he began again, "is to swallow the truth about ourselves."

Their eyes were glazed with polite indifference.

"Our obsession with comfort makes us indifferent to the deprivation of others. We do not listen when others are in need."

A few nodded like placid drunks who would endorse anything for a handout. Through the window of the doorway he saw her signaling. He excused himself and stepped into the hall.

"It happened again last night," Lorraine insisted. "But this time it was a different voice."

"You've been smoking again."

"Seems the first message was an error or something."

"Lorrie, I really wish you wouldn't smoke when I'm not around."

"I know it sounds like a joke but...."

"Lorrie...."

"... but the new voice said I should ignore the previous message, that a new one would follow. Listen to me, another message did follow."

"What is all this religious crap?"

"It's not religious and it's not crap."

"Lorrie, I have a class."

"Big man, big man. So you have a class."

"All right, what did the voice say?"

"I can see by your face you don't give a flying fuck."

"Don't be silly. What did the voice say? Come on, now."

"Well, I don't want to take up your time. But I do have some news that will interest you. If you care to listen."

"Go on."

"The voices; big mystery, right? Well, this time I found out who was talking. I mean I know who it was, this time."

"OK. I'll bite. Who was it?"

"Thomas Jefferson."

The day before Lorraine went off to college, her parents arranged a going-away party in her backyard. Sally Ranslick gave her a box of pink writing paper with the initials L.B. inscribed. Nick Columbo gave her a box of white writing paper with the letter B inscribed. Sexy Viola Testi offered the gift of a pair of pink panties with small black stitching that warned: "If you can read this you're too damn close." And from her parents she received a watch with an inscription on the back reminding her that a man's reach should exceed his grasp or what's a heaven for? Several ladies from the Mission gave a dictionary with a note reminding her that she had once given them a box of cookies. All remembered and smiled. Sally Ranslick was moved to tears. Years later, Mrs. Durkee, who that day gave Lorrie a box of pencils, would say, "She was always such a good girl." Then with a shake of the head: "Who would have guessed she would do what she did."

Going to college meant buying her own books and reading them in poor light. It meant the muffled torture chamber of libraries where she took notes to keep the sea-edge of ignorance from washing the hours away. It meant larger classrooms and the fear of humiliation. It meant the self-conscious glory of her first miniskirt. It meant meeting handsome men and watching the armored faces of lovely women. It meant Negro rights, a boycott of grapes, and peace now. It meant guitars in the park, and songs that ask where all the flowers have gone? or shout of John Henry and his hammer, or tell of how you long to be in your bed again with your true love in your arms.

Lorraine's bed was a narrow one on the third floor of a brownstone in Brooklyn Heights. It was there that she continued that other study not mentioned in the school catalogue but which she had begun with Nick Columbo in her parents' living room. Her experiments in this field resulted in conflicting conclusions. In outline form her results were these:

One, that sex was the loveliest of man's discoveries, so much so that it threatened to make all his other discoveries unimportant.

Two, that sex was a pain in the padukie.

Three, that sex had really very little to do with sex, that it was simply a way for a girl

    (A) to insure that she did not spend too much time sitting alone in an empty room.

    (B) to build a buffer zone, by the use of one man, between herself and all other men.

    (C) to get a bulb in the ceiling changed or a drip in the sink fixed.

    (D) to cook for two instead of for one which otherwise meant not cooking at all.

    (E) to be cherished again as she had once been long ago.

    (F) to know that she hadn't been abandoned even if she did have to spend too much time alone in an empty room.

Further research, she decided, was clearly called for.

In the hallway of Main Building she often noticed a distracted, intellectual-looking young man—a senior most probably—wearing eyeglasses as if they were a scholar's badge of honor and who always walked swiftly but calmly as if late for a seminar in satori. Here she decided was a wonderful opportunity for further research. Sadly he never slowed down long enough for the experiment to start.

One day when she began a course entitled *The American Enlightenment, 1687–1765*, she noticed him, glasses and all, sitting in the back row talking with some other students. At last I'm in the same class with him, she thought. Others entered and the room filled up like a bus. Galoshes and cigarette smoke. Books and springbinders. The dull blur of voices. The bell. All are now waiting for the professor to arrive. At that point, the terribly intriguing and very intellectual-looking classmate of hers walks down the aisle, places himself in front of the desk and says: "I am, as luck would have it, the professor for this course. Or as Alexander Dumas once said in defense of his novels, 'If I rape history it is only to give her children.'"

The class replied with a diffused belch of pleasure.

"Later on many of you might want to write the Dean praising my wit and charm. Others, to demand my immediate dismissal. Either way you will need to know the correct spelling of my name."

In large chalk letters he wrote: Justin E. Warmflash.

Lorraine decided she didn't like him.

It was hard teaching history when the mind kept dissolving to problems of panning, splicing, fade-in, fade-out, cut. And when the 8th Street Cinema was having a Godard Festival it was particularly difficult to go home and correct sixty dull papers on the Reconstruction from a class that sat through his lectures like a montage of death masks. One of his tricks was to play the clown, then switch to the body count at the Little Big Horn, explaining that "our boys" had died there for nothing more than a national lust for gold and because of General Custer's presidential ambitions. The montage of death masks frowned. Nor was teaching made any easier by having to ignore carelessly unveiled legs, sensual lips, the promise of a warm tongue, the fantasy of a gentle plunder; zoom in, pan along her flank, close-up of the eyes, slow fade, cut.

But his despair at ever reaching their minds was broken occasionally by an intelligent and totally unexpected question.

"Sir," one student asked him, "when the slaves were first brought to the Colonies how did they learn English? Was someone assigned the job of teaching them? Whose was the first voice they understood?"

For years he had hunted for the answer to just this question. He had to admit he didn't know, that no one knew. But he was impressed and made a mental note. Benglesdorf. Pretty. And bright. And bulging.

Justin understood that a teacher seeking love, or any of its component parts, should never approach the girls in his class. He didn't have to. They would always approach him. Those who were interested would mingle at his desk after class to confide their questions with soft voices, with yielding eyes. And during his office hours they would appear for guidance counseling when in truth the only counseling they needed was to be guided the hell out of his office. There was always something simmering in their calm attention and when they laughed it never involved a hearty falling back from the thrust of his wit but rather a sudden leaning closer as though to achieve conspiratorial contact. All this, of course, while discussing the Alien and Sedition Acts or the causes of the Great Depression. Yes, he had only to wait and the best or at least the boldest would come to him. This was not to say that New York University was supplying Professor Warm-flash with a harem. Often, in fact all last year, he strove for happiness with women he met outside of school: a talkative librarian, a self-centered modern dance instructor. But in class there were always those simmering gazes of ripe young ladies who worshiped knowledge or perhaps only him. In the coeducational college the left-wing instructor was king. Or as close to it as he would ever get.

There was one young lady, however, who did not come to him and he was intrigued. In class her comments were stimulating as was her energy, her perigee, her callipyge. He made a special announcement. "All those who wish guidance counseling should see me during office hours." This got him nowhere. "All those who felt they could have done better in yesterday's test and would like to take it over again come up and talk to me about it." She never did. "Miss Benglesdorf, would you see me for a moment after class." That did it. Up she came, soft and fresh as new bread in early morning. And smiling, too, and staring, with her hard hazel eyes. He didn't know what the devil to say.

"Was there anything in my lecture that gave you any trouble?"

"Why? Did I look more stupid today than usual?"

"You looked, I don't know, puzzled."

"My shoes are killing me, is all."

"I'm sorry to hear that."

"Your lectures are very clear, really. Even for me."

"I also want to say that you're doing very well."

"Am I? Thanks." She was beaming.

"And don't be shy. Speak up more. It helps when bright students ask good questions."

"Wow. Can't you just see me getting a rupture tonight trying to think up good questions?"

"Just stay loose."

"Tell that to these shoes."

She walked away increasing her perigee, giving a gentle swing to her callipyge. He had her not and never would, yet to lose her now was something close to heartbreak. Then to see a dull college deadhead, his arm on her waist, guide such loveliness out of his sight was something close to torture.

As consolation he scheduled a cozy dinner with his old friend and irritating companion, the self-centered modern dance instructor. Then his father called reminding him of his promise to attend his mother's only professional singing engagement that year in New York. Both dates fell, of course, on the same evening. So he asked dark-haired Susan, who had once appeared with Merce Cunningham, if she cared to listen to his mother who had once appeared with Ye Good Ol' Days Quartet on the "Ed Sullivan Show." Susan, who was overjoyed at the invitation, at once visualized marriage, motherhood, wealth, grandchildren, a golden wedding anniversary in the ballroom of the Waldorf-Astoria Hotel, and gentle death in that order.

The festivities, at which his mother was to sing, were sponsored by the Veterans of Foreign Wars Counter-Protest Fund-Raising Committee. Justin sat beside long, lean, marriage-prone Susan with her black hair pulled tightly back and with her legs double-crossed at the knees and ankles. But before his mother could sing of the joys of sailing along on Moonlight Bay, there preceded her a series of angry speeches in which pudgy, proud, uniformed survivors of past wars stood solidly at the podium and announced loudly their total disbelief and complete rejection of the recently published stories of American war crimes against innocent civilians in Vietnam. The truth of the matter, they explained, was that the enemy troops took dope which turned them into crazed murderers as compared to our boys who were really good boys because they were trained by the U.S. Army to be courteous and polite to all foreigners and to respect their elders as well as their commanding officers. Susan whispered how wonderful these speeches were and applauded with a stiff-backed American pride which immediately disassociated him from everything about her which he had previously found to be even remotely sexual.

The tirades from the podium finally drove him to the bar where he stood, clinging to a double bourbon, advising himself to bolt from his bony date and his show-biz mother. Go on, big shot, down the stairs and run. He sipped his drink and considered the repercussions.

Then he noticed her coming from the ladies' room looking as he had never seen her in class, hair vivid, eyes gleaming, sculptured in shining satin from just below her head to just below her hips, as if the touch of a wand had brought her into focus. It was almost as though she were up for sale.

Trapped in a den of Neanderthals, he wanted to run to avoid having to explain that the large lady who was about to entertain this reunion of maudlin war lovers was none other than his baritone mother.

Too late. Lorraine's face went dim just as it did in class when she was asked a question she couldn't answer.

"Dr. Warmflash. Oh, wow. I was hoping I wouldn't meet anyone I knew."

"Same here, actually."

"Well, getting caught in a bordello might be worse."

"The clientele might be better."

"So how are you? How's that for keeping the conversation going?"

They quickly explained their reasons for being caught where they were. She said an uncle in the army had begged her to go with him which she finally did only as a favor to her father. He claimed a friend had dragged him here and that he was amazed at what he had gotten himself into. They joked of making a break for it, but at last filed back into the auditorium where a veteran of Pearl Harbor was saying that all the cowardly bastards who wouldn't defend America by going to Vietnam should all be brought home from Sweden or released from prison and shot. This won him a standing ovation which Susan would have joined except that Justin forcibly held her down. Across the room he saw a seated Lorraine eyeing him with a whimsical look while standing beside her was a slim, well-preserved, military bigwig applauding with slow, loud, ostentatious strokes.

Then Mrs. Warmflash in a splendiferous bouffant hairdo and a silver lamé dress sang of sailing along on Moonlight Bay and of K-k-k-katy b-b-b-beautiful K-k-k-katy plus all those other songs which he hated and everyone else hummed, rocking to and fro. Suddenly it happened. It was something he could not have foreseen or else he would have run down those stairs indeed.

"And now," said his mother's magnificent voice, "I want to introduce you to my own dear son who" (applause) "who is doing so brilliantly over there in NYU College teaching everybody all about American History and what a great country we have, and how" (louder applause) "and how proud we should all be to call ourselves Americans. My son, Professor Justin Warmflash. Gosh, I love 'im." (Loudest applause) "Come on everybody, give him a big hand for doing such a wonderful job. Stand up, honey, so everybody can see you, cause I'm so proud of you. Come on, honey, stand up . . . ."

The air thundered. He sank low in his seat. But nimble Susan sprang up like the evil witch in *Swan Lake*. She pointed him out and led the applause. He was forced to surrender. He rose from his shallow trench and faced the painful volley of their love.

With a final chorus of "Good Night, Irene" (this after a stirring rendition of "The Battle Hymn of the Republic"), Mrs. Warmflash threw her arms wide in a final massive stage kiss to one and all crying, Bless you, Bless you, Bless you! She waved. The pianist bowed. She waved again. The pianist bowed. Justin tried to drag Susan away. She insisted on a backstage visit to see "Mama" as she called the woman she had yet to meet. When he noticed Lorraine and her aging army uncle exiting with the crowd, he decided that a backstage visit might not be a bad idea.

Many others had the same plan, however, and they were stopped dead in a squeeze of shoulders. Several jolly war veterans crushed his hand and pounded his back. Justin, in a quick retreat, pardoned his way to the bar. It was closed. He wanted to go home. Susan still wanted to meet Mama. He sat on the couch while she went to the restroom to enhance her narrow face. A second wave of war veterans charged across the lobby to shake his hand and bark clichés. Justin strolled to make himself a moving target. Wrinkled women splashed him with warm smiles. He went to the cloakroom to claim a cigar from his coat pocket and mostly hide. There he saw Lorraine who he had dearly hoped was miles away. She stood hands raised as if in surrender, holding that graceful, defenseless pose of a woman waiting to receive a cape to cover her shoulders. She sweetly thanked her army escort who bowed slightly, grinning charmingly and, from behind, cupped her breasts. She lurched, hissed, her cape slipping from one shoulder causing her to slap her other shoulder to stop the cape from falling to the floor which it did anyway where her escort kicked it coming forward, this time with apologies. But now she saw Justin who she realized had seen everything, for he was backing out numbly mouthing a soundless excuse me.

The next day there was a note on his desk.

Hi,

What a fumble of fibs! Loved your mother. How'd you like my "uncle"? Wanna trade? Some people live for applause. Not you, boy. Should have seen your face. Look who's talking! Bet mine was a beaut. Well, perhaps we'll meet again. Maybe at a fund raising dinner for the Ku Klux Klan. Or the Martin Bormann Centennial.

Sieg Heil,
Lorrie Benglesdorf

He sent a postcard.

Dear Miss Benglesdorf:

You are cordially invited to attend a surprise orgy and buffet dinner in honor of Juan Peron and sponsored by the Woman's House of Detention to be held at noon Wednesday in the office of Pro. J. Warmflash. Costumes will be optional. Fingerprints mandatory.

But she didn't come.

The next of his classes in which she was due to appear was not for another two days. And Justin was the type who waited badly. He bit his nails, counted the hours and rose early each morning to get in a full day of anxiety. In his great impatience, he all but stopped the passage of time. He did prepare for his next lecture, however, for he was determined to dazzle her with his profound grasp of the labor movement in America. He readied charts and jokes. The charts, at least, were new. When the hour arrived, she didn't.

"Damn it," he said, "I need a distraction."

His bankbook indicated that after a year of scrimping he had saved almost enough to finance his first film. He was too impatient to wait any longer. He chose as his subject a social protest passion play that he had once seen performed in pantomime by a strolling group of amateur players in Washington Square Park.

The story told of how American Big Business wages war and pollutes the planet all in the name of patriotism and profits. But that it doesn't have enough patriotism to spend enough of its profits to wage a war on pollution.

His idea was to shoot without sound and afterward dub in a Beethoven Quartet. Now with the $1,400 he had saved (plus a loan from his bank), he rented his equipment, bought his film, reassembled his actors and had them perform again in front of a Sunday crowd. At the end of three hours and after several repeated performances, the film was finished and he, exhausted. All had gone well. The movements were hypnotically stylized, the satire whimsical, the message blunt. In fact, that afternoon, despite the influx of uptown people, with their neat haircuts and striped ties or their matching pumps and pocketbooks who came to "slum" through Greenwich Village, there were, now and again, slowly curling smiles, quick nods, an ensemble of laughter. All had gone well and best of all, for him, was the act of shooting film. It made him feel like a benevolent god selecting, touching, and christening life.

He was Justin E. Warmflash, the soon to be much respected scholar, teacher, and lecturer. Yet he was still in a state of heat over a silly, bulbous coed. Scholar, teacher, and lecturer whose list of published works will be held in awe in the cold academic world and whose powerful films (truly a two-letter man, that Warmflash), whose powerful cinematic accomplishments will, in time, become landmarks of the art form. He decided to abandon his plan to seduce the elusive L. Benglesdorf. He was too big for that kind of game. Instead he would work out the questions for Wednesday's test.

Write an essay answering one of the following:
(1) Why was James Buchanan a worse President than Franklin Pierce?
(2) Why was Thomas Jefferson's second term in office a failure?
(3) What does the lyric "I was sailing along on Moonlight Bay" have to do with the U.S. foreign policy in Vietnam?
(4) Will Professor Warmflash ever be able to control his manic lust for female students?
(5) Are all self-centered modern dance instructors poor in bed?
(6) Why does the excellent mind of Professor Warm-flash run rampant this way as he walks through the halls?

He reached his office and found a cute, blinking L. Benglesdorf engrossed in a fashion magazine.

"You're a tough professor to get a hold of."

"Yes, well I've been trying to locate someone and it's kept me kind of busy."

"Can I help?"

"No, no, it worked itself out, finally. Well, Miss B., what can I do for you?"

"Nothing, really."

"Sit down."

"Well, actually, there is something."

"I was afraid of that."

"So was I."

"Care to talk?"

"It's difficult."

"Take your time."

"OK."

"I'm listening."

"Well, this is it. I didn't dig you at first. Not really. But I dig you now. That's all I wanted to say. Thought your lectures were kind of…oh…arch, stilted. In a nice way. But, you know, cutesy. I was really wrong, though. You're great. More honest than any teacher I've ever had. And challenging, wow. The whole class just loves you. They think you're great fun. Well, that's all I wanted to say. Don't know why I had to say it. Felt guilty, I guess. So that's it. Speech over. Now if I can just get out of here before I faint. I'm taking up your time, I know. I should leave. I am leaving. I've almost left."

"Move from that chair and I'll break your arm."

"And you're forceful, too. The kids in class like that. Forceful in a gentle way."

"You didn't care for me at first. Now you do. What made the change?"

"Massive doses of vitamin B."

"OK. I withdraw the question."

"No, really. I was sick and run down and my doctor gave me a whole lot of shots of B 1 and B 12. I don't know if this changed my outlook but I feel, you know, like my whole outlook's been changed. That make sense? I think I may have said something very stupid."

Staring at this smooth assemblage of bulbous beauty, he found himself smiling and biting his nails at the same time.

"I thank you for being honest," he said.

"Oh, hell, that's OK."

She stood up, dropped her books, picked them up, gave a sigh, a lopsided grin, her thigh a slap with the rolled magazine and said, "Well, so long."

His throat hardened. With considerable effort he opened his wrought-iron jaw and with an arch and stilted naturalness squeaked out: "*Lorraine!* Will you have. Lunch with me?"

She looked immensely sad. "I already brought a sandwich." She produced something in wax paper from the depths of her leather shoulder bag. "Ham and cheese."

"So I see."

"Plus a real sour pickle."

"Throw them out and I'll buy you all the Moo Goo Gai Pan you can eat."

"Done," she said and the heavy ham and cheese hit the bottom of his empty trash bucket like a padded brick.

Whenever she was with him she felt as relaxed as a Buckingham Palace guard: a catatonic most of the time and a poorly programmed robot the rest. Her normally free and easy lopsided grin now bent its way into one cheek while the rest of her face, to her chagrin, maintained a steady status quo. When she caught sight of herself in the mirror of a theatre lobby giving one of these woe-besmeared smiles, she thought she looked like a drunken waif about to give one last wave goodbye and then pass out flat on her back. And he was so damned informed that any discussion dwindled into a lecture as if they were both back in class. In an Indian restaurant on Carmine Street she made the mistake of saying that it seemed logical that violence on television breeds violence in life. He asked if it wasn't also logical, as the sixteenth century believed, that different weights would fall at different speeds? Yet Galileo, on the Tower of Pisa, proved otherwise. Wasn't it equally logical that the death penalty had successfully reduced the numbers of murders? But as each state abolished capital punishment the percentage of murders also dropped. Lorraine was silent. Would she ever learn to keep her mouth shut? she wondered.

Their first kiss took place in the IRT. The lights in their car had gone out and everyone was speeding along together in semi-darkness. She said it was spooky like a nonstop express to Hades. He put his arm around her shoulder; he would play the part of Charon to make sure she arrived safely. She made the mistake of asking who Charon was. Justin described him as being that myth-ological gentleman who ferried the dead across the River Styx. Then he asked:

"What was the name of the dog who kept him company in the ferry?"

"Look, we're not in school now. We're in the IRT."

"His name was Cerberus. Not a pedigree probably. Had two heads."

"Must have been some fun when he barked."

"What was the carfare on Charon's boat?"

"A box of Dog Yummies? That's just a guess, you understand."

"The custom then was to place a coin in the mouth of the dead before they were buried. God knows how they pay the fare these days."

"This is the last time I ride on a train with you," she said, shifting her sourball so it bulged in her cheek like a walnut. Her other cheek rubbed against his itchy, manly suit. His arm tightened around her. Something is about to happen, she thought. She caught a glimpse of his face in the flying tunnel light. His arm pulled her still closer. Something is about to happen. She was right. And after it happened it was he who had the bulge in his cheek.

He would, of course, want to sleep with her next. She waited eagerly for the nerve-wracking, exciting, slightly frightening scene to begin. Then he stunned her by announcing they would wait until the term was over. It was the ethical thing to do, he explained. He didn't want it said that her final mark had anything whatever to do with sex. This was the kind of charity she could do without. And she was annoyed that he took so much for granted. His self-control also bothered her. She was, she decided, pissed off.

So whenever they went to her Brooklyn Heights apartment—which her father paid for but had never seen—with its thin walls, its slanting stove, and its dripping faucet, or whenever they went to his more comfortable West Village apartment with its floor to ceiling phalanx of books and his precious record collection whose disks he treated like delicate crystal, touching them tenderly with moist cloth and referring to the album covers as sleeves (over his AR speaker he would occasionally pick up mumbled police calls whose intrusions she found hilarious, which made him all the more furious), whenever they went to either apartment and the usual labyrinth of discussion had been successfully traversed, they would watch movies on TV at her place, listen to Paisiello or Galuppi at his place, smoke pot at either place, neck like teenagers everyplace, and wait for the school term to end.

Then, tragedy. It was a late winter afternoon. Lorraine phoned to explain that the history course she had planned to take had closed before she could register. Another class, which she might have taken, conflicted with intermediate French. As a result she was forced to sign up for a course given by, guess who? Professor Justin E. Warmflash. He didn't speak. She held on and bit her lip. A sign in the phone booth advised her to dial 411 for emergency.

"Well, that's just fine," he said, grim and sarcastic.

"I had to take it. I really did."

"Well, that's just fine."

"Look I'll drop it. I'll—I don't know—I'll take a summer makeup. Or something."

"No, don't drop it." There was a bruising silence. "Well, that's just fine. OK. Look I've got to—run. Got a committee meeting in five minutes."

She was alone. The door to the phone booth became stubborn and to escape she needed the outside help of an old lady with a hard shoulder. Freezing wind forced her down the street as she held the nickel she had meant to use for the next five minutes. The terrible fear was that now, and perhaps forever, all love in her life was at an end.

Her mother, who had the flu, greeted her from bed. Her father, overjoyed to see his daughter for a few days, took her on a round of local parties during which they both got drunk. Sheriff Honeycutt put his only arm around her waist and gave her an exuberant kiss on the left eye. Mayor Kinch commented on how nicely she had filled out. Sally Ranslick, who had lost her husband that year, took the girl's hand at the buffet table and give it a lingering squeeze. Lorraine even got a chance to see Nick Columbo who attended one of the parties with Viola Testi. He was the first man Lorrie ever kissed and he had become fixed in her memory as being a gorgeous swarthy male who any woman must surely want. Now he seemed only boyish at best and talked about such things as the greatness of Michigan State by which he meant not the University but only one of its teams, and about something called Dreyfus which she thought was a reference to the famous French scandal but which turned out to be a mutual fund.

Getting home was an odyssey in itself. Her father sang "The Battle Hymn of the Republic" and drove as though leading a suicide squad into battle. Twice he stopped along the road, threw his arms around shivering Lorrie, produced a bottle of Canadian Club and toasted his wife, his only child, and shitty life in general. After that he rammed a snowbank, said the hell with it, and sang loudly of how he wished he were in the land of cotton, o' times darn and not forgotten. When he got safely back and had negotiated the narrows of his garage, he turned off the engine (the abrupt silence was like a premonition), he kissed his daughter (she meant more to him than even his life), and began to cry. He was a bad father, he said. He should have sent her to a finishing school in England but the truth was he couldn't stand the thought of his baby so far away. She told him how very much his love meant to her and how glad she was that she hadn't been sent off to England. Now that they were speaking quite openly of love, he asked her if she had ever given a boy what he called the last full measure of her devotion. Not thinking of Nick Columbo who hadn't received it, or the half-dozen equally clumsy ones who had, she offered a temporary, semihonest answer of no, thinking, at the moment, only of that damned elusive professor. Good, her father said. But it wasn't good at all, for she saw herself as having lost her only love forever. Now she would be exiled to the cold wastes of spinsterhood where she would die old and lonely, gumming her last pathetic curse to a Spanish superintendent who would misinterpret her words as being a social outcry for "La Justicia," when in actual fact she would be trying to shout: "The hell with Justin." Such was her drunken vision of things to come.

When she returned to New York and he didn't phone, she took courage and phoned him. He wasn't home. Nor was he the day after. For his first class of the spring term she decided to walk in looking her very best. She hated the game that ruled she must display her body to catch a man's soul. She much preferred to display her soul to catch a man's body. But she didn't know how this was done, exactly. So she dressed herself in boots that reached just above her knees and a skirt that hung down just below her hips. Masquerading in false lashes and Revlon war paint, she stood in front of a full-length mirror with hair that a beauty parlor had done absurdly sensual things to and the mirror said, "Ridiculous!" She agreed. She was the very image of a modern female astronaut ready for an intergalactic orgy. Had she allowed the latest fashion farce to make a total fool of her? A non-objective view was needed. She closed her eyes and opened them again. Well, she was either a complete success at transforming herself into a mindless instrument of instant arousal or she was simply one hell of a clown. And she would never know which. But did she have the courage to let the outside world decide the answer?

A maxi coat got her safely to school. She waited until the bell sounded and then, removing her shield of imitation fur, she entered his class with everything a mod, well-dressed girl should have—everything but a police escort. There was, thank God, a stir. Pleased, she adopted for safety's sake that old American female stone face. Only when she sat down did she realize that the teacher up front was someone other than the man she had expected. "Dr. Warmflash," the intruder said, "will miss today's class due to the sad fact that his father just had a heart attack." Lorraine stood up and caused another stir as she left the room. She went directly to a phone booth, called the only Warmflash listed in Brooklyn and got him on the third ring.

He seemed startled, then faintly pleased. No great reunion of lovers, this. He informed her that his father would survive. She extended her heartfelt commiserations, hating herself for the cliché, but not sure to what extent his father's illness might help her future. As to his feelings toward his mother, she was on firmer ground. Yet these uptight intellectuals were hard to fathom. Only one-tenth was above the surface and surely that part was as much ice as the rest.

"I got all dressed up for your class," she said, hearing in the electronic distance another couple on another line arguing faintly and fiercely. "I put on a micro skirt, got my hair all done and then, *zap*, you didn't show."

In that other conversation a man was shouting that he didn't want to see her ever again.

"That was sweet of you to go to all that trouble," Justin told her.

In the sad, dim distance a woman was weeping.

"You should see the skirt I'm wearing," Lorrie said. "Don't know what I'll catch first, rape or pneumonia."

The man called her a bitch and said he really disliked her.

"I hate to have you get dressed up for nothing," Justin said. "Where are you phoning from?"

The woman said, Oh, sure, now that you've slept with me you don't want me anymore.

"Where are you calling from?" he repeated.

"In a phone booth in school."

"Right now my parents' place is filled with relatives. Same as when my brother died. Look, let's get together."

And you think going to bed settles everything, the man shouted, you think it's like signing a goddamn contract.

"Get together where?" Lorraine asked. "Or do I sound too anxious?"

"You mean too eager, not anxious."

"Upps, we're back in the IRT."

The woman was crying with soft, helpless sobs. If you didn't like me why did you keep coming back?

"Sorry," Justin said. "It's hard to forget I'm a teacher. Maybe you can help me forget."

"Where shall we meet so I can start helping you?"

The other man on the other line said something Lorraine didn't catch and the woman answered, I hate you, I hate you, I hate you.

"I can be at your pad in ten minutes," Lorrie added.

"I can be there in twenty," Justin replied.

"A dollar says I get there first."

"OK, you're on."

"And hurry 'cause I really miss you."

Off in the great void, the man was laughing faintly. And you even had the nerve to reverse the charges, the woman said. You really are a total shit.

"I'll be there as fast as I can, sweetheart," said Justin whose words sent Lorrie sailing with a broad grin through the great sky of hope and love.

If you didn't like me, why did you have me over in the first place?

"Justin, can you hear another couple talking?"

"No, why?"

"That's funny. She raised her voice. "Other couple ... Hello ... Oh, other couple. Look don't be so mean to each other, OK?"

The tiny sobbing female voice kept on about not knowing what it was she ever saw in him.

"Lorrie, are you all right?"

"Yes, oh, yes, if you meet me real soon."

She felt like a Russian countess in her long black coat as she waited on the top step of his three-flight walk-up until she heard the stomp of his eager (perhaps even anxious) steps. In tune with her tsarist mood, he poured her a glass of something named Stalichnaya and put on a glorious, loudmouthed cantata called *Alexander Nevsky*. Still cold, she sat for a while on the couch with her coat on. When she removed it at last and he saw the hard-sell display of her thighs, he pretended to be overcome, and as in the novels of a certain Russian author, he fell rather than sat into his chair. He called her his little Nutcracker Suite and let her push his rump with her right boot as he bent to pull off her left one. Displaying a soulful smile and deft fingers, he began to undo a row of crucial buttons. Nyet, she said, and reminded him of his pledge not to bed down with a student until she was no longer registered in any of his classes. He took a deep breath and thought of all the highly career-damaging repercussions that might arise out of this helpless obsession of his. Then he exhaled and said, "Ah, what the hell."

She, in turn, saw scandalous headlines in *The Village Voice* resulting in her immediate expulsion from school and relegation to the rank of slovenly waitress in an all-night diner in the depths of New Jersey. She thought of all this, exhaled and said, "Ah, what the hell." Then by way of a final commitment, she undid the rest of the buttons herself.

After all these months of waiting and maneuvering they made love as if it were a rehearsal at best, a hurried run-through with the mistakes left in and the dialogue left out. They lay in bed holding hands and telling each other how wonderful it had been. Yet it had been much the same as his other encounters. And it had promised to be so very much more. The delightful discovery of her smooth, indented body turned him into a self-conscious explorer rather than the confident landowner he longed to be. And her industrious prologues, those intense, melting, fearless kisses in subways, hallways, doorways, were replaced now in bed by a languid, hesitant passivity. As far as she was concerned, this new beginning was nothing more than the old nerve-racking ending. What would he think of her numerous collection of bodily imperfections? And why here in her committed nakedness was she further than ever from passion or even love? When it was over, if not done with, they were secretly convinced that each of them alone was responsible for this moderately pleasing failure.

Some time later, even as they lay in bed holding hands, she discovered he was lecturing again. She had made the mistake of saying that America was obliged to halt the advance of communism around the world. Justin shook his head. The social reform movement that drove the French from Vietnam, he said, was stronger than the one that had backed George Washington. The peace treaty negotiated by Mendès-France provided for a temporary division of the country until an election could be arranged to unify the entire nation under one government. When President Eisenhower learned through the CIA that 80 percent of the Vietnamese were prepared to vote for Ho Chi Minh, he decided, as his memoirs state, to circumvent democracy and set up in the South a pro-American Saigon puppet government. When this government failed to defend itself against the majority of Vietnamese who for over thirty years had been fighting to rid their country of foreign influence and bring about agrarian land reform, the United States was forced to send in troops to defend it. Our excuse was that we were fulfilling our treaty obligations when actually no such obligation for us to send an army into Vietnam exists. In fact we were breaking our tacit agreement to respect the Geneva Accords of 1954 which provided for the very unification election which President Eisenhower chose to deny the Vietnamese people. This, Justin said, was often the way we fight communism around the world.

There was a silence.

Lorraine sat up, frowning. "Wow," she said. "If you're right...."

"Yes?"

"If you're actually right...."

"Yes, well?"

"Holy shit."

The next time they were alone was in her cramped apartment in Brooklyn Heights a few days later. He had suggested that they attend a lecture on air pollution when, actually, she had hoped to take another crack at his bottle of Stalichnaya. Cautioning herself against becoming aggressive, she said, "Why, yes, I'd be delighted to go with you to hear a lecture on air pollution," immediately wanting to kick herself for using the word delighted. Not because it was a lie; because it sounded so Radcliffe-phony.

The lecture proved to be a two-hour exercise in terror. She was told that every day 90 million cars belch forth 100,000 tons of sulphur dioxide, 180,000 tons of carbon monoxide, 33 tons of hydrocarbon, 17 tons of nitrogen oxide. Among the many diseases this aggravates was one called emphysema (the destruction of lung tissue), which had risen from 1.5 per 100,000 people to 8 per 100,000. Next she was told about the corresponding increase in bronchitis, lung cancer, the common cold and the phenomenon called black lung.

She came away as though from a funeral and in the street she had trouble breathing. She also had trouble understanding Justin's complete serenity. He lounged in the taxi enjoying a cigar like a suicidal clairvoyant in a deck chair on the *Titanic*. She held a frown all the way across Manhattan while he maintained a whimsical grin as if his vision of history had, at last, been vindicated.

Now, more than ever, she longed to continue the battle of Stalichnaya. Instead, they went to her apartment to retrieve a book he had lent her (Zola's *Germinal*) which he wanted to quote from in his lecture on the labor unions. They sat in her kitchen drinking beer while her depression widened like a canyon between them. Kicking off her shoes, she slumped in her chair and studied a paper clip while he printed rings on the table with his glass and studied her thighs.

He was absorbed in the logistics of getting the two of them together into the back room onto her bed. He remembered her once referring to it as a "prim, single job," which she had selected for appearances' sake in case her parents ever paid her a visit. This never happened, however, though her father was often in town on business. He would take her to dinner and afterward drop her off in front of her building. When she invited him up, he always begged off. She thought perhaps he was being discreet but Justin had another interpretation: her father, he said, didn't want to see four-walled proof that baby daughter was now a woman. Lorraine praised his insight. He suspected it was his use of the word "woman" that impressed her. Of course none of this was getting him any closer to her bed.

But her gloom was so chilling that he actually considered canceling his passion and rescheduling it. Why should someone he had recently slept with behave as if nothing between them had happened? Could it be menstrual cramps? Intestinal flu? A bad memory? It was as though he had lost not only the future but, doubly sad for a historian, the past as well.

Perhaps a witty line might loosen things up. He tried one out in his head. Miss Benglesdorf, did I ever demonstrate for you my guaranteed cure for hiccups? You need two people and a bed.

He coughed and wisely kept silent. There was nothing to do but sit and resist, as best he could, the magnetic field of her thighs. Soon he had created for himself a gloom as deep as hers.

"Disgusting," she announced without warning. "Even people who don't smoke will have their minds fucked up by car fumes. The earth's atmosphere is being turned into a sewer. The sea is dying. We're being poisoned by the very foods we eat. Life on earth might well be ending. And still no one is alarmed."

"Yeah, right."

"Did he exaggerate?"

"The lecturer? No."

"Then not enough is being done. At this rate we're lost."

"I think so."

"Well, what the hell do we do?"

"Complain."

"Does it do any good?"

"Sometimes."

"Complain how?"

"Oh, write letters."

"*Letters!* You're telling *me* to write letters? Look."

She dashed out of the room. The faucet tapped four slow beats. She returned tousled-haired and angry. She plunked down a large box.

"Look," she cried, "just look."

The first carbon was dated 1959. It read:

Dear Mr. Editor,

I wish to praise Mayor Kinch for turning Lindbergh Boulevard into one direction because this makes ....

He skipped a few and stopped at

Dear Mr. Eisenhower,

In your speech about the U2 being shot down over Russia you said that what we Americans must do in the future to prevent this kind of thing from happening is for all of us to be more vigilant. The trouble is that I am not sure what I must do to become more vigilant so as to help my country. I talked to my Daddy and to my current events teacher and ....

He found one that began

Dear Mr. President,

I watched your inaugural yesterday on television and I want to wish you and your beautiful wife the very best of luck. I am thirteen years old. I will be nineteen at the end of your second term. As my current events teacher said, I will learn a great deal about government by reading the newspapers everyday and by watching all that you do while you are President. In the next few years you will face many problems at home and...

Keeping in chronological order, he glanced through some of the others.

Dear Mr. President,

I am very unhappy over what happened at the Bay of Pigs. You said you hoped that most Cubans would rise up and support the men of the invasion force. But recently most Cubans rose up and threw out these same men and the government they represented. Why should most Cubans suddenly rise up now and support them? I know it is your job to oppose communism all over. But I had hoped that you would find more intelligent ways to do this.

Yours very truly,

Dear Mr. President,

I know you are very busy at the moment with the Cuban missile crisis. But I hope you have time to read this because I just thought of a suggestion that might help you avoid a war. I just learned that we have missiles located in Turkey which are as close to Russia as their Cuban missiles are to us. I suppose you know all about this. Well, why don't we offer Mr. Khrushchev a trade? You give up your missiles there and he gives up his missiles here? Then, you see...

Dear Senator Goldwater,

I don't really see what using nuclear weapons in Vietnam will accomplish and neither does my current events teacher, Miss Swarthson. If a people fighting for their democratic freedoms can't win a war on their own, then they are just not fighting hard enough and so how can killing innocent women and children and trees with atomic bombs solve ...

Dear Mr. President,

I worked hard to get people in my town to vote for you because I liked what you said about not sending American boys to Vietnam to do what Vietnamese boys should do. But now I read in the paper that you are sending a whole lot of American boys to ...

Dear Mr. Vice President,

My father tells me that you are a very liberal and understanding person. Would you please talk to President Johnson and tell him that I do not approve of the way he is now bombing North ...

Dear Mr. President

You may remember in my last letter ...

Justin skipped to the very last one. It read

Letters to the Editor The New York Times
Dear Sir,

A danger exists to our national security that no one seems aware of. The U.S. capacity to deliver nuclear warheads is four times greater than that of the Soviet Union. If Congress passes President Nixon's ABM proposal we will so outdistance Russia in nuclear strength that the military just might lose their chance someday to build still another, bigger and better rocket system. There will simply be no need. Thus we are in grave danger of winning the arms race.

I have a proposal. What we need is a foreign aid agreement whereby we sell missiles to the Soviet Union as a way of strengthening their nuclear deterrent and enabling the vital arms race to continue. Such a Rockets to Russia deal will accomplish four things. 1. It will continue to boost our Gross National Product. 2. It will satisfy the hawks by giving them cause to worry over our national security. 3. It will satisfy the doves who believe the only way to increase the chances of world peace is to allow Russia to feel secure in their military defenses so they will cease being as terrified as we would be were we as far behind in the arms race as they. 4. It will encourage the Chinese to adopt a less belligerent stance in the hope that some day they too will be allowed to purchase missiles wholesale. This will calm many of their fears concerning a possible first-strike attack from the "warlike American imperialists," who keep extending to even greater lengths their missile lead over everyone else.

I therefore urge all patriotic Americans to make known to President Nixon the need for this important Rockets-to-Russia-Cold-War-Peace-Move Breakthrough.

Yours truly,

"Hey, this last one is good enough to be published."

"Tell that to the *Times*."

"No luck, huh?"

"I got a note saying they had considered it."

"Well, these letters impress me very much."

"Except no one did a single thing I asked them to. They even turned Lindbergh Boulevard back into a two-way street."

"Did you write another letter?"

"Didn't have to. Spoke to Mayor Kinch personally this time. I'll have you know I'm real big in Salemville."

She made a circle with thumb and forefinger, turning down the ends of her mouth.

"What did the Mayor say?"

"Said I had filled out nicely."

"Bastard."

"Oh, he's OK I guess."

"OK? He exploited you."

"Me? How?"

"He talked down to you. Flattered you so he could change the subject. Treated you like a pet and sent you away wagging your tail behind you."

"Think so? And I was all proud of myself for having filled out so nicely. Wagging my tail is right. Wow. It was only later I realized that he hadn't answered my question. Bastard."

"See?"

"I should have written an angry letter."

"That's the spirit."

"What am I saying?" She punched the cardboard box. "All these letters over all those years. You know what that was?"

"What?"

"Masturbation. Political masturbation."

He had no answer. The kitchen window rattled pathetically. A leak in the city's water supply filled the void with a faint, slow beat. A radio from the floor above gave off the blurred sounds of a woman singing. Lorraine opened her mouth and let a strand of beads fall to a soft landing on her chest.

"So how's your mother?"

"Oh, Christ." He looked away.

"What's wrong? Come on, what is it?"

"She just accepted a stupid engagement."

"But she's married."

"Dummy. A singing engagement."

Lorraine jackknifed with silent laughter.

"You can see how much I know about show biz."

"A singing engagement," he repeated soberly. "And you know where?"

"OK, where?"

"Vietnam."

"You're kidding."

"To entertain our boys. I've never held a gun, but my mother's off to Vietnam. My brother Howie was killed in Korea. During World War One, in a trench in France, my grandfather was bitten by a rat. In World War Two, in the Pacific, my father caught malaria. And now my mother's off to Vietnam."

He looked away.

"Don't tell me that you're guilty that you're not off somewhere killing people? Or letting them kill you?"

"Of course not. But why do I always escape the absurdities while my family suffers them?"

"Doesn't your mother want to go?"

"Are you kidding? She can't wait to leave. We're supposed to protest the war, I told her, not to go over and help out. She said it was her patriotic duty to support our gallant fighting boys. I reminded her of her hatred for certain German opera singers who performed for Nazi troops."

"What did she say to that?"

"She said I sounded like a Commie fink."

Lorraine laughed. "You know what? My depression is gone."

"No it's not. I have it."

She slipped into his lap and kissed his nose. She whispered "poor baby" and patted his hair. Justin said it was bad enough not having influence in Washington. He looked out her window at her sweeping vista of wall. "But you'd think in my own home."

"Sometimes I think if only I could, like, *talk* to the President. But I can't even change my own father's mind. Do you realize he refused to sign a petition to turn Lindbergh back again into a one-way street."

Now he laughed. He lifted the all but empty can of beer and shook it like a dead bell. She apologized for not having more. She was about to suggest (the hell with not being aggressive) that they go to his place and uncork that bottle of Stalichnaya. But he put his cold hand on her sweeping vista of thigh and asked: "You know what I really want right now?"

She smiled, mentally corking the bottle again.

"What, Mr. Warmflash? What would you like right now?"

"Lorrie, would you mind if… do you …"

Shyness? From him? She was delighted.

"Do you," he finally asked, "smoke?"

"Me? No."

"Any special reason?"

"Lung cancer, mostly."

"I mean smoke pot."

The sink dripped once. It was her turn to talk.

"Oh, pot." She was stalling. "Well, no actually." She was frowning. "Why?" Biting her beads again. "I mean why do you ask?"

He removed his hand from her thigh to produce from his jacket a golden pocketwatch. When he snapped it open there was oddly enough something that looked like loose pepper inside.

It didn't work. She inhaled a bitter cloud of smoke, wheezed, produced tears, coughed, held her breath, waited, shrugged. Swallowing a spoonful of Kaopectate—that chalky witches' milk—was easier than this. She tried again. All she was aware of was a strangely disappointing sensation like a headache without the pain. He, on the other hand, savored the smoke, letting none escape. As far as she could tell nothing happened to him either. He didn't seem to mind. She tried again.

It just didn't work. Yet sitting on his lap, as though waiting for a bus, she was aware of, yes, of something somehow different. He spoke to her: his handsome lips moving, his simple words forming, her lucid mind grasping and holding everything except what it was exactly he was saying. At work was a kind of instant erasing of memory. That was all she could recall. 'Twas a nice sound. Think it again. OK. And that was all she could recall. Again. And that was all she could recall. How funny it was. And that was all she could recall and that was all she could recall and that was all she could recall. It was so good she had to share it with him. What are you laughing at? he asked. She explained it, this totally erased thing that was, in itself, all that she could recall. He smiled. Lorrie, you're high. Nonsense, she replied from the two places in which she was sitting, from his lap with her thighs all showing and from up there in the corner by the ceiling looking down benignly at herself sitting there on his lap with her thighs all showing and him busy inhaling even more of that bittersweet cloud, drawing it in like a miser from his absurd, hunched-back, hand-rolled cigarette.

And she said, "*Look!*"

For there, running across the kitchen table, were three small Disney cartoon characters with top hats and flapping tails running furiously yet moving slowly their blurred legs whirling like wheels and their little hands holding onto the tops of their stovepipe hats as they scurried gaily and gradually across the kitchen table with such startling vividness that she had to reach out and take hold of them to verify their absence. And although her hand closed upon nothing she was as certain of their presence as ever because, look, there they were making her laugh and there he was, Jaundiced Justin, blandly pretending he couldn't see them.

"I am not high," insisted both Benglesdorfs.

But yet something had changed. Merciless life, normally so anti-Benglesdorf, had suddenly gone slack. No longer was there that relentless, anonymous interrogation of her essence, of her laziness, her emptiness, her dumbness, her unworthiness, her not-nearly-pretty-enoughness, her what-are-you-trying-to-beness? you with your big-boobness and your fat-assness and your failing-marks-in-bed-despite-an-occasional-warmflashness. Yes, all this ridicule and humiliation vanished as if everyone in the whole world had all at once lay down and stretched out on soft grass in the warm sun.

"I'm not. Really, I'm not."

"OK. You're not high."

"But Justin, baby."
"Yes, Lorrie."
"Am I ever glonged."

He had, of course, smoked pot before and made love before and both together before. He had even had the smooth, indented Miss Benglesdorf before. Now it was vastly different. The judges and referees were gone, the Scoreboard, too, all fears dissolved, and there was nothing more to prove. They were no longer a human pair of component parts mouthing and grappling through the secret semifinals of possession and vanity. Without effort they both became precocious children, lecherous, saintly, audacious, playful. He swam in sex like the sea. Lorraine hung on and was swept away into the deep.

The morning's sunlight infused the room. Wearing a top hat and gripping a fan of five poker cards, which he eyed suspiciously as if he didn't even trust himself, was a cautious, deceptive W. C. Fields. Close by Paul Newman offered a relaxed and bawdy smile. To his immediate left was a poster showing the offbeat, beat-up, baby face of Jean-Paul Belmondo:

FOR A GOD TO DO SOMETHING
GODLIKE IS NOTHING

This was tacked to the door. It opened as Lorraine entered fully dressed and with a bag of groceries.
"I got more beer," she said.
"In the morning? Why?"
She shrugged. "The A&P didn't have any pot."

From then on she was all his. In return, he assumed a few small added tasks. He became her protector, debaucher, analyst, father, mind reader, pot supplier, cockroach-killer, depression-eradicator and the Court of Appeals in matters of fashion, term papers, family diplomacy, and art and literary criticism. The rest she took care of herself. Except changing light bulbs in the ceiling.

On her part she encouraged him to continue filmmaking, for which he needed no encouragement, only money, and she assured him that she would be his severest critic though, in fact, she loved without reservation every film clip of his she was ever shown. She also became, in a sense, his appointment secretary. That is, she would say to him twice a week, lest he forget: "Isn't it about time we ... r ... " and they would go to his apartment, ignore the Stalichnaya and open instead his golden pocket watch. They would sit together and hand the joint back and forth, drinking in its endless puffs of magic. They would compare and discuss impressions or simply smile and watch as the uptight world went slack.

She was all his to do bold, prolonged, sensual things to. But in the time left over during evenings of untrammeled solitude, when she wasn't there, evenings which often were for him the better part of past affairs, he became aware of something wrong. His concentration, while reading through a tenacious stack of student papers, would pan to smooth Lorrie stepping out of a pair of once-blue dungarees to unveil for their joint amusement bikini panties with a warning stitched on in black thread. He remembered attending a history conference in the Sherry Netherland Hotel amid a stuffy assemblage of college peers and getting his rump pinched by primly dressed Lady Lorraine who immediately postured a farcical look of astonished innocence. Once she came dripping out of the shower wearing his terry-cloth robe, her hands lost in its sleeves, and announced with a flapping salute: "Sir, they have just fired on Fort Sumter." And he replied: 'Let 'em have it. Let 'em have it. A house divided I can live with."

Annoyed at his wandering mind, he threw himself back into work. Yet there they were again standing together at the funeral of one of his fellow professors, a gray-haired man with a hacking cough whom she once had for European History and whom Justin admired as a colleague and a friend. The burial, during a late afternoon snowfall on Long Island, was oppressive and the air painfully cold. As they drove back in Justin's rented car he couldn't rid himself of the sight of the ponderous coffin or the feeling of what it must be to lie at last, arms folded, inside. He drove toward home more depressed than when he had started. The familiar sight of a turnoff on the expressway ignited an old memory of a dingy street in Williamsburg where one could park with a girl near the water and be alone. He went there at once to purge himself of the chill of life's terrible omen. The street was more dingy than he had remembered and the car trembled in idleness. The snow continued to fall on the windshield and into a river as dark as iron. As the wind blew and the heater moaned, he removed her slacks despite a delicious, half-hearted resistance and made her kneel on the seat, astride his lap, where she too trembled and moaned while he strove to delay all that he knew was coming.

Again he was back home alone, trying hard to stay there. But a dozen naked Benglesdorfs were dancing all around him. He reached out. It rang before he could touch it.

"This is Lorraine. I think I'm in trouble."

"*You're* in trouble," he replied.

But he promised to come right over, relieved to get away, and not really worried by her tone of voice. It was simply another depression perhaps or that old crisis whenever she begins writing a new paper.

Though the night was mild, he shivered strangely. In the train, as he continued reading, he wondered why now, at last, he was able to work.

All things considered it had been a lousy week. It began with his realization that he hadn't done anything with the film he had shot in Washington Square Park, six months ago, and guilt was beginning to erode his self-confidence. He promised himself to do the editing soon but he recalled too many dead promises to really take heart. For his own edification, he found himself saying to one of his classes, "In life as in politics, you can't even have a meaningful defeat without a meaningful beginning." But neither he nor his class quite caught the brilliance of this remark.

Another thing that happened that week was Lorrie's jolting awareness of the population explosion. She had previously believed that this Malthus business, as she put it, had been pretty much discredited, that there would always be meat for most of us, fish for the rest of us, and rice for Asia. Something like that, anyway. But Justin sat her down and recited some facts. There were a billion people on the earth in 1830. There were two billion in 1930. Three and a half billion in 1970. There will be seven billion in the year 2000. The rate now is a billion more every five years. She stared at him with her beads in her mouth. He gave her another fact. If all the people who had ever lived in the whole history of the world were brought back to life today their number would equal all the people who were now alive and walking the earth. More people, he explained, mean more factories and more cars to pollute more of our air and water. More people would jam our cities just at the time when they were all crumbling. More people would mean more poor people with less means to help them and greater tensions breeding more hate at a time of global famine, mounting revolution, and endless war.

She was too sick at heart to speak. They sat on a park bench watching two laughing children climbing through a maze of monkey bars. Nearby was an empty pint bottle of cheap wine standing in the grass. Several minutes passed.

"So then family planning is very important," she said.

"To put it mildly."

"That settles it."

"Settles what?"

She slapped her knees with her hands. "Let's plan a family."

Her grin implied it was all a joke. Her hazel eyes implied it wasn't. The empty park, it seemed, was very crowded now with just the two of them.

"Lorrie, aren't you late for a class or something?"

❧ ❧ ❧

And that week the voices began as well. It all started when she swiped his pocket watch in retaliation for his giving her a B-minus on one of her tests. When he first realized it was missing he had a few bad moments wondering if he had lost the damned thing in class. Inscribed on the back were the words: *And when you see clouds upon the hill, They may just be clouds of daffodil.* Signed, Mother. Harmless enough, he decided. Fingerprints? Nonsense. Nothing to worry about. Then he received a typewritten postcard in the mail.

> Dear Professor Warmflash:
> If you ever hope to see your golden timepiece again, put on a black hat and a rabbi's beard and park in a rented Good Humor truck in a certain side street in Williamsburg, Brooklyn. There you will wait for a piquant blonde to amble by doing a third-rate imitation of Betty Davis. This stunning creature will have with her the item in question. You will offer in exchange the broken pieces of a Spiro Agnew watch in an old pepper shaker. Do not notify the police. Do not cry out. Do not try to sell ice cream or in any way attract a crowd. Sincerely, Piquant Blonde.

"Got your card," he said over the phone minutes later.

"Deserves at least an A-minus, don't you think?"

"Stealing grass from a poor boy whose mother is off in Vietnam is a terrible thing to do."

"I know it. Oh, I know it. OK. I'll give it back."

"Now you're wising up, kid."

"Come up and see me sometime," she said in her third-rate imitation of Mae West, "and you'll get your golden timepiece."

Although she let fly a flurry of hints, he made a concerted effort to stay at home. This wasn't one of their scheduled meeting days and Justin was one of those who stuck to schedules. After all, keeping to schedules avoided disruption and they allowed him a peek into the future. In return all they demanded was that you stick to them. Once she accused him of being uptight and he replied, "Me? Why?" in that slightly uptight tone of his, she let him have it. "Because you wear those stuffy shit-brown vests. And because," she added, fumbling for the coup de grace, "because you stick to schedules." He was wounded by the vest remark. But the other made him feel rather proud. Surely schedules made sense. Even their love affair throbbed to a schedule. She would attend his afternoon class on Wednesday. When it ended at five she would leave the building alone, meet him in a restaurant and then spend the night at his apartment. She slept over on Friday and Saturday nights. Sunday she went home. Next week it began again. So when her postcard arrived on Thursday and he phoned and she let fly a flurry of hints, he made a determined effort to stay at home. He said goodbye and hung up. Time passed and visions of Benglesdorfs danced in his head. He decided to call back. She beat him to it. But her mood had changed.

"This is Lorraine. I think I'm in trouble."

It was a lousy week, indeed.

When he arrived that night and told her that hearing a strange voice was nothing but the side effects of being stoned, she sort of believed him. Then he berated himself for having come to see her in the first place. No doubt about it, she was becoming a problem. Her body was his three times a week. But his mind was mush for the other four. No good. You've got an armful of tests. Idiot, go home. You'll end up in her bedroom if you don't show some restraint. Look, her hips are swaying through the door. And that goddamn dripping is enough to drive one mad.

"Oh, I meant to talk to you about that," she said, when she returned to find him at the sink.

"I've got to go," he explained after his *mano a mano* with the faucet. She snapped her fingers as if to say, Tsh, that's life. As he prepared to leave she announced she was hungry—stoned out of

52

her mind—but hungry. He offered to go down and get her some food. He could have kicked himself when she accepted.

He found some chickens roasting in a window. And there was a full tray of rice pudding, a food which always seemed to him both mundane and magical. He bought enough for three.

On the way back he spotted a man coming out of Lorraine's building. It was the same slim, well-preserved bigwig who had grabbed little Lorrie in the cloakroom. The man stopped and looked up at her window where the lights, for some strange reason, were turned off. The firm arrogant Army face looked from side to side and up again. Then he marched ramrod straight directly at Justin who was shuffling along with his hot chicken and cold rice pudding. They passed on the sidewalk without incident or apparent recognition and Justin entered the building to push her downstairs bell. There was no answer. Again, harder if not louder. No answer. Push, push, push. Very, very hard. Nothing. What the hell is this? He rang someone on the top floor and was buzzed in at once. He climbed the stairs to Lorrie's door and rapped the knocker. Silence. He hammered now hard enough to stir the dead. A terrible thought occurred. Had that Army bastard done some foul deed? Justin was torn between running after him, calling the police, or breaking the door down. The last of these he dismissed for he knew it would be his shoulder and not the door that would break down first. Puzzled and stalling, he ventured a tentative and half-hearted, "Lorrie?" The door popped open.

"Thought it was you," she said. "Couldn't be sure."

She explained it this way: "I stood by the window to watch wonderful you march off with bow and arrow to shoot me a chicken in the local deli. Then I noticed coming up the street one Wyatt Nimols, Colonel Nimols to you, and to me Hot Pants Nimols or rather Hot Bra Nimols. I went zap!" She struck a cross-eyed pose of horror. Normal again, she explained that Hot Bra Nimols had phoned dozens of times trying to arrange another date. Now, evidently, he had decided to attack without warning. But when he rang downstairs, she didn't let him in. When he got in anyway and knocked, like fate, on her door, she didn't answer. She just sat there in the dark as did the brave English during the Blitz. (All references to history were carefully included to impress him.) She was also afraid that Justin would return while Madman Nimols was pounding away. In that event she would have to keep both of them out or let both of them in.

"Sad part is I sort of like him, Nimols. No, not that way," she quickly corrected, seeing the old jealousy equation forming in Justin's eyes. "All I feel *that* way is *blech*. But he's, how shall I say? kind of mentally cross-eyed, if you know what I mean. Semi-insane is a better way of putting it. But he has energy, and you know how I love men with energy. Look," she added quickly, seeing the old equation again, "look, I'm as lecherous as the next girl, but to me this guy is just a big placebo. Also a comic madman. But he's obsessed with me and I sort of have to be polite because of my father. Actually I don't even like him, Nimols. See my dilemma?"

They ate semiwarm roast chicken with semicold rice pudding and bemoaned his failure to buy wine or beer. She made coffee instead and afterward the faucet commenced dripping again. Once more he berated himself for not having stayed home or for not going back there right now. But her loaded, double-barreled sweater dared him to make a move for the door. Oh, well, he thought, by way of conclusion, fuck it. He asked for his pocket watch. She handed it over, empty. Again he reached the same conclusion. He entered her bedroom on his way to the toilet. Belmondo and company were gone. Surrounding him now were the huge faces of Che Guevara, Malcolm X, Bobby Kennedy, Martin Luther King, and Gene McCarthy. Tacked to the bedroom door was a quote from the great bank robber himself.

In my time you had to get up at 5 A.M. or 6 A.M. on cold winter mornings and case a job for a month or two and lay out perfect plans. It was hard work. The young kids don't go for all the work, time, and preliminaries. All these kids want to do is run into a bank, grab the money, and run out.

—Willie (The Actor) Sutton

54

On the mirror above the bathroom sink was taped another quote.

Just outside the village was this big pile of bodies. This really tiny little kid—he only had a shirt on, nothing else—he came over to the pile and held the hand of one of the dead. One of the GI's behind me dropped into a kneeling position, 30 meters from this kid, and killed him with a single shot.

—Army Correspondent Jay Roberts From Mylai.

When Justin came out of the bathroom—the toilet rearing up like the North Atlantic in a storm—he found Lorrie sprawled on her bed, hands behind her head. Sex, he thought. She has only to call you on the phone and you rear up like her bathroom plumbing or "Sneak Attack" Nimols or any would-be Jack-in-the-Box who comes within leering range of her twin spheres of influence or pauses to read subtle interpolations in the lilting of her hips. He moved nearer, unbuttoning his brown vest. She sat up and punched the mattress.

"You know what's wrong?"

"With us?" Fearing the worst.

"No, with life," she said.

"Oh, that. No, tell me. What?"

"We're doomed, that's what."

"Yes, I know."

"I mean all of us."

"Yes, I know."

"You're being flippant."

"Hey, I'm not."

He sat down to show his seriousness. She stood up to show hers.

"Doomed on the same day, I mean. It's too much all at once, don't you see. Inflation, pollution, and the population explosion. Wow, that's enough, right? But then we have the military complex, power lobbies, Negro rights, the Middle East, Vietnam. Do you know that when the kill count comes over the radio I'm rooting for the other side? I don't want to, but hell, if we're wrong, how can you root for the side that's wrong? My country is bombing and burying innocent people to death everyday in Asia and I'm sitting here counting calories and studying Colonial History. I feel sick."

"I know."

"Big man, big man. You know. But what do I *do*? How do I stop all this? And now. Not by the second centennial of the Alien and Sedition Acts. I mean now. And don't tell me to write letters or vote or wait or pray. I want to straighten things out right now. I feel awful. Shit, why did I use up all the pot? And don't tell me to march. I marched. Up and down I marched. I even bought an ugly pair of shoes at the Red Cross Store. On 14th Street. Comfortable posturepedic shoes for protesting against the government in. God, I feel sick. And ugly. And lied to. And cheated."

"I understand."

"Big man. He understands. But what can I do that will work? Tell me, O Big-Time-Political-Type-with-a-Brown-Vest. Tell me."

He leaned back on the bed. "All right. I'll tell you."

"And don't tell me revolution."

"I won't."

"'Cause they'll slaughter us."

"I know."

"He knows. Yet you say you have the answer."

"Yes, I do."

"Well, what is it?"

"Rebellion."

"I don't get it?"

"A revolution overthrows everything. In America this is impossible plus impractical. Rebellion, however, is civil disobedience. It is organized resistance against organized stupidity. It's riot, a roadblock, an occupation of a building, the refusal to carry out an order. It's local defiance with univeral purpose. It means working for change inside *and* outside the government."

"People might get killed."

"A few, perhaps."

"I'm against killing."

"So am I."

"Well?"

"Don't worry, the government will do all the killing for you."

"I'm against *all*, repeat, *all* killing."

"I agree with you."

"Then *why*?"

"Because time has run out. The normal channels for change are too slow. It'll soon be too late."

"Shit, I don't like violence."

"The people who complain the loudest against violence here at home are all for it in Vietnam, which is, of course, someone else's home. And those who feel that any violence for whatever purpose is illegal must then agree with the King of England that George Washington should have been hung."

"Oh, wow."

"Thoreau said…"

"Jesus, I'm back in school again."

"…that all men have the right to resist the government when its tryanny or its inefficiency are great and unendurable. He added, and I quote, But almost all say that such is not the case now. But such was the case, they think, in the Revolution of '75. Unquote. I love that one."

"Look, I don't care for violence."

"Neither did Jefferson but in 1787 he wrote a letter in which…"

"I feel I should be taking notes."

"…in which he said and I quote, God forbid we should ever be twenty years without a rebellion."

"Hypocrite."

"You're right if you mean how the author of The Declaration tried to justify keeping slaves."

"I don't mean him, I mean you."

"Why?"

"I don't know. Maybe in time I'll figure it out."

"Maybe my answer scares you."

"Maybe your mother was right. Maybe you're a Commie fink bastard."

Hurt, he turned to face her and collided with her teasing smile. Annoyance sat askew on his head like a party hat. Quickly he was himself again: cool, bomb-proof, professional.

"Hey, I was only kidding." He said nothing. "By the way, how *is* your mother?" He didn't answer. "Oh, don't be angry. Come on."

"She's fine. My mother's fine."

"Did she write?"

"Yes she wrote."

"What does she say? Oh, Justin, what did your mother say? Come on."

"She had one complaint."

"Tell me."

"Seems the humidity in Saigon is even worse than New York."

After class he hurried away, cutting short his conversations with bed-worthy coeds to march to an Italian restaurant on Thompson Street to meet her for lunch and to ask, without a greeting or a smile:

"Now tell me exactly what happened?"

"Just what I said. Thomas Jefferson."

"Are you serious?"

"Absolutely."

"He spoke to you?"

"Scout's honor."

"All right, what did he say?"

"Do you want a drink first?"

Justin looked up and said no to the waiter.

"Then what's your order?"

Justin informed him most emphatically that they weren't ready to order. Lorraine broke in, however, to request a green tossed salad and minestrone soup.

"I'm on a diet," she explained to the waiter who seemed unhappy with the sparseness of her lunch.

He made quick pencil strokes on his pad as if sketching her portrait. He turned to Justin who was deciphering the purple scrawl of the mimeographed menu.

"Veal Saltimbocca," he said in a fluster of indecision and looked up at the waiter whose dead hair and white face reminded him of his father.

"Fried potato or veg?"

"Veg."

The waiter tossed off an action painting on his small pad.

"Plus a glass of red...." But the waiter was gone. "OK. Now, finally, about Tom Jefferson. What exactly..."

The man with the tired face was back. "Saltimbocca finito," he said, tapping his pencil on his pad as if Justin were at fault.

"Oh, spaghetti and meatballs then. Plus a glass of..." Again he was gone. "OK. Now, at last, about Tom ...."

"Wait." She frowned. "I've got to go to the john."

Left alone with his frayed patience and basket of bread-sticks, he drifted with the lingering image of a white face until he was back there again with a cluster of relatives who stood like voyeurs to enjoy someone else's illness and reflect upon their own good health. Lying in silence in a bleached bed in the middle of the day made his father look suddenly frail. They said hello to each other and shook hands but all Justin could think of were the symptoms he detected in his own chest. Now other things occurred to him. The shape of his father's hands bore a striking resemblance to that of his own, as did the old man's habit of adjusting his glasses with a twitch of his nose. Even the chart on the foot of the bed bore the name Warmflash. Again he felt the chill of life's terrible omen.

Justin stood by the bed and tried to be cheerful. No one smiled and the chill grew worse. He tried to pull himself out of it by remembering Lorrie late one afternoon reading *I. F. Stone's Weekly* in the Carmine Street Pool. She, lying in a bikini in the dim city sun, making a public display of her tender indentations, of her bulbous annunciations, and her obscene good health. He tried to recall the way she walked in the street carrying with her everywhere she went all that she had in lovely abundance beneath a scarcity of clothes, not like one of those disinfected debutantes with arthritis of the spine, but with a slightly winning waddle as if Lorrie were a lovely swan purposely marring her classic image with an irrepressible sense of fun. Then he remembered that he had probably lost her; lost her because of his bombproof schedules, his high and mighty sex-postponements, his haughtiness on the phone, and his goddamn brown vests. He felt the chill worse now than ever.

He announced to the bedside gathering that he would send a telegram telling his mother what had happened. This was traditional and proper and besides it was a good way of getting her the hell home from Vietnam. But he was outvoted. His father, as always, wished to avoid a fuss, and the others followed his lead. Or was the old man simply afraid of his wife's theatrics?

A doctor appeared indicating politely that they would have to leave. Justin shook hands with his father again who attempted to smile to cheer up his son.

Feeble old men in bathrobes made sliding sounds with their slippers in the hall and there was the stink of everything having been made thoroughly clean. Justin thought he was free at last when he stepped into the filthy street but his relatives insisted on going back with him to his father's home in Brooklyn. It was part of that cruel assumption that those who grieve should never be left alone. So he and six of his least-loved kinsmen journeyed back to South Ozone Park where some did the dishes and others opened the mail and the rest took Justin aside and infected him with their morbid and condescending encouragement. He had had enough. He selected Aunt Pauline who frequently borrowed money from his father and never paid it back, who gossiped about his mother when she was away from home, who was the least loved of all these endured grotesques called relatives; yes, he selected Aunt Pauline who was sweetly babbling her non sequiturs with her rich gold teeth, and he prepared a handful of eloquent insults with which to run her through. At the last minute, a family scandal was narrowly averted by the ringing of the phone and the sound of Lorrie's charming voice.

"OK. Now, finally, about Tom Jefferson," he said in the restaurant. "What exactly *is* this nonsense?"

"You really don't have what I would call the right attitude." And she bit off a piece of breadstick with a haughty, clumsy crack.

"He talked to you in private, you said. In private, with my girl. Well, at least it wasn't George Washington. We all know what a womanizer George was. Franklin wasn't much better though he insisted on writing about it, which was worse. But Tom was tricky. We don't know much about those smoke-filled bedrooms up at Monticello.

"You're making fun of me."

"Of you, never."

"You're making fun of my voices and I don't like that."

"Sorry."

"Here I am in trouble and you're joking around."

"What trouble?"

"Never mind. Besides, if I tell you, you'll just joke around."

"OK. I'll suspend judgment. What did Tom say? I know him through his writings. You know him in person. Let's compare."

"No."

"Oh, come on, for crissake."

"Ha, you don't like that, do you? The historian without his source material. Well, I have a right to keep certain things private."

"Then why did you pull me out of class to tell me all about it?"

"Because I thought you were a good guy who would take seriously certain private things."

"I do take them seriously."

"Ha."

"And besides, it was my pot you were smoking."

"Big man. I'll pay you back."

"I didn't mean that. Look, you were on some weird kind of trip with my own private stuff and you haven't even the common courtesy to describe it to me."

"A junkie's right of privacy," she announced as if reciting a state law.

"Oh, balls." And he adjusted his glasses with a twitch of his nose.

"Balls to you too."

"Meat balls and spaghet," shouted the waiter.

"Yes," said Justin. It was placed in front of Lorrie.

"Minestrone soup?"

"Here," Lorrie answered. It was placed in front of Justin.

"And a glass of red …"

Again too late. They exchanged plates and ate in silence.

"OK. So don't tell me. I don't care."

"Balls," she said and cracked a breadstick so loudly that a lady at the next table actually turned and frowned.

It was when he was most certain that she belonged only to him that he lost her. As summer arrived with its ice cream wagons and school dwindled away with its endless chatter, it became time, finally, for their long-planned escape. A friend of his had offered to lend him a cottage on a lake in Vermont for their use alone for two whole months. When Justin viewed in his hothouse mind the coming attractions of their feature-length vacation, he saw them arriving at dusk in a damp and hollow woods, building a fire that snapped like breadsticks and, leaving their luggage unopened on the porch, undressing in the chilly air to hurry and try out their strange new bed. They would cook all their meals outdoors, even their morning eggs, read a few of those semi-portable Russian novels that took too much time for city consumption and, of course, swim nude at night in perfectly motionless moonlit water. It would be like all the bad romantic films ever made and some so bad they hadn't ever been made. It would be *Tarzan and Jane on Walden Pond*, it would be *Apollo Carrying Aphrodite across a State Line and into the Woods*, it would be *The Fourth Army Band vs. Phil Spitalny's All-Girl Orchestra*. It would be a blast.

And he would bring a camera in hopes of finding here, at last, a full-length motion picture subject. He wanted something stunningly visual, completely original, amazingly inexpensive, and requiring a cast of one. But which, of course, would make his name. The life of a simple fisherman, perhaps: a dawn to dusk odyssey of patience and loneliness showing the oars of the rowboat dipping and dripping in the dancing light, or the tale of a hunter seeking food to eat as he stalks through the muffled chamber music of the woods until at last, like a snapped breadstick, the crack of the gun.

First, however, Lorrie had to visit her parents to keep things calm on the western front. It would be a brief, formal appearance of just one week at home. Then she would say goodbye and travel with a girl friend to Vermont—or so her story would go. All this, too, he saw in his coming attractions. One short week in her quiet hometown (honeycake and tea with friends on the front porch), a ride back to New York in a borrowed car (one of the two that belonged to her "Dad"), then he, Justin, climbing in behind the wheel, squeezing her in a bearhug kiss and taking the Thomas E. Dewey Thruway nonstop to Vermont.

Lorrie rode the train to Salemville with the glee of a child. She took a list in shorthand of the summer things she would need by the lake. Also a gift from her lover: *Walden* by Henry David Thoreau. Included in the same volume was an essay Justin hadn't noticed: "Civil Disobedience."

Justin completed his packing three days before she was due to return. He suffered her absence poorly and spent most of his time amid gunfire and love scenes in local movie houses. Then the day and the hour arrived: but she didn't.

Time stopped and piled up like traffic. Neither doorbell nor phone rang. No mail from anyone. It was as if somewhere in his life a fuse had blown. A four-day-old postcard stood on his artificial fireplace. It was of little help.

Hi! Just arrived home. Miss you already. Stay away from all those evil city ladies. See you next Monday at noon. Look for a sex-starved blonde doing a third-rate imitation of

Betty Davis driving a Good Humor Truck. I love you, I need you, I miss you.

Regards,
Lorrie

On the other side was a color photograph of empty Lindbergh Boulevard looking like an ad for a science-fiction movie about the capture of a community by superior beings who came to the earth in sophisticated spaceships from millions of light years away to suck blood.

Finally, on Tuesday afternoon, angry and desperate, he phoned long distance and heard the maid answer in a long, sibilant, slightly British, "Yesssss?" He asked for Lorrie. He was told with impressive enunciation that Lor-raine (rhymes with your-train) was indisposed. Whom should she say was calling? He mumbled his name. With Christian generosity she offered her own.

"This," said she with deadly diction, "is Mrs. Benglesdorf, Lorraine's mother."

"Ah. " Which was all he could think of at the moment. Fate took its time saving him.

"Oh, wait, Mr. Warmflash, it appears that my daughter is finally here."

The receiver touched something hard like marble. There followed a silence implacable as death. The phone was scraped up, a hand cupping the mouthpiece. Words were mumbled. Perhaps secrets exchanged.

"Hi," said Lorrie, a bit too sunny, a bit too bright.

"What the fuck happened to you, for crissake?"

"Why Justin, what a pleasant surprise."

"Why didn't you show up, damn it?"

"How sweet of you to call, really."

"Look, don't give me that shit."

"Yes, things have been just wonderful here. And how have things been with you?"

"Your mother's still in the room, is that it?"

"Uh huh."

"Great. How do we talk, then?"

"Now that you mention it, I *was* hoping you'd come up and pay us a visit."

"Visit you? Are you crazy?"

"How very, what's the word, gallant of you to say so."

"Look, this is impossible."

"Improbable, I grant you."

"Lorrie, I'm serious."

"So am I now that—wait a minute—yes, now that my mother is gone. Wow. You won't believe this but she was dusting ashtrays."

"Lorrie, why didn't you show up? Why didn't you phone?"

"Oh, baby, I couldn't."

"Couldn't? Why?"

"I was told not to."

"Who? Who told you not to?"

"Sam."

"Who?"

"Sam Adams."

"From your hometown?"

"Big historian. From 1776."

"Holy Christ."

"Him I haven't heard from yet."

"Lorrie, you've been smoking again."

"Viola Testi brought some good stuff back from school. She's the one who gave me those underpants, remember?"

"So this time it was Samuel Adams, eh?"

"I like him best, I think. He's really nice. Even if he is a bit intense."

"You're very big these days with the signers of the Declaration."

"Jefferson didn't sign it, did he?"

"Dummy, he wrote it."

"I know *that*. But in this business you write a lot of things you don't sign."

"Lorrie, I know you're high but concentrate. What did Sam Adams say to you?"

"The weather's been beautiful this spring, hasn't it?"

"Lorrie, don't evade the question. Are you going to Vermont with me or not?"

"My mother's garden is starting to bloom already. You should see it."

"Has you mother come back into the room by any chance?"

"Affirmative."

"Lorrie, will you call me back in an hour from a phone booth?"

"I have to do something first. Then I can, yes."

"OK. I'll be home and I'll be waiting."

"Good guy."

"Don't forget."

"And thank you so very much for calling, Mr. Warm-flash."

"Up yours."

"Likewise, I'm sure."

He kicked off his shoes and poured himself some Stalichnaya. He took down her postcard again with the picture of a truck parked in front of the drugstore and read it three more times. For no reason he could think of, he became happy and started humming. But his mood splintered when she didn't call. He was furious and verging on eloquence. He paced the floor rattling his ice and stumbling twice over his shoes. He stopped dead as an idea struck him in the groin: *she has a lover.* That was it. That was the answer. *Now* what should he do? He paced and rattled his ice some more. Three hours had piled up and the pressure was enough to make him scream. He shouldn't phone her. That was the smart way to play it. Go to a movie and the hell with the bitch. He even picked out the film he wanted to see. But before he left he called to make sure she was all right. The line was busy. Ten minutes later it was still busy. Finally he got her mother again.

"Oh, dear, I'm afraid you can't speak to my daughter now, Mr. Warm-flash. You see, she has just been arrested."

"What?"

"Some silliness about trees. My husband, who's an attorney, claims there's nothing whatever to be alarmed at. In fact, he says it might even do her some good. It will teach her to respect the law and not descend into the streets. He's down there now. At the jail, I mean. Is there any message?"

"I commend you on your calm, Mrs. Benglesdorf."

"Oh, it's not the way it seems. Sheriff Honeycutt is a friend of the family and Lor-raine is getting the red-carpet treatment. My husband made sure of that. My husband makes sure of everything."

"But then why was she arrested in the first place?"

"Because she broke the law."

"How exactly?"

"Oh, it's not what it seems, Mr. Warmflash. It's just one of the games of youth. Please don't concern yourself with it."

After much difficulty he got the operator to connect him with the sheriff's office. Adam Honeycutt, the Chief Deputy Sheriff, had a pleasant-sounding voice with a slight Southern accent.

"Can't bring the young lady to the phone right at present. She is in custody at present. And in another building altogether. Who might I say is calling?"

"This is James Reston of *The New York Times*. I want to make sure that persons taking part in your recent demonstrations involving those … trees get the best possible treatment."

"The young lady is a friend of mine and I wouldn't let anyone harm a hair on her pretty head, Mr. Reisner."

"Reston, James Reston of *The New York Times*."

"Good-o. You a friend of the family, or what?"

"I'm a columnist."

"Is that a fact?"

"When will she be released?"

"That's for the judge to decide."

"When will she go before the judge?"

"When he comes back from fishing."

"Will you deliver a message for me to Miss Benglesdorf?"

"Well, that's not allowed a-cording to regulations."

"But I'm a friend of the family like you said."

"Well, I'll have to take it verbal instead of in writtin' 'cause I ain't got but one arm and I need that one to hold the phone."

"Would you tell her that her old history professor is coming up to pay her a visit after all."

"Sure 'nough."

"Thank you, Sheriff."

"Don't mention it, Mr . . . ."

"Reston. James Reston of *The New York Times*."

"Don't mention it. And leave everything to me."

Justin put on his shoes and dialed Grand Central Station. The line was busy. He dialed again and the line was busy. When he realized that it would take something close to a miracle to get through, he dialed the operator but she wasn't home. Deciding this was impossible, he dialed again and finally got an answer. He requested the number of the out-of-town information operator, jotted it down, and dialed the out-of-town information operator and found the line busy. He dialed several more times before he finally got through to ask for the number of the railroad station in Salemville, New York. He jotted it down, dialed, and found no one at home. He tried again and waited two whole minutes before someone answered. He asked when the next train was scheduled to arrive from New York City. Five ten, he was told. When would it leave New York? Three fifteen. Wonderful, he said and hung up. He tried to call the operator again but couldn't get a dial tone. When he finally got one and dialed he heard a busy signal. At last he reached the operator and asked for the number of Western Union. He jotted it down, dialed, and found he had awakened an old lady taking a nap in Staten Island. He apologized, dialed more carefully, and got the same old lady again. Her mood was somewhat worse, now. So was his. He dialed the operator again and as he listened to her phone ringing endlessly, he wondered if someone like himself who had been dialing for days, had perhaps given up, gone over and killed her. A different operator answered this time but she sounded the same as all the other robots of the New York Telephone Co. He told her that someone in her office had given him the wrong number of the Western Union office. Unconcerned, she gave him a new one. He jotted it down, dialed, got a busy signal and screamed. On the fifth try he got through and sent two telegrams, one to the jail and the other to her home, both explaining that he would arrive on the five-ten from New York. He finished his drink and carried his luggage down to the street where he signaled nine empty passing cabs before the tenth stopped and grudgingly took him to Grand Central Station. The man next to him on the train was reading *Playboy* magazine. Eyeing its parade of boobs and bottoms, Justin was reminded of just how long it had been since he had last fondled L. Benglesdorf.

The railroad station was a concrete slab with an overhead of rotting timber. There were a number of advertisements for musical comedies now playing in New York or long since closed. Lorrie was standing at the end of the platform in a pleated skirt that hung to her knees and a little girl's blouse with a rounded collar primly buttoned at the neck. She was holding up a sign that read WELCOMEWARMFLASH. Her grin was triumphant, self-conscious, and, as lopsided as always.

"I got both your telegrams," she announced proudly. "I never knew jails forwarded mail."

He leaned in to give her a wolfish kiss long overdue but made contact instead with a pristine cheek as Lorrie said, "Hello there, Mrs. Durkee," who in reply said, "Why hi, Lorrie, is this your gentleman guest from the big city? Hope we get a chance to meet him 'fore he leaves." And Mrs. Durkee heaved her bundles into the train like a longshoreman and waddled aboard.

Justin heaved his luggage into the back seat of the open Buick convertible (one of the two that belonged to Lorrie's "Dad") and slipped into the front seat to try for her lips again when she said, "Why, hello, Mrs. Swarthson," to a woman in a flowered hat driving an old Ford. "Hi there, Lorrie," the woman replied, "so he finally arrived, did he?" Then turning her steering wheel as if trying to unscrew it, she managed to maneuver her Ford around the corner and out of view. Justin, about to speak, had his head snapped back as Lorrie launched her father's convertible, bringing Mrs. Swarthson's flowered hat back into sight again, passing it swiftly and swinging hard into a wide street where a number of cars stood parked at an angle to the curb and whose flat, dreary, two-storey shops struck Justin like a recurrent nightmare until he remembered the picture on the back of Lorrie's card.

Just as he was becoming accustomed to the trajectory and acceleration of the convertible, Lorrie swung it to the curb and climbed out. "Hi, Mr. Defreeze," she said to a tall man in a plaid cap sitting on the porch of the Salemville Hotel. He stood up, put away his magazine, nodded, said, "Hi, Mrs. Swarthson," to the passing Ford and carried Justin's luggage up to the second floor of the hotel and into a room where nothing had been changed since the Hoover Administration, except perhaps the sheets. There was no radio, TV set, or phone. There were three sagging, diamond-shaped, wire hangers dangling from the long crossbar of a tall, four-wheeled coathanger. There was a bureau of drawers, a sink just the size of a football, and a mirror that reflected his face from below his nose to just above his head. There were two pillows side by side on a double bed. But Mr. Defreeze took one of them with him when he left.

"Isn't this just great? she whispered with a conspiratorial delight. "When they first showed me this room I nearly fell down."

"It's awe-inspiring."

"They say John Dillinger slept here."

"I believe it implicitly."

"Thought you'd dig that, being a big-shot historian and all."

"I'm more concerned with who's *going* to sleep here," he said taking her around the waist.

She explained that she couldn't, not here, not now, not with the town so small and she so well known, not with her parents waiting right this minute for them both to come to dinner and certainly not with Mr. Defreeze downstairs knowing that Mr. Benglesdorf's little daughter was upstairs, unguarded and alone with an actual man. There was a knock on the door. It was Mr. Defreeze who tipped his cap and said, "Towels," hanging one small one and one large one over the back of a chair.

"Look, Lorrie," said Justin when the door had shut again, "there's a lot we have to talk about."

"Agreed, but this is not the place, believe me."

Another knock. Mr. Defreeze seemed most perplexed with himself and deeply apologetic. "Clean forgot to ask you to sign in."

The office was down behind the stairs. It was hopelessly somber with scale drawings of locomotives behind glass on the wall. Everything seemed as dry as a tomb, and time hung like incense in the air. In a cardboard box on a roll-topped desk were a dozen postcard pictures of a pickup truck on Lindbergh Boulevard. The last entry in the register was an A. Mottle (Mr. and Mrs.) from Nyack, New York. The ballpoint desk pen had *Disneyland* inscribed along its length.

"What line of work you in, Mr. Warmflash?"

"I'm a historian, as luck would have it."

"There's plenty of history 'round here, all right. Don't know if it's interestin' but there's sure plenty of it."

"I bet there is."

"I hear you went and got yourself arrested, Lorrie."

"You heard right, Mr. Defreeze." And she led Justin by the hand into the street where busy Mrs. Swarthson drove by again in her vibrating Ford heading now in the opposite direction.

"Lorrie, what's all this about?"

They drove past the barbershop with the barber asleep in the chair.

"I told my father we're engaged," Lorrie said, waving to someone leaving the drugstore.

"Engaged? What you mean engaged?"

They passed the butcher shop and the hardware store and a black cannon mounted like a toy in a triangular park.

"Oh, I just said that so I'd be able to get him to lend you money for your next film."

They passed a bar, a bowling alley, and, on the corner, a drinking fountain. No one waved because no one was in sight.

Justin was staring at her. "Lend me money? For my…"

"If it involves family, my father, when he says lend, means give."

"Lorrie, I never proposed marriage to anyone."

"But it's best for him to think so or else he'd run you out of town for encroaching on his property, meaning me. He's a lawyer, my father."

"But we're deceiving the man. It's unethical."

"See these houses? The old, tall ones? They were built when Salemville was a flourishing lumber town. Beyond this point the houses are all smaller and less attractive."

"Lorrie, are you sure you're not just trying to trick me into marrying you?"

"Would I marry a man who thinks we lost the War of 1812?"

"Lorrie, I'm serious. Why are you doing all this?"

"Because I have to stay in town and since I have to, well, I want you to stay here with me. Besides, I told my father what a fabulous filmmaker you are and now he says he wants to lend you ten thousand dollars."

He stared at her again. "Are you … Ten thousand …"

"Ah, here we are." She swung her father's treasure ship through the open gate and up the driveway across a large lake of grass, snapping his head as she halted the car on a dime smack in front of a door that looked like the gnarled entrance of a medieval castle. "This hyar's de home uh ma pappie," she said, cutting the engine and giving a sigh.

It was while sitting at the table at the conclusion of dinner, sipping his second cup of coffee, that he realized he had said essentially nothing since he had entered. His side of the conversation had gone something like this.

"How do you do, Mrs. Benglesdorf.... Yes, a most pleasant trip.... Yes, it had come early this year.... Oh, I agree.... Ah, how do you do, Mr. Benglesdorf.... And I've heard a lot about you too, sir.... Oh, whatever you have the most of.... Bourbon on the rocks is fine.... Yes, I am, as luck would have it.... Oh, she's just saying that because she might end up in one of my classes again, ha, ha.... Yes, films are my real interest.... I believe you mean *The Sound of Music.* No, I didn't see it.... No, I didn't see that one either. But I've always liked Barbra Streisand.... No, I'm afraid not. Was it good? ... Uh huh.... Uh huh.... I know what you mean.... Yes.... Exactly.... Really? ... Oh.... Yes, I will, thank you. Ice, no water.... Much obliged.... Well, in my opinion I.... Yes, I am hungry, as a matter of fact.... After you, sir. Thank you.... Would you pass the salt, Lorrie.... The steak is delicious, Mrs. Benglesdorf.... You were saying, Mr. Benglesdorf... Uh, huh.... Uh huh.... My opinion? I feel that student riots are less likely to occur in more enlightened universities and more likely to occur in less enlightened universities.... Uh, huh.... Uh, huh.... Uh, huh.... Well, I guess I have a different perspective on the problem, Mr. Benglesdorf being, as you know, a member of a university and so... Uh, huh.... Uh, huh.... Yes, Mrs. Benglesdorf, I think I will have another cup of coffee. And it was an excellent meal, it really was."

He had plenty of opportunity to notice the house. Imitation Louis XV furniture stuffed as if with money. Glass ashtrays clean as soup bowls. Cigarette lighters shaped like silver seashells. In a gold frame was a young Lorrie with a desperate, waxen smile. Another photograph, also framed in gold, but taken somewhat later, showed a serious girl peering into a plush future. And on several walls were paintings of lively dolphins leaping from a waxen sea. These last held his eye.

"They're very nice," said Justin with effort.

He and his host were sitting alone over their third cup of coffee. Justin accepted a cigar but the silver seashell failed to light.

"Paid five hundred for each painting. Here's a book of matches. I'm told they're worth twice that now."

Lorrie appeared from the kitchen, said the paintings were ugly, collected some silverware, and went away.

"I got news for ya," her father yelled over his shoulder, "you're getting them for a wedding present."

While the women did the dishes Lorrie's father stood up to show his guest a place he called "out back." He was a big man in a gray silk, custom-made suit with a cream-colored tie and he walked as though testing the construction of the house. The tassels on the lamps shook, a table quivered, the floor creaked. Together they thundered down to the cellar, banged open a glass storm door to emerge beside a long, luminous swimming pool, vivid as crème de menthe.

"Cost me three thousand to build the damn thing and another nine hundred to fix the leak."

They sat in reclining deck chairs like self-satisfied financiers and tapped ashes onto wet flagstones causing an abrupt, brash hiss. In the exhausted light, the host's cigar flared like a warning button on an instrument panel.

"Well, young man, I understand you're out to marry my daughter?"

Justin cleared his throat. "Yes, well one hates actually to jump into something too quickly. That is I think marriage is a very important thing, Lorraine being a very special person, you'll agree, therefore caution is, don't you think, somewhat," Justin cleared his throat again, "advisable." He adjusted his glasses with a twitch of his nose. "Don't you think?" He chewed on a thumbnail.

"I got news for ya," said Benglesdorf making the flagstone hiss beneath him. "When I was your age I felt the same way."

"How do you mean?"

"Scared shitless. What did I do? Went and made a lot of money, that's what? Know something? I wasn't scared anymore."

The evening began to drift pleasantly, and in the direction of an orgy. Cognac was offered in elegant snifters the size of cannonballs.

Seductive music slithered through loudspeakers from the paneled den. Soon Justin was having another cognac which joined the whiskies and the wine and the anisette in the coffee to unleash in him a rambling love for all living things.

Cathrine Benglesdorf sat beside her feverish guest and poured praise on top of alcohol. Though she had also been drinking, she continued to speak as if appearing on the BBC. Now he actually liked it. She confided how often her daughter had spoken of him. In a recent letter she even said that Justin was the only teacher who had ever excited her. The mother repeated this with a straight face. Yes, he liked it, indeed.

Hirum Benglesdorf appeared large and naked in a flesh-colored swimsuit and leaped off the low board as though trying to hug the entire pool. He landed in a flat, fearsome plunge of tonnage sending shockwaves up onto the flagstones. Lorrie appeared next. She was pleasantly accentuated in her terry-cloth bikini as she dipped forward into a clean dive through illuminated crème de menthe.

His empty glass cannonball had somehow been filled again and he began in the private lecture hall of his mind an exegesis on the odor of chlorine and the possible reasons why it smelled like pot. He was interrupted by Lorrie's father who, after toweling himself off, insisted on leading an almost maidenly Warmflash to a damp dressing room in their newly built cabana where several guest bathing suits, each too small, awaited his forceful commitment.

Lorrie cried, "Hip, hip, hurrah," when he reappeared in the surprisingly raw night air and Lady Cathrine, like a magician's assistant, relieved him of his cigar and eyeglasses, which he had forgotten about completely, and then left him alone on the stage.

He decided to make up for his modest physical presence with a bullshit racing dive which he executed from the edge of the pool into freezing water and then swam to avoid frostbite with a clawing, slapping stroke as if he were squinting his way through a nightmare conga line. He stood up at the shallow end, his hands to his eyes, like a surrendering warrior. Then he focused in on those penultimate spheres of influence made to seem even smoother by the roughhewed terry cloth in which they were almost encased.

"Made it all the way across. Big man, big man."

He tried to dunk her like the tasty doughnut she was but she spun free, playful as a dolphin, leaving him standing knee-deep in water as he watched her swim away jabbing at the sky with her elbows and churning up a fuss with her feet.

Since they both had had plenty to drink Lorrie decided to walk him back and leave the car behind. The town was asleep and the old trees shrouding the street stirred listlessly while the shadows of their branches quivered like giant cobwebs. Justin stopped on a dim sidestreet and kissed her. She made sounds as if swallowing something good. When their lips parted she said:

"Yes, I remember you."

"And do you remember Vermont?"

"Which one is he?"

"Are you coming there with me or not?"

"Yes, but can we please go next month? That'll still give us four weeks. Oh, please."

"I don't like the idea."

"Neither do I. But can we, please?"

"Lorrie, what's happened to you?"

"I'm sorry. I really am. There's nothing I'd like better than to go off into the woods with you."

"But?"

She didn't answer.

"You'd rather stay here and get arrested, I suppose."

She looked at him. "It isn't much but it's a beginning."

"You're being flippant again."

"The sad part is I'm not."

As they walked, she told him the story and there was a seriousness in her voice that he had not heard before. When she arrived home to visit her parents and borrow the car, she learned of a small protest group whose cause attracted her. It seemed a local industrial company planned to enlarge the town's only factory in such a way as to needlessly destroy a number of acres of fine old trees. Lorrie had often gone there as a child on picnics and she even remembered hearing talk of turning this area into a public park. But the idea was shelved because few people could see why Salem County, which was made up mostly of woods, needed a park in the first place. During the Korean War, when the factory was built, the idea of having a park side by side with the noise and smoke of industry seemed even less practical. But the trees remained and they were very beautiful. In fact some people still went there for Sunday picnics. Then plans to buy the land and expand the factory were announced in the press. Since more jobs would result from such industrial growth, few people cared to listen to those who argued for conservation. The protest group presented alternate plans to the board of directors but were told it was too late; the papers had already been signed. This later proved to be a lie, for the lawyers, who were drawing up the necessary documents, were not expected to complete the job before September. Then someone, hoping for a *fait accompli*, paid a contractor to remove the trees at once. The protestors uncovered the plan and went to court to seek an injunction. At 8 o'clock in the morning on the day after Lorrie's arrival, the bulldozers came to clear the land. Since the court was to convene at 10 o'clock to pass on the injunction, Lorrie suggested they try to stop the bulldozers themselves. They went, six people in all, and stood among the trees with signs and water guns. Three were arrested, Lorrie among them. The injunction arrived three quarters of an hour after the trees were cut down.

She picked a leaf from a shrub and placed the stem in her mouth as she walked. She said she had been so depressed at what had happened that she and Viola Testi went off and smoked pot. This time the voices told her quite clearly what to do. She was not to leave town. It was here that her first battle would be fought. It was here the campaign to save her country would begin.

Lorrie stopped speaking and blew the leaf from her mouth. They paused at a crossroad. The silence was as fixed and implacable as a stopped clock.

"How," he asked, "is one girl supposed to save a whole country?"

"That's what I said. Me? I said. You've got to be kidding. Like I get nervous just going shopping."

"And how did your ... voices answer that one?"

"They didn't. It happens sometimes. They kind of fade in and out a lot. I decided they were letting me think it out for myself."

"And?"

"I decided maybe there are many people in many places hearing the same kind of voices." She shrugged. "Look, what do I know?"

He stopped and squeezed her shoulder. "Lorraine, listen. Hearing voices is not normal. I cannot stress that too strongly. Perhaps you are overworked or something."

"If I am, it's from all those damn tests you kept giving us."

She started walking again.

"Lorraine, you must stop smoking. I told you that before."

"I like smoking. It relaxes me when I'm overworked."

"Balls."

"Ah. Again eloquence."

"For you pot is a bad habit. You use it to cop out."

"Shit, you introduced me to it."

"But I don't smoke to cop out."

"Oh? Then why do you?"

"To intensify my personal sense of existence."

"Big man, big man."

"I'm serious."

"You're a riot."

"Lorraine, damn it, listen to me, will you please?"

"Shhhh, not so loud."

"That first time when you heard voices, they said go to the Dauphin, take his army and drive out the English, remember? Now what was that supposed to mean? That's fifteenth-century crap.

And how come your voices sent you the very same telegram five hundred years late?"

"I asked them that question."

"And of course they didn't answer."

"They answered, all right. I hope I can quote them correctly. They said it was a kind of test, a symbolic sort of thing, to establish a historical perspective."

"That's crap."

"No, I think I understand. I mean if I had heard a voice say, Hi there, you don't know me but I'm old Tom Jefferson himself from your high-school books, remember? Well, I have a little errand for you to run. Zap. I mean if I had heard that I would have jogged to the nearest hospital. But the way they did it, being historical and all, it made me think for a minute. After I calmed down, I mean. I was scared, sure. But afterward, I thought, you know, it's like when you get a wrong number. It may be a real crazy person calling but it's not for you so it's O.K. But then the next time the phone rings…" She stopped. "Look, what do I know. Upps, here's your hotel."

The windows were as dark as a gutted building. Then, far away, he heard it.

"My God, just like in the movies."

"What is?" she asked.

"The mournful sound of a distant train."

"I used to listen for it as a child before I fell asleep. It seemed more cheerful then."

"Lorrie, when am I going to see you next?"

"Soon. I don't know when, exactly."

He heard the wail of the train again and he slipped his arm around her waist. She stiffened and glanced about for signs of surveillance. He felt helpless in this silent town and so, it seemed, did she. Around him all was dead and yet caution was needed more than ever. Surely noisy cities were better places in which to hide, at least from life's long mournful sounds. His subversive palm slid down over the firm fruits of her rump. She swung away in a full turn like a girl doing the lindy. Widening her eyes, she mouthed the word no. He invited her up to his room. She said she couldn't. He suggested they go back for her father's car and drive somewhere and park. She said she would try but couldn't promise. Hell, it's only eleven o'clock. She frowned; eleven already? She must hurry home to receive a phone call. Who from? A girl friend, she said. A warm hit-and-run kiss. In the distance she turned once to wave. Then he lost her in the grillwork of giant cobwebs.

His rented cell was like the waiting room for a crematorium. The bathroom down the hall was bristling with heat in June and the knob on the radiator came off in his hand. Back in his room he studied his face from just below the nose to just above the head. It was the portrait of a man peeking above a picture frame. He sat down and engaged himself in the boring torture of waiting fifteen minutes. After what was surely forty-five minutes of soundless agony, a quarter of an hour had somehow passed. He descended the soft stairs to emerge into a hushed night. A few blocks away he found a live phone booth beside a dead gas station.

"Is Lorrie there, Mrs. Benglesdorf? Sorry to bother you. This is Justin Warmflash. How are you?"

"Oh, dear, she left about two minutes ago I should think."

"On foot?"

"Oh, no. By car. It's much safer."

"Did she say where she was going, by any chance?"

"I believe she went for a drive to unwind from all her schoolwork."

Tingles of pleasure alerted his groin.

"Thank you, Mrs. Benglesdorf, and thanks again for a most splendiferous evening."

"Oh, you're most welcome, Justin, I'm sure. And you must come back to visit us again very soon."

He sat in the rocking chair on the hotel porch and tried to outlast the stubborn quiet. As he leaned back there was the rowdy creak of a floorboard. The night held its breath. Nothing at all moved. The fixed, dry silence reminded him of an old colleague lying now in a box beneath the earth.

Her automobile approached from the distance. Justin stood up, his chair rocking gaily behind him. The headlights splashed downward as if searching for something lost. There was the brief glimpse of a gray-haired man at arm's length from the wheel. Justin sat again. He opened his gold pocket-watch and rolled himself some relief with nature's chlorinated pepper.

In the rent-free lecture hall of his mind he was deep in an exegesis of the nature of small-town silence and how it reflects small-town thinking, when his eye caught sight, above the line of two-story rooftops, of frightening, livid, orange flames.

He arrived out of breath and stood among a dozen attentive citizens to watch a storefront become engulfed in smoke and fire. A sign now vanishing in the yellow fury said UNITED STATES SELECTIVE SERVICE CENTER, NUMBER and the rest unreadable. Members of the fire brigade were busy wrestling a python hose into position while others were having some difficulty attaching the other end to a hydrant. Meanwhile a few old-timers were busy passing pails of splashing water toward an open window with the ceremonious pleasure of children playing at adult work. Justin was moving forward to help with the buckets when a hand took hold of his arm and tried to crush it.

"Who started the fire, did you see?"

Speaking was Mr. Benglesdorf wearing a sports jacket over his undershirt, his hair wildly uncombed. Justin said no, he hadn't.

"You sure?"

He said he was sure.

"There's a lot of funny things going on in this town," Benglesdorf hinted, his face alive with shadows.

"An electrical short can start a fire, sir."

"I got news for you. So can arsonists."

"What makes you think it's that?"

"Because an electrical short can't bribe an army guard to unlock the door."

Justin was incredulous. "The army had a man guarding ... *this?*" And he pointed with amazement at the pathetic shop that had been turned into a Selective Service Center and then into an inferno.

"What do you mean *this?*" snapped another voice as another hand tried to crush his arm. The slim, well-preserved army bigwig whom Justin had last seen in civilian clothes exiting from Lorrie's building in Brooklyn Heights, was standing now in full dress uniform like a forest ranger watching Oregon in flames. "This, I'll have you know, is government property. And this fire is the work of a leftist fink. Got that, mister?"

"Justin," said Benglesdorf, "I'd like you to meet a good friend of mine, Colonel Wyatt Nimols. Colonel Nimols, Mr. Justin Warmflash. A friend of the family."

"A pleasure," said Nimols, smiling politely.

"How are you, Colonel?" asked Justin in return.

"Fantastically well," he replied.

"Wonderful," Justin shouted over the mounting noise of the holocaust.

The colonel's smile fell like a stone. "Sure you didn't start this fire, mister?"

"It's all right, Wyatt," said Benglesdorf, "he was with us all evening."

"If you say so, Hirum," Nimols shouted as the fire snapped like a million breadsticks. "Tell me, did anyone see who did it?"

"Did what?" asked the sheriff. He was wearing a vest that couldn't have been buttoned even if his aides had helped him try. A badge hung from his shirt, more or less facing the ground, while on his head was a blue postman's cap with the printed stitching removed. There was a holstered pistol on his right side; on his left an arm was missing. The empty rolled sleeve was held in place with a rubber band. "Got to sign me up a whole lot more of them citizen volunteers and that's a fact. They took so long gettin' over here, the town's liable to burn down and them in it 'fore they even get their pants on and start work. Howdy, you new in town, son?"

Hirum Benglesdorf introduced Justin to Sheriff Honeycutt and the sheriff said:

"You willin' to join up and become a member of the Citizen Volunteers of Salemville?"

He said he was and the sheriff copied the volunteer's name and address on the inside of a book of matches, using a pencil stub and the volunteer's back. As he wrote he explained that Justin would be expected to answer the call night or day in any emergency involving a fire.

"I got news for ya," Benglesdorf told the sheriff. "We average a fire every two years. By the time the next one comes due this boy'll be back in Manhattan where he comes from."

The sheriff stopped writing for a moment. "He's still liable to get here faster than some of them from across town. Fact is, some of my volunteers won't know there's been a fire till lunch tomorrow when hunger drives them out of bed and they notice a building's missin'."

Justin asked how he'd be notified.

"Son, this town's too small to keep a fire hidden 'less you're in bed all boozed out."

The pencil pressed into his back again while Justin stored away in his mind a motion picture idea about the Civilian Volunteer Department of Salemville. He regretted not bringing his Bolex with him from the hotel but by now the building was mostly glowing ashes anyway.

Colonel Nimols was bemoaning the loss of all the files of all the young men who would have been drafted that month and sent to Vietnam. Hirum Benglesdorf said he had news for Colonel Nimols. The fire was the result of bribery and arson, and such things damage our commitment abroad. The sheriff insisted the fire was an accident and that it shouldn't make much of a dent on the American military posture in Asia. Nimols snarled at the sheriff.

"Listen, mister, I represent the United States Army. In these here parts I *am* the U.S. Army. And it's my job to protect our Selective Service Offices wherever they might be. I don't intend to let this kind of activity continue. Do you read me, mister? And when I catch that son-of-a-bitch soldier who was supposed to be on guard duty here, I will have his ass on a platter."

"No need. I've already gone and checked him out. Just a little service we perform free of charge so that the army don't go and hurt itself none. The boy's ass you want was lying in sick bay all night. Seems the army just plum forgot to send someone in his place. Right careless, if you ask me."

"Listen, mister, I'm going to have someone's ass for this even if it's yours for not guarding the place yourself, got me?"

"Wyatt, for God's sake," said Lorrie's father.

"Local elections comin' up real soon," said the sheriff, scratching a kneecap. "You're free to vote if you can prove you're a citizen."

But Colonel Nimols had marched off to shout orders at some soldiers he noticed fraternizing with two girls in bathrobes who had appeared in the street to watch the excitement.

Hirum took hold of the sheriff by his only arm and insisted that an investigation of bribery be conducted. It seemed that one of the volunteers found the front door wide open when he arrived. Someone had the key, he concluded ominously. Or picked the lock, the sheriff suggested. Or picked the lock, Benglesdorf agreed.

"Except no one in this whole town knows *how* to pick a lock, including me," the sheriff said.

"Then I got news for ya. Someone had the key."

"Or the door was left open out of plumb carelessness."

Hirum didn't see it that way. What he wanted was a thorough investigation of the possibility of bribery and he wanted it started now. In his opinion there was something very funny going on in this town. The sheriff didn't see it that way. He said that investigations uncovered the damnedest and most embarrassing things sometimes, and he pulled his postman's cap more tightly onto his head as if to demonstrate his rightful intransigence. Mr. Benglesdorf asked Justin to pardon them a moment and led the sheriff away to continue the discussion in private. It didn't take long. About two minutes. With another squeeze of his arm, Justin was led away.

"Let's get out of here," Benglesdorf growled, "these hicks drive me batty."

He opened the vault-thick door of the Cadillac and soon they were purring toward Lindbergh Boulevard.

"He didn't want to do it. How do you like that? Either he's lazy or he's covering up. Well, I got news for him. He's going to investigate for bribery and that's that. In fact, it's all settled. If you keep your eyes open, my boy, you'll learn a lot in this town. For instance, you know how you go about getting a sheriff to investigate for bribery when he doesn't want to?"

"How?" Justin asked.

"You bribe him," said Benglesdorf, "that's how."

He was still high on the peppery extract from his golden pocket-watch when he climbed out of the cream-colored treasure ship and watched it speed off into the cobwebs. It was then that he noticed someone standing on the porch, someone who had been curious about the fire but loath to leave his post as guardian and owner of the Salemville Hotel. Justin had to describe the calamity in detail before Mr. Defreeze was satisfied. Then he said: "By the way, Lorrie was here a while back askin' for ya. Said I didn't know where you was at."

"What'd she do then? Did she say anything? Where'd she go?"

"Drove off. No. Said goodbye. Then she drove off. Don't know where she went. Home I guess."

"Shit."

"Only place to be when a pretty girl like that comes a looking for ya is right smack in the middle of the road. Don't pay to take no chances. 'Cept a big fire is a real attractive sight. Yes, sir. Knew a man once. Was real taken by the sight of a prairie fire. Went off to have hisself a better look. We never did see him again."

Next morning he phoned several times and, after suffering the bruises of an impenetrable busy signal, hurried off on foot. He felt more confident now because of what Lorrie's father had said last night before dropping him off at the hotel. He had promised to support Justin in any film project he might decide to enter. Hirum would demand only 10 percent of all profits and he would earmark the loan as a capital gains investment. He said he was pleased that his daughter wanted to marry so bright and creative a lad because if his creativity ever failed him he could always fall back on teaching history again. Justin, who was stoned out of his head, smiled and said nothing. His glazed speechlessness seemed to Hirum to be the highest form of awe and gratitude, and that was how Justin Warmflash, who saw himself as the Marijuana King of the American Colonial Period, became a financially solvent motion picture director.

The house was empty. At least no one answered the bell. In back, amid the perfume of newly cut grass, he found a cloistered Cathrine Benglesdorf doing delicate things to a row of lilacs. In the once magical swimming pool an empty bottle of cognac bobbed slyly. "Lorraine is not here," said the clearly enunciating woman after commenting clearly and distinctly on how his presence had startled her. However her daughter had left an address where one could contact her. Number Six Cedar Lane. The puppet strings of compulsion pulled him toward the street but he fought to stand still and make polite comments on her lovely flowers while she in turn knelt, as though in happy penance, to pronounce for him their multisyllabled Latin names. Finally leaving, he pointed at the bottle in the pool. "Who threw that in?" And she, with a pleasant smile, said: "I do believe you did."

Cedar Lane was within walking distance as was everything else in Salemville. Yet people drove everywhere, even down the block to buy a paper. When he got to Seven Cedar Lane, the row of houses ended and only the road continued. A small Negro boy, standing and peddling, came by with two foxtails flowing from his handlebars. When questioned, he pointed to an empty lot and peddled away.

What looked like a coffin in the middle of a roller rink became, on closer inspection, the foundation of a building that had never been completed. It had a square wooden floor and no walls. A sign read THE REORGANIZED CHURCH OF JESUS CHRIST OF LATTER-DAY SAINTS. Several parked cars surrounded the rink as if it were a waterhole. Justin opened the coffin and descended into darkness.

He tossed a greeting into the void. Nothing happened. He called hello, again, loudly, and listened. Still nothing. He said: Lorraine? The lights snapped on. Rows of benches with black hymnals left haphazardly on the seats. There was an old piano, its soundboard missing. Also a large cross above the pulpit with a sunburned Christ like a bored lifeguard leaning back and watching that the kiddies didn't drown. Lorrie in slacks behind the pulpit was waving happily. A boy and a girl seated in the front pew had turned their heads toward the stairs. Another young man, standing by the wall, had his hand on the light switch.

Introductions. Nick Columbo, the lighting technician, was in army uniform. He was a good-looking, dark-haired, articulate young man who had just learned a new word. The word was Justin. Hello, Justin. How do you do, Justin. I'm pleased to meet you, Justin. To tell you the truth, Justin, we've heard a great deal about you. Justin, I'd like you to meet David Fenskie.

David was engulfed in a hysterical shirt. He had a brownish beard and blond hair straight to his shoulders. He could well have been Jesus returned to earth disguised as a hippie but remembering too late that he didn't know English. So far he had learned only a few words: man, bread, crazy, cool, stoned, split, freak, and funky. His progress seemed slow.

Last and mentally least, or so was his first impression, was a tantalizing provocateur named Viola Testi. The skin of her wide, carnal face had a permanent maple stain that made the sun obsolete. To prove that the rest of her was equally well varnished, she wore a bare midriff that invited lengthy appraisals. She smiled at Justin with ripe lips as if she had just been told all the details of his private life and had found them vastly amusing. Lorrie proudly informed him that Viola was part American Indian. He now knew how some of that oppressed tribe would achieve their revenge.

Justin gave Lorrie a kiss, made everyone sit down among the scattered hymnals and asked what this place was and what the hell was going on? Lorrie, evidently the leader, took the floor and explained things this way:

When construction was halted some years ago due to lack of funds, the decision was made to use the church as it stood, or rather as it lay, half-hidden beneath the earth. Between services, she and her followers borrowed it for meetings. They secured permission under the pretext of forming a local theatre group.

Now, first, on today's agenda, said Lorrie plunging right on, was the question of how to acquire more members. Beside the four present they had only four others of whom just two were expected to attend. The second question was how to stop the expansion of the factory. Lorrie gave statistics to prove that the air pollution would be four times worse after the expansion was completed. Justin remarked that Salemville didn't seem to be suffering from air pollution at all. Nick Columbo said yes, Justin, that was true because all the pollution went off toward Port Madison. The wind had been blowing in that direction for the last fifty years and so Port Madison, which had no factories of its own, became the garbage dump for all of their aerial dirt. Viola Testi shook her head sadly. Fenskie nodded in agreement. Chewing her beads as if she hadn't been listening, Lorrie dropped them from her mouth and said, "If there was only some way to get the wind to change." She pondered.

Justin took a chance and mentioned the fire. When four rascal smiles resulted he knew he had come to the right place. Lorrie tried to explain but Fenski interrupted. "Cool it, already. Like we don't rap with every tie and shirt who wanders in here, dig?" Private Columbo said that if Lorrie felt Justin was OK, then as far as he was concerned Justin was OK. Viola was not so sure. She was at twenty-one a grand-master at anticipating man's rampant treacheries and she studied the supposed historian as if he were a suspect in a police lineup.

"I knew a guy once looked just like 'im. The jerk-off stole some hashish right from out of my purse."

"Hey, now wait a minute. Justin's my lover." Lorrie's protest carried some weight, but not much. "I mean he was the first to turn me on." That did it.

Fenskie said, "Peace."

Viola smiled and Nick leaned forward. "You want to know about the fire, Justin? OK. I'll tell you."

"Let me," Lorrie said. "I need the passing mark."

Fenskie turned to Columbo. "Schmuck, it was her idea."

Viola told Lorrie to go ahead.

Justin noticed how courteously they treated her. He had held seminars that gave him more trouble. In fact, now, when she spoke it was as if to a classroom.

"We were getting an ulcer from doing nothing. I felt like a housewife home from a long vacation with the place a mess. We tried to clean things up. We campaigned for peace and Johnson against war and Goldwater and what did we get? Stabbed in the back. We've decided to give ulcers to those who gave them to us."

"And you started with the Selective Service Office," Justin added.

"The army posted a guard there. We decided to get him sick."

"How did you ever do that?"

"I," said Columbo, lighting a cigarette, "was the guard."

"Don't smoke," Lorrie scolded.

"You know I can't help it."

"You want cancer of the lungs, you big boob?" Lorrie gave him a left to the right epaulet.

Viola was gleeful. "Oh, how ex-lovers will quarrel."

Nick Columbo looked at Justin. "I'm not an ex-lover."

"You're an ex-lover," Viola insisted, "live with it."

"What I mean, Justin, is that I didn't ever qualify as lover."

"Hey, man, such modesty," said the hippie Christ.

"Anyway, Nick hid out in sick bay which left us one last problem," Lorrie continued. "The key was in the pocket of a Lieutenant Locke. Crazy, no? Well, to make a long story short we bribed him."

"With what?"

"With me." Viola smiled as if remembering another Little Big Horn.

"Would you care to tell the story of you and Lieutenant Locke?" asked a polite Miss Benglesdorf.

Miss Testi shook her head in disbelief. "I've met rapists with more suave than that bastard. What a come-on. Said he'd teach me the art of self-defense using government-approved wrestling tactics. Must have got them from an army rape manual. Lots of breast grabs and thigh holds. Slipping the keys out of his pocket was easy. Avoiding a fractured rib was something else again."

Justin was about to speak when Columbo jumped up and ran toward a wall like an outfielder chasing a triple. Lorrie hurried to the pulpit, Fenskie killed his cigarette and before Justin knew what had happened he was slapped into darkness and told to shush. There were feet on the stairs, then a pause.

"Bunch of horses' asses," boomed a deep baritone, "turn on the mother lights."

Columbo snapped the switch. Fenskie waved. He got nothing in return.

"What are you savin'—'lectricity?" shouted Willoby Brown.

He was a huge black man with his head shaved clean. The sleeves of his T-shirt were gone, the threads still showing. A belt buckle on his dungarees was the size of a small picture frame. And he looked angry enough to knock out a wall. When introduced he said nothing. A church pew creaked under his weight and there he sat as if daring the world to utter just one more phony word.

Nick Columbo again dashed for the wall switch when Willoby boomed: "It's only Briggs. Stop wetting your pants."

A young lady descended with matching shoes and pocketbook. She wore a prewar crinoline dress, white beads, and a thick magnifying glass on each eye. She was the only one in the church who didn't seem out of place. Her features were stamped: neuter gender; her manner: meekness and dignity. But when she spoke she throbbed with uncontrollable petulance. Fenskie waved at her as well. She, too, paid no attention.

"And just what do you mean by not turning out the lights? Our rules are very explicit. They state that if anyone should go down into..."

"We know the rules," Nick said amid ascending cigarette smoke. Fenskie nodded.

"Be quiet!" Briggs looked like a furious monkey. "In point of fact, Mrs. Durkee went down into the church just yesterday and she nearly caught you. And today I go down and what happens?"

Viola smiled sweetly. "The day you go down I enter a nunnery, that's what happens."

"You have the world's filthiest mind." And Briggs seated herself with her purse on her lap.

"Like who doesn't these days," Fenskie said.

Willoby exploded. "I seen you comin' up the fuckin' street, that's how we knew who it was."

"I fail to see what purpose is achieved by cursing," Briggs replied.

"You virgins get me sick," he boomed.

"Now, Willoby, you mustn't discriminate against minority groups," said the appetizing Miss Testi.

The Negro's lurch and laughter threatened to shatter his bench. He pointed a long log of an arm to show his delight.

Viola continued. "And you thought it was only us poor colored folk who've been left out in the cold."

Briggs called her a bitch. A rumpus followed. It ended with a knife jab in everyone's ear. Sitting cross-legged on the stage, Lorrie removed her index fingers from her lips as silence fell like a collapsed tent.

"Briggs, you're late," said Lorrie quietly. "Willoby, you too. And Viola like save your wit for Honeycutt and Co. OK? It was Briggs remember who got us a lawyer free of charge when we were trying to save the trees. As far as I'm concerned she's done more for the cause than anyone here. Briggs, I'd like you to meet Professor

Justin Warmflash. His field is the American Revolutionary period and he's come to help us to destroy the factory."

Justin gave Lorrie a startled look. Briggs stood up to formally shake his hand. "A pleasure to be sure." She sat down again with her purse in her lap.

He was led behind the pulpit and left there, a droplet of sweat sliding down his spine. He studied the face of proud Lorraine seated expectantly in the front pew. He cleared his throat. He jiggled his nose to adjust his glasses. Then he gave all the reasons he could think of to use restraint. They must try every possible means of peaceful persuasion. They must plead with whomever they found to be the offenders. They must win the people to their side, seek justice through the courts, and peaceful change at the polls. The law must be preserved. The federal elective system must be preserved. Sanity should be their goal. Not more madness.

His lecture was over but the wall remained. Faces listening for the bell again, faces waiting for freedom. Lorrie looked stricken. Somebody coughed. Somebody said: So what else is new? But it was Briggs who finally helped out.

"In point of fact, Mr. Warmflash, we have already tried all the legal and political means we possess."

Fenskie stood up. "Pollution, man. If we sit and make nice, the earth ends up a gas chamber, dig? There won't even be anyone to turn us into soap, like it shouldn't be a total loss."

"Professor," said Willoby to the ceiling, "you're a horse's ass."

"You teach the American Revolution?" Viola asked. "What does the American Revolution have to learn from you?"

"Look," Justin pleaded, reaching out with both hands for Lorrie's attention, for she had turned away, "things are not as bad as we think."

This time even he heard the noise. Nick made for the light switch as if intending to go right on through the wall. Willoby dug his arm into his side pocket. Viola leaped onto the stage but Lorrie had beat her to it calling desperately for the lighter which Willoby had already thrown and which hit her in the stomach where she trapped it with both hands and grunted. Fenskie had produced a large box from under one of the pews and was hurrying forward, Briggs running with him opening the box and pulling out what looked to Justin like sticks of dynamite. Then he was slapped into darkness again. Strong hands lifted him as if rearranging an end table and dumped him into a front pew. On stage he saw a small flame giving birth to three other flames that burned, each with the deadly calm of a slow fuse. Justin decided to run but two log-sized arms held him in place.

"Double, double, toil and trouble," Briggs burbled.

"Fire burn and cauldron bubble," Lorrie trebled.

"When will we three meet again?" Viola murmured.

"I'd like to have the lights turned on in here and that's a fact," said a familiar voice from the rear. Nothing happened. "Hop to it, son, cause the darkness makes me real nervous."

Someone snapped the switch to reveal three crouching figures holding candles on the stage in what looked like a rehearsal of the weird sisters scene from a summer stock production of *Macbeth*. The performers consisted of a Las Vegas Pocahontas, an innocent-looking buxom blonde with a lopsided smile, and the local school-marm who had never acted before. Evidently the management had to make do with local talent.

Sheriff Honeycutt came marching down the aisle with a deputy behind him, a dazed, all-American crew-cut type holding a wicked nightstick. He used the end of it to touch his forehead, his stomach, his left shoulder, his right.

"Sorry to come bustin' in on you like this but I'm lookin' for Private Nicolas Columbo."

"He's in sick bay," Lorrie said.

"Not any more, he's not." The sheriff was glancing around the room. So was Justin.

"Well, if he ain't there no mo'," said Willoby, turning it on a bit thick, "then dar's only one place dat Lazy Nick could be."

"Where's that?" Honeycutt asked.

With a black hand over his heart and a sad upturned face, he said: "In dat big sick bay in de sky."

The sheriff pointed angrily with his only arm. "Button that lip, boy. We ain't had no racial occurrences hereabouts and that's a good record for a town to have. So you just button that lip tight shut or we're liable to have all kinds of occurrences that you won't be too keen about. See what's in back, Moe."

The young deputy, stunned by the obscenity of Viola's naked pelvis, went reluctantly out of the room and came back. He shook his head and became engrossed again in her sculptured abdomen. The sheriff, still angry, asked what everyone was doing here. Lorrie explained that they were rehearsing a play and that they had permission.

"And you, son. What are you doing here?"

"I'm a film director," Justin said. "I came to see if I could put it all on film."

"That a fact?"

Justin nodded.

"Where's Columbo at?" the sheriff barked. No one spoke. The sheriff moved about the room, stopping now and then to scratch his knee. "I said where's Columbo at?"

"In point of fact, we haven't seen him in a week."

The sheriff wasn't listening. He had maneuvered himself near one of the empty pews and now thrust his hand inside Lorrie's unguarded shoulder bag.

"That's private property," she shouted but too late for Honeycutt had fished out and held up a large dirty silver key. Everyone knew what door it belonged to. Willoby reared up to decimate the sheriff. Moe brandished his club and backed off as Lorrie jumped from the stage to throw her arms around the enraged black man.

Briggs stepped forward. "We demand to see your search warrant."

"You got a big pair of balls, buddy, reaching into a chick's bag like that." And Viola snapped her fingers at him.

Fenskie agreed. "Yeah, man, you're outa line."

The sheriff achieved quiet by stamping his foot. "This here key is the duly authorized property of the recently deceased Selective Service Office. You, young lady, are charged with arson. Come with me."

Much hubbub and clashing of voices until Justin shouted: "*Hold it. Everybody hold it.*"

"You hold it, son. You're a stranger around here. Now don't go hurtin' yourself none."

"Sheriff, may I speak to you a minute?" Justin walked off into a corner of the room. "Privately, that is."

"You horse's ass. What've you got to say to pigs you can't say right out in fronta everybody?"

"Yeah, man, we rap together or we don't... "

Lorrie interrupted. "Sheriff, please go and speak to him. He may help."

"Don't need no help and that's a fact."

"Sir, I am one of your voluntary firemen. Surely you'll extend to me the courtesy of a private word. I am unarmed and, in the presence of violence, I tend to faint a lot. There will be no danger to yourself, I assure you. I also have some vital information that I'm sure you'll want to know about."

They were like actors on stage when no one knows the next line. The sheriff loosened and tightened his cap. He strolled over to where Justin was standing, his hand on his holstered gun, his oatmeal face puzzled and curious. They spoke together softly.

"I ain't got much time, son. I gotta make an arrest and then I gotta referee a softball game, so make it fast."

"Fast it'll be. The man who bribed you to conduct this investigation has no intention of paying off if it results in the arrest of his daughter. Her second arrest in a week, in fact. Now don't look so shocked, Sheriff. There was a bribe and you accepted it. So far it was only verbal. My assistant was photographing the fire and has a revealing sequence of you talking privately with Mr. Benglesdorf. Your lip movements are particularly readable. Now I understand this is an election year, Sheriff, and I've heard you've done a sterling job. You certainly don't want a lot of damaging charges concerning you and bribery. My suggestion, sir, is for you to take that key and talk with Mr. Benglesdorf before you do anything official. Nothing will be lost. Lorraine won't hijack a plane to Cuba and Mr. Benglesdorf will be most interested, I assure you, in who it is you intend to arrest."

The sheriff studied this smooth-talking Manhattan wise-ass who kept twitching his nose to adjust his glasses and who looked as sickly pale and helplessly intellectual as someone who collects books instead of women or prefers wine instead of beer. The sheriff bent to scratch his knee and stood up straight again.

"Son, you ain't no fun at all. I could pull you in right now for bad-mouthin' an officer of the law as to his moral conduct and that's a fact. But I'll talk to Hirum first, like you say. But if he gives me the green light then, son, I'm pullin' you in, too. Now is that understood?"

Without another word he and his deputy together loudly ascended the stairs. Justin fell, rather than sat, onto a stack of hymnals. Lorrie hurried over and kissed him. The others moved closer. Honeycutt was gone. How did he do it? Columbo was gone, said Justin. How did they do it? There was a kennel of cat smiles.

"Well?" he asked.

"Hail Columbo," Lorraine cried as though summoning up the patron saint of army privates, "appear to us so that we may worship thee."

"Like dig, man," Fenskie said, pointing, "you'll plotz when you see this one."

From behind the Lifeguard Christ, stepping away from the hollowed-out back portion of the sunburned facade (incomplete due to lack of funds) appeared, miraculously, PFC Columbo, a perfect fit, arms still outstretched as if frozen in the act of transmitting semaphore.

"You know, without nails it's really tough to stand like this."

There were no new days in Hirum's life. Each was a rerun of a day already lived through. He had once been obsessed with wealth.

Yet the more he had the more it increased his need for all those things that weren't for sale. He once possessed a lusty appetite for a pretty girl named Cathrine Rose who spoke with more elegance than any woman he had ever known and whose calm and unflustered self-respect made him take her at her word, made him value her as highly as she did herself, and eventually made him marry her. But later he found he had allowed into his life forever a woman who loved plants and Simenon novels and her husband, in that order; a woman who was, as no secretary of his ever was: reliable, calm, and unflustered. She had sex the same way. She even had a child that way. Later when he made a great deal of money, she was pleased. But she was just as pleased with a new plant or a new Simenon. If one of her plants died she took it calmly. When she read a Simenon and didn't like it, she simply bought another. She had his novels sent to her two or three at a time from Paris. There were hundreds of novels in all, and she read slowly; she read French very slowly. If she ordered a book and the wrong one came, she didn't really mind. She sent it back with a note. She never became agitated. Even when things did bother her, as when she and Hirum disagreed on what was best for Lorraine-Louise, she remained unflustered.

Meanwhile her husband, with each daily rerun of his days, felt more and more as if he were going to explode. He took a mistress. It was an attempt to keep all suspense in his life from fading away completely. She was the third in a series of secretaries: one was fired for incompetence; the other left to get married. The new one, whom he hired because she had excellent references from New York, was almost as bad as the one he had fired. But he let her stay because she was young and small like an oyster you swallow whole; because she had excellent legs, pale as ice cream; and because she laughed at anything he said that was even remotely funny. Sometimes she even laughed at things he never intended to be funny. Finally, he let her stay because at first she seemed nervous, which made him feel confident, and because one day when he knelt to pick up a fallen page of notes and kissed the knee of the leg she had crossed to support her steno pad, giving himself a mild electric shock, she even laughed at that too.

At the end of the day he offered to drive her home. She said OK and sat beside him in the car ready to laugh at anything. But instead, he told her a long story of the landing in Normandy during the great invasion and how most of his company had been killed on the very first day. He described how the enemy fire had kept them tied down on the beach and how the ocean's waves that morning had turned dark red. She shook her head many times and said what a terrible, terrible thing the Korean War had been. He thought it best not to correct her as to the exact war he was talking about.

Meanwhile he was getting dangerously close to her home. He turned quickly into a side road of dark woods and held his breath. She said nothing. He stopped the car and cut the engine. Still she said nothing. He stared at her. She was like a work of art which he couldn't decide whether to own or where to place her once he did. She made a comment on how still the night was. He cut the lights. It had been fifteen years since he sat maneuvering this way with a girl in a car and he realized to his chagrin that he had forgotten all he knew. How does one get close? How does one get the arm around? Silence exposed his stupidity. The hell with it. He asked if he could kiss her. As if he had requested the next dance, she gave her polite and formal permission. A few moments later she said: Isn't this dangerous? He said he had news for her. In life, one way or the other, everything is dangerous. She thought this over, or at least didn't reply. She allowed him to kiss her again. Yet an important part of her was absent as if she didn't care. What was missing gave him room for guilt. He dropped her off in front of her house, said Adios, and drove back.

Waiting for a red light a few blocks from his home he noticed her pocketbook on the floor of the car. He could have put it in the trunk compartment and returned it to the office in the morning. But fear listed it as Exhibit A and advised him that it was highly incriminating. So he drove all the way back to the office and placed it on her disorderly desk. Then a delicious curiosity made him open her purse and reach in. He had all the time in the world yet he hurried like someone who had climbed through the window. A letter! But it was only from a pen pal who lived in India: evidently someone with whom she had corresponded since high school, or so the letter implied. The boy's English suffered from bumps and collisions. One line even made the lawyer smile. "You should stay proud to being an American," it said, "for American is the greatest country of the Twentieth Century Fox."

Not so pleasant was what he found when he opened her wallet. There to his disgust when he glanced quickly at the date on her driver's license was the same date of birth to the year and the month as his daughter Lorraine. He stuffed everything back into the bag and decided that two kisses and a car ride were as far as he would go. Wait, there was her knee. Three kisses, then, and a car ride. Could that be considered adultery? Or worse yet, a kind of symbolic incest? Nonsense. He recommended that charges be dropped. Tomorrow he would tell her that a mistake had been made. It was all a misunderstanding.

He lurched as if stuck with a pin as the door to the office popped open and into the room she walked. When she saw him she gave a sigh of relief. Her mother and sister were away, she said, and without her key she couldn't get in. She had phoned his home and asked Mrs. Benglesdorf to please have her husband return to the office because she had left her purse on her desk. Mrs. Benglesdorf said she would refer the message. The secretary frowned. She hoped she had done the right thing. He assured her she had. He held out the purse. She told him how very wonderful he was to have gone to all this trouble for her. Very, very wonderful, she purred, approaching to put both arms slowly around his neck. She kissed in a way she hadn't dared to in the car. She kissed in a way that proved to him she knew a lot of things at eighteen that his daughter at eighteen surely didn't know and would hopefully never learn.

Next she unbuttoned her coat and let it drop to the floor as if she never intended to use it again. You're only eighteen, he said nervously. She thanked him for the compliment but she was much,

much older than eighteen, she said. Much. And she laughed. He was forced to tell her of the date he had seen in her wallet. "Well, you forgot to look at the name," she said, "because that driver's license belongs to my sister. I lend her mine when she wants to go drinking." Then taking his hand and placing it on her cashmere-coated soft left breast, Camilla Epps smiled.

Cathrine Benglesdorf believed her husband to be a jovial man. His desperation was something neither she nor anyone else ever suspected. Yes, he was remote at times; at other times, filled with a splendid rage. Yet he was energetic and a good provider always. Rigid in his ideas about children, but a fine example of success in the eyes of his community. Never would she have believed that he was just as unhappy as she.

Whenever business beckoned from New York he took Camilla along. He ensconced her in their hotel room, met Lorraine-Louise in some elegant East Side restaurant, fed her a three-course dinner while he remained faithful to a diet of salad plus yogurt, and imagined with delight that the waiters considered her his paramour. He drove her to her home in Brooklyn Heights, refused to go up because he was late already, hurried back to his hotel to turn off the TV set Camilla was invariably watching and ordered two splendiferous steaks with red wine and dessert.

When she was away at school, he and Lorraine talked by phone and wrote long letters to each other. But there was no substitute for having her with him, however infuriatingly argumentative those meetings had become. The hours spent with his daughter were simply the most important in his life. Cathrine knew this and didn't mind. Camilla also knew and pretended not to mind. When he had to choose between spending an evening with his wife or with Camilla, he chose Camilla and called it work; and his wife, who knew how often work occupied a lawyer's evenings, didn't mind. But when he had to choose between an evening with Camilla or one with his daughter, he always chose his daughter and Camilla knew and hated it. She was more jealous of his daughter than of his wife because she knew he considered one a chore and the other a pleasure. What she wanted was that in his life she, Camilla, be the only pleasure because he provided so little in hers.

One weekend she decided on a test of strength. They had planned to visit Philadelphia but he changed his mind when Lorraine-Louise phoned to say she was coming home to see her mother who was sick with the flu. Camilla presented him with an ultimatum. Either he take her away for the weekend as promised or she would accept an invitation to go skiing with a "young gentleman who is so very, very eager to reinstate himself," as she put it, "back into my romantic interests." Hirum raged like a wounded beast and even threw an expensive ceramic ashtray against the wall of his office.

But that weekend he saw his daughter. Thinking herself defeated, Camilla went off to the movies with her sister, Ellie, while Hirum went off to several parties and got drunk with his daughter and drove off the road into a snowbank because all he could see was Camilla Epps in Stowe, Vermont, absorbed in the endless movements of a moist copulation with an imported Bavarian stud. Singing how he wished he were in the land of cotton, o' times darn and not forgotten, he still couldn't forget the two of them up there in that bed having changed positions in his mind so that she was on top now beginning that several-times-fast and several-times-slow and several-times-fast again teasing movement of hers that he and God knows how many other men knew only too well. And by the time he had backed the car out of the snowbank they had changed positions again and she was now backing herself up to him, gripping the bedpost and moaning and pleading for the Bavarian stud never to cease bucking and skewering until she had exploded into that star-studded oblivion which were the words she had used to describe what she felt on the leather couch of his inner office after she returned to retrieve her purse on the day he kissed her knee once and her lips twice and then decided never to touch her again.

Strangely it was not during the act of love that evening in his inner office but afterward as he sat on the couch and watched her bend and shoulder her impressive breasts back into a bra and watched her decorate her pelvis with that flimsy, artful, tight lace doily and watched her wrestle up into her sweater and step down into her skirt and put on her shoes and comb out her hair and color her lips and then watched her just sitting there so innocent, as if waiting for another session of dry dictation; it was not until then, with the admiration and pity and need he felt for her, that he realized that he, a small-town lawyer, was already way out over his head and being swept away by something unpredictable and dangerous and terribly long-lasting.

But then the Canadian Club washed Camilla away and Vermont, too, in a sudden 100 proof wave of guilt and grief causing him to hug his virgin daughter in the safety and misery of his dark garage and swear through his tears to protect and defend her forever.

Yet only once did he get a chance to physically defend his little girl. Usually there was nothing more he could do than provide a protective shield of wealth between her and the world's truth, a truth she usually refused to be protected from anyway. His big chance came, however, during a walk one night from the restaurant to his car. Camilla was waiting for him in a hotel on Central Park South and Justin was waiting for her in his apartment in the West Village. Both father and daughter informed each other of how pressured they were by work and Lorrie said that this time there was really no need for him to drive her home. At dinner there had been more of that infuriating argumentativeness. Now in the street they were talking again about pleasant things. Hirum paused in front of a shirt store while his daughter, seeing a dress boutique up ahead, kept walking. At that moment a drunk appeared from a doorway, spotted Lorrie's anti-Vietnam war button, and denounced her as being a degenerate Communist shit. Lorrie, made happy by the wine and guilty by the opulence of the food, replied that the gentleman was himself a bag of freeze-dried, grade B Pentagon vomit. The drunk pushed her and she nearly fell. Hirum lurched forward.

Physical turbulence, sudden and angry, stabbed her with fear. In a moment the drunk was leaning against the building with a baffled look and a bloodied cheek. The act of violence (the first she had ever witnessed closely) was like a terrible crack of thunder that hammers painfully at all the nerve ends in the body. She turned away and with both hands at her mouth, fought to hold down her dinner.

Cathrine Benglesdorf's Lady Aurelia needed transplanting. She broke a small clay pot with a carpenter's hammer and placed the pieces in the bottom of a larger pot to allow for drainage. She lowered the plant inside with enough fresh soil so that the base of the stem was half an inch below the top of the pot. Then she pressed down with her thumbs to depress the dirt but not the roots. It gave her pleasure, when she was finished, to see her hands coated with earth.

When Lorraine came home her mother took one look at her filthy baggy slacks and stained sweater and asked her to please shower and change because they were having a guest for lunch. Lorrie moaned when she learned who their guest was and begged to be excused. She had important things to do, she said, but her mother insisted. In retribution Lorrie called her guest a dirty name. Cathrine said, now really. Lorrie tried an even worse name and her mother chased her from the kitchen with the spray she used on the plants. For a moment the older woman felt like a giggling school-girl. Her daughter, she noticed, hadn't joined in the laughter. In fact, even when she first came in, she seemed rather sad.

Upstairs, Lorraine selected the ugliest dress she owned. It was puffed out at the shoulders and had a choke collar like a constant admonition against sin. Its pleated skirt hung low enough even for a preacher's wife. This frightening ensemble she had worn to a high-school dance and now she stared at the mirror in bemused silence at the gawky, tasteless child she once had been.

Everyone at lunch said how lovely she looked. Her father meant that at least she wasn't all naked thighs and braless breasts. Her mother had to say something nice because it was she who had made the dress. But she knew it was out of fashion by two decades at least and worried what their guest might think of their daughter's taste. Personally, their guest liked naked thighs and braless breasts not to mention thousands of other erotic images his tireless mind could summon up at a moment's notice, and yet he felt that flattery was the best weapon against such blatant camouflage, at least in front of her parents it was, so Colonel Nimols said that she, Miss Lorraine, was the only young woman who could look succulent or saintly and still not lose sight of that little girl inside.

Lorrie uncorked her red-wine-turned-vinegar smile and snapped open her napkin. When Hirum asked their guest how things were going with him and how things were going at Fort Guilbert, the colonel replied, "Fantastically well." And indeed from his handsome appearance it would seem that this smiling army career man lived a life in which truly everything went fantastically well. It would seem so if one didn't know him. Unfortunately, Lorrie did.

She had occasionally allowed herself to be escorted by him because he was her father's friend and business associate and because her father considered the colonel's interest in her to be that of a doting uncle. Also the two men had a big business deal in the works and her father had news for her; he didn't want his relationship with Nimols placed under strain just because his daughter was unwilling to be polite to a lonely army career man who wanted nothing more in this world than a little companionship. But Lorrie still refused. Then her mother considered the problem with her unshakable calm and announced this subtle interpolation:

"It can even be said that, in fact, the colonel looks upon our daughter not so much as was previously suggested, that is, as an uncle but, indeed, rather as a father. Don't you agree?"

Whenever her mother talked this way Lorrie, as a child, would go into the garage, close the door, and shout, "Goddamn shitty fuck, Goddamn shitty fuck," until she felt better. Yet since her mother, now, for the first time in years, actually agreed with her husband about something concerning their daughter, Lorrie thought to herself, Goddamn shitty fuck, and then with a smile said, OK, Mother, I'll be nice to him. Her father clapped his hands and said wonderful. Her mother nodded once, solemnly, like a monk, and Lorrie, just to be sure she was keeping a healthy psychological grip on herself, said two more shitty fucks and went to bed.

But the truth is, she was interested. Not in him as a man, although he was surely attractive enough, but in making the most of that rare chance to fraternize with a member of the enemy, to rap with and psych out, as Fenskie would say, an actual living representative of the dreaded Pentagon. Of course she never dreamed that the Pentagon, or its representative, despite that department's many nefarious ploys, would ever make a bold power grab for her boobs. Actually she had decided long before this happened that the good colonel was mad. But even madmen sometimes behaved themselves and so for a while his hands had remained those of an uncle or even a father. The reason she had decided he was mad was that when they were alone together he babbled like a monkey who knew three subjects only: war, money, and sex. For example, he described to her in detail all the newest weapons their government had invented so that our boys could kill more quickly and easily and in more and more horrible ways. Lorrie took as much of this as she could and then politely asked him to change the subject.

He then told her all about his business investments which his many connections through the army had enabled him to secure. He had bought land in Vietnam, which he expected to triple in value when we won the war. He was also involved with a number of foreign firms that traded with Hanoi and which would make great profits should we ever lose the war. Finally he had vast stockholdings here in America which could not fail to make him rich should the war never end at all. Lorrie asked him to change the subject.

He then enlightened her as to the latest sexual news from around the world: of naked women wrestling in mud on the stage in Hamburg, an act followed by five people having group sex who, when needing a sixth to even things up, called upon and always received at least one male volunteer from the audience; or of a powerful organization dealing in slave traffic that abducts young females who shop alone in Paris boutiques by dropping the floor out from under them in private dressing rooms after first inspecting the victim's physical qualifications through a one-way mirror; or of six American soldiers giving a helicopter airlift to two Vietnamese women who were forced to engage in a sexual gang-bang under threat of being pushed out high above the jungle and then, when the rape was complete, being pushed out anyway. Lorrie asked him to change the subject.

But that only brought him back again to his description of the army's newest weapons. A smooth date, he wasn't.

But when he grabbed her in the cloakroom with Justin standing there to witness some on-the-spot sexual news from around the world she decided that she had had quite enough of Colonel Nimols and would never see him again. But Thomas Jefferson advised her not to be so hasty. Colonel Nimols, he said, would be of great use to her in the grand design.

"And how is your cousin doing down in Washington?" Hirum asked, as they ate their hors d'oeuvres.

"Fantastically well. I received some classified information from him just today." There was a pause while he flaunted his secrets in silence. Abruptly, and with great charm, he gave an exhibition of how a good man pulls himself free of the worrisome problems of America's survival; that is, he complimented Mrs. Benglesdorf on the table setting. Before she could thank him, her anxious husband asked if he had received, from his cousin in Washington, any inside information as to what was really happening in the nation's business community.

"They're having a run on swords," said Lorrie, buttering a piece of bread.

Everyone laughed. But the men were laughing uphill.

"My congratulations, sir," said the colonel to his host, "your charming wife is the greatest cook in the world and your beautiful daughter is the greatest wit in the world."

Cathrine smiled. "That's quite a compliment, Colonel, coming as it does from the greatest critic in the world."

Lorrie applauded and the colonel said: "Miss Lorraine, I see now where you get your wonderful sense of humor. Hi-rum, you are a lucky man. I drink to the charm and beauty of your wife and daughter."

Cathrine, pleased with herself, nodded graciously. Lorrie released a sour smile. Four glasses were raised, tapped together, and the wine that Colonel Nimols had brought as a gift was tasted and found to be vinegar. Apologies and counter-platitudes were thrust politely back and forth. Hirum went down to his wine cellar for reinforcements while smiling Lady Cathrine went off into the kitchen to assemble the second course.

"Miss Lorraine," the colonel asked, now that the two of them were alone, "do you know where I've been for the last half hour?"

She shrugged. "I give up."

"With my head between your legs."

The clock could be heard in the wood-paneled den.

"You're a smash at the dinner table, let me tell you, boy."

He grinned with gleaming teeth. "There have been women who were charmed by my directness."

"Well, you certainly don't beat around the ... " She held her brow. "An unfortunate choice of words."

His grin widened. "Oh, lovely maiden, open thy willowy legs for beneath that ridiculous dress I sense the delights that await me."

"Shall I tell my mother what you just said?"

"It would place her, I fear, in a state of cardiac arrest."

"My father, then."

"He wouldn't believe you. He'd lose too much money if he did."

"Fuck you, Colonel."

"Ah, that, in brief, is my fondest hope."

"Oh, wow."

"I pray that beneath that stern expression I have touched a chord of genuine response."

Despite herself, she burst out laughing, which caused her mother to remark upon entering the room: "My, what a charming conversationalist you are, Colonel. I haven't seen my daughter enjoy herself this much during a meal since I don't know when."

She decided to become infuriatingly argumentative. Turning to Colonel Nimols in the midst of an overly amiable and resplendent lunch, she asked if he didn't think the U.S. Army's infiltration into South Vietnam was an act of interference into the internal affairs of a sovereign state equal to, let us say, the Vietnamese infiltrating an army into America to support Jefferson Davis and his fight for freedom against the infiltration of Lincoln's Army of the Potomac? Lorrie smiled like a satisfied pyromaniac as she forgetfully buttered a piece of bread and then put it aside mindful of life's never-ending infiltration of calories. Cathrine cleared her throat nervously. Hirum's face crumpled into a frown. The colonel unveiled his obscene teeth.

The discussion that raged for the next full hour ended in a standoff. On one side was the still-smiling Colonel Nimols and his very angry host. On the other was inflamed Lorrie and, to everyone's surprise, the long-winded Mrs. Benglesdorf. Lorrie could have kissed her mother for her support even though the height of Cathrine's fervor was the statement: "My dear Hirum, as regards Southeast Asia and our flouncing about there, I say, really now, enough is enough."

But Lorrie wanted more. Her next question for the colonel was how should those who are against the war respond? Should they, as a minority, respond as the German minority did against Hitler, by doing nothing? Or should they respond as a minority of Colonialists did who opposed King George III, by taking up arms? That, shouted her father, was a loaded question. Nimols cautioned her against talking treason.

"If this be treason..." Lorrie began.

"Bullshit," Hirum shouted.

"Hirum," Cathrine admonished.

"One should not deal in violence," said the unsmiling colonel.

"Look who's talking," Lorrie countered with a thrust of her fork which sent a piece of boiled potato into the breadbasket. "Just look who's talking."

They all turned and waited for the ramrod warrior to give his reply.

"Violence is wrong," he threatened. "Johnson said it. Nixon said it. It's wrong, goddamn it."

"One cannot make an absolute value judgment on violence," Lorrie said, "any more than one can on passivity."

Her father slapped the table. "What the hell are you saying?"

After spearing another piece of boiled potato, Lorrie held up her fork and shook it like a finger. "Civil disobedience, local rebellion, anything but this willingness to be led like sheep, that's what I'm saying."

"I'll tell you what violence does, buddy boy," Nimols said to the young blonde in the puffed sleeves, "it pollutes the life's blood of the nation."

"Exactly," said Benglesdorf.

"Look what it did to the Selective Service Center. American property destroyed by Americans. Ugly, ugly. Violence is wrong, I tell you, and if I ever catch the son of a bitch responsible. Excuse me, Mrs. Benglesdorf. Oh, the whole thing is ugly."

"Exactly," said Benglesdorf.

"Civil disobedience has a glorious history," Lorrie continued. "Read Thoreau."

"I don't have to read Thoreau," said both men, proudly.

"I can't imagine you disobeying anyone," said her mother.

"What about that business of the trees?" Nimols asked.

"That's over and done with," her father announced.

His wife was about to say something.

"I wonder," the colonel put in.

"Well, I got news for ya." Eyeing his daughter sternly, Hirum picked up the phone which was now ringing. "That's all finished.

Over and done with. Period. Hello ... Oh, hello, Sheriff. What can I do for you?"

First the sheriff and his deputy left the church. Finally everyone else did, too. Only Lorrie and Justin remained. She was still furious at his treacherous speech though she knew he would say it was concern for her safety that had made him do it. So she kept still, deciding to try a different tack.

He, on the other hand, saw her universal concern for the world's well-being as a rejection of the specific needs of Justin Warmflash. Thus he was forced to repeat the error all men make: he would prove she was still his by the simple test of taking her to bed. And as luck would have it, in the back room, there was a bed. Actually, only a cot. Something for a tired preacher to use after a long sermon. But Justin was determined to decide this business of her love now, on this cot, once and for all.

OK, she said, provided first they smoke some grass. Absolutely not, he said. No more free pot until she returned with him to the city or went as planned to that cabin in Vermont. She played the time-honored role of the outraged woman whose purity (read loyalty) was questioned, or when attempts at impurification were tried. She threatened to march up and out of that saintly place if he refused to make available to her the means to achieve her spiritual freedom. This presented a problem. He solved it by reaching into his watch pocket.

Soon she was sinking into a cloistered world of calm pleasures and unwinding tensions while he was inhaling an aphrodisiac that seemed to inflate her breasts with helium. She was a solid state, hi-fidelity, ear-pounding outpouring of symphonic sensuality. Then she became a three-dimensional, technicolor sexploitation film of erotic derring-do. Next she was simply Lorrie Benglesdorf sitting innocently on the floor smoking peacefully but longing secretly to be exquisitely ravished. Or so he thought, for his mind had become a late night discotheque of gymnastic passions. There was a thunderous ovation as succulent Lorrie climbed to her feet to answer his need. She swayed toward him with those soft indentations and firm protrusions. She knew what he wanted, she said, but it was not, at that moment, what she herself wanted and she was sure that he respected her own needs enough to delay his until some other, better time.

The hi-fi blew. The film broke. The discotheque stopped. And all love perished until there was nothing left but her hard, hazel eyes. And his anger. You've been in touch with your goddamn voices again, haven't you? he demanded. She could not deny it. And I suppose they told you not to sleep with me? No, no, they didn't, she lied. Just not in the mood, was all. She almost smiled at that one. A definite escalation in lying, she thought. To balance things out, she injected a bit of truth. The voices had told her to go to where the trees had been cut and stand vigil. She had to go now and make preparations.

"Stand vigil?" he stormed. "That was old hat ten years ago. That's like bomb shelters all over again and, and, and victory gardens."

"What's a victory garden?"

"See, see."

"If a vigil is old hat that means you prefer something more effective."

"Well, yes."

"Then why the hell did you tell my friends to use restraint? Restraint, my ass. You mean we should allow the establishment to instruct us as to how to protest against it? Well, that's not what you said in New York. I think you're a hypocrite, Mr. Warmflash. Like how'm I doin'?"

"Lorrie, I just don't want you to get hurt."

"I should stay in bed, safe and sound. With you, that is."

"Balls. But if you keep setting fires you'll get burned."

"So?"

"I don't want you hurt 'cause I love you."

"Hey, you never said that before."

"Well, it's true. I love you. Shit."

"So you love me. Big man. And I suppose that means no one who is ever loved should ever take a chance on getting hurt?"

"Look, what do you want from me?"

"Help."

"In New York, OK. But I will not help you get slaughtered out here fighting this small-town mentality."

"Then this small-town mentality will choke us all. Look, I am trying to stop a war, help the poor and clean the earth. That's all. I love my country and I am trying to help it. If we don't do something soon those hotshot patriots who want us never to lose a war will fuck us for good."

"I see I've taught you too well."

"I'm doing OK, huh?"

"I haven't laid a glove on you."

"Or anything else either," she teased.

"That can be corrected." He tried to move her toward the cot.

She broke away. "I've got to scat. Oh, baby, be a good guy. Understand."

"Damn it all." He kicked a chair and it screeched in pain. "If you leave me now I'm going back to New York. That's final."

She stood with her mouth slightly open. "You don't mean that."

"I mean it, I really mean it."

"You're going … you'll go home?"

"Yes."

"Really?"

"I'll take the train today."

"Oh, God, I hate you."

Feeling tears coming fast, she took it from her purse and flung it at his feet. She turned away. "There."

"What's that?"

He looked down and saw an envelope. He looked up. She had left the room.

"I mean it," he yelled, feeling as hollow as the echo of his voice in the empty church.

Lightly stamping feet hurried up the stairs.

"Screw her," he said without conviction. He picked up the envelope. In it was a letter.

Dear Mr. Warmflash:

I have instructed my daughter, Lorraine-Louise, to forward this letter to you pursuant to our recent agreement of the 10th inst. Therefore consider the enclosed to be in the nature of a gift but with the profit-margin stipulation as was verbally agreed upon in our discussion.

Yours sincerely,
Hirum Benglesdorf

Justin looked inside the envelope and found a check for ten thousand dollars.

"Am I alone? Sheriff, I got news for ya. At the moment we're having the eminent Colonel Wyatt Nimols for luncheon, as my wife would say. What can I do for you?...Yeah?...Yeah, and who was it?...That's not funny, Adam.... You've got to be crazy.... Like hell it is. Circumstantial evidence, that's all that is.... Who the devil is Lieutenant Locke?...For crissake, what do I care what some crummy army man says.... What do you mean, more?...On film? What the hell have you been drinking?...Sheriff, who told you that? I want to know his name.... No, no, I'm still here. Just thinking.... *I said I was just thinking*.... Sorry, didn't mean to shout. Listen Adam, suspend the investigation. You got that?...Adam, I said suspend the investigation.... For crying out loud just suspend it, OK? I'll get back to you later. Just do what I say and don't tell me no different.... Yeah, yeah, don't worry.... Look, I'll even throw in the dime you spent on this call."

Justin emerged from the coffin in the middle of the roller rink but Lorrie had disappeared. Even the cars were gone. There was only the warm silence and a stern sunlight. Down the street came the Negro boy on the bike fluttering his fox-tails. He peddled in a slow circle in the road as he paused to talk. Had he seen a good-looking blonde making a getaway in a speeding automobile? No, the only person he had seen was Lorrie driving along in her father's car toward Lindbergh. Justin said thanks and walked in that direction. Hey, Mister, you know who's pitching for the Mets today? Justin said he didn't and kept going.

It was lunchtime and Lindbergh Boulevard had come alive. There was diagonal parking, he now realized, and a good number of the vehicles were trucks. Lorrie was still missing. Yet here, in exchange, was everyone else. A stranger swung his arm upward and Justin flinched before he heard "Howdy." Others greeted him and it became less startling. Since they were so damn friendly he felt like asking them where the hell Lorrie was so he could slap the check back into her hand and inform her that as of the 11th inst. their phony engagement had come to an end.

He glanced angrily through the window of a luncheonette named EAT. People with dazed expressions sitting at the counter looked as if the food had weakened their brain. Farther down the street was a sign that said QUALITY SNACKS. Tables and chairs, this time. Yet the same dazed look. Courage, he said, and walked in.

Seated, he took a paper napkin from an empty glass and placed it on his lap. It fell immediately to the floor. As he bent to pick it up, he noticed, a few tables away, a pair of attractive legs as pale as vanilla ice cream.

"Good gracious," said Mrs. Benglesdorf, "what was *that* all about?"

"A business matter," mumbled her husband, after he had hung up the phone and returned to the table. "Not important."

He didn't look at Lorrie. His face was flushed. Only the women understood how agitated he was.

"Well," said Wyatt Nimols, pouring himself some more wine, "we were talking, I believe, about civil disobedience."

Lorrie was as agitated as her father and frightened at his smoldering anger. Since she expected to run into much anger these next few weeks, she decided she might as well get used to it. She thought: I have burned my bridges behind me and the Selective Service Office as well. So take courage girl and don't snivel.

"Yes," she said, "we were talking about civil disobedience."

"And the burning down of government property," the colonel added, "whose protection, incidentally, is my responsibility. Mark my words, Miss Lorraine, when I find the person who did it…"

"Hirum, are you all right?" Cathrine asked.

"I'm all right," he nearly shouted, as he chopped with his fork at a boiled potato sending it flying off the plate. "I am all right."

When Lorrie excused herself from the table, Nimols protested. Such charm should not be taken from them. Though her voices had told her to be polite to him, they had also told her to go and stand where the trees had been and so now she didn't know quite what to do. And as she climbed the stairs to her bedroom, her father called out: "Don't leave the house, young lady. I want to talk to you later."

Lorrie's hand was trembling when she dialed Briggs Smith to convey the instructions the voices had given her. Briggs was the treasurer of the Woman's Lib of Salem County and though she didn't approve of pot or God, she liked to believe that if there were such things as voices and if they deigned to speak to anyone at all, then that anyone, if there was any justice, would be a woman.

But standing vigil? In point of fact, vigils were proven ineffective. Maybe this one will be different, Lorrie suggested. Sure, said Briggs, you'll lose all your followers, that's how it'll be different. If you don't want to go with me, I'll understand, Lorrie replied. But would you please help with the posters and make a few calls? You see the sheriff spoke to my father, as Justin had suggested, and I think I'm under house arrest. Briggs gasped and agreed to help. Lorrie told her in detail what she wanted done, thanked her, and hung up.

She changed from her ugly dress into black slacks and a new blue sweater that came down snugly over her hips. She put on a wide belt, loosely fastened, that held up only her pride in her narrow waist. She studied the blonde in the mirror who was studying her. Hell of a revolutionary you are, boy. See what the well-dressed Viet Cong will wear. Go light on mascara, girls, advises veteran

Lorraine Benglesdorf, so the tear gas doesn't ruin that lovely natural look. She smoothed her sweater to augment her bazooms. She put her comb to work disarranging her hair the way Justin liked it. But she felt worthless. What's the good of glamour if the man you love is gone? Face it, he's gone. It's the end. Tears threatened. Oh, hell. Hollow and worthless. Ugly. And, on top of that, abandoned.

To cool down, she placed her forehead against the mirror and studied her stupid, giant, bulbous nose.

With her coat still lying on the floor in the reception room, Camilla allowed herself to be hurried into his private office and across the newly laid carpet to the old leather couch. It was all very amusing just as it had been in his car in the woods when he kissed her for the first time. And now, just as then, she didn't dare laugh. What was funny was that this man, many years married and the father of a grown daughter, was acting like one of those desperate teenagers who strove to make love as if their windpipe had been cut off and that the only way to breathe again was to penetrate immediately. He had unzipped his fly and was trying to consummate with their clothes on when she said no, and again no, firmly, until finally he stopped. Then she began to undress him. He was shocked. What are you doing? My very best, she replied and snapped off his tie. We don't have the time. We have all the time in the world, she said, and removed his jacket, heavy with valuables. When she got him down to his funny striped jockey shorts, she noticed that his erection had gone the way of all flesh (a book her sister had read in college and whose title Camilla had always thought funny) and she hoped she could get it to salute her again. She had been married once and remembered such problems although it was the daytime agonies and also poverty that had forced her to get a painful divorce. But once single she was just as unhappy, for now she knew that marriage was no longer that glittering escape she once had thought it to be.

Well, aren't you going to undress me? Of course, he said, a little too loudly, and once again, as so often before, she allowed her clothes to be fumbled with. He worked hard and mostly in vain as if she were a safe whose combination he had forgotten. She helped for fear that his ten thumbs and her many hooks and snaps would keep him busy all evening. It was just like being a virgin again on the grass in Prospect Park. At last her naked back felt the cold leather of the couch and his weight was like the sum of all the worthless men she had ever known. Again and again "creeps in this petty pace from day to day" (a speech she had learned in high school whose lines had seemed so funny) to the last slobbering syllable of making time. He labored and plundered and totally discomforted her, but she was happy for he was someone important and he had money.

Her happiness lasted a week. Although he gave her gifts and books (which she never considered as gifts) and best of all a second-hand auto to drive anywhere she wished, and although she cared for him and he for her, she became steadily and unhappily herself once again. It just wasn't what she wanted. Nothing in life was what she wanted, no gift or place or man, at least not for long. And certainly she didn't want the rigid life of the mistress; the couch in Salemville, the hotel in New York, the occasional lunch or dinner together, or even the gifts. Though skimpy with her salary, he was amazingly generous with his gifts. Yet it just wasn't what she wanted. It was too secret. No one knew of the victory she had won in catching the top lawyer in the county, and everyone else had first call on his time. Even a Colonel Something-or-other who Hirum had to invite to his home at the last minute when he and Camilla had planned a drive to Bear Mountain to have luncheon outdoors on white linen with chilled glasses of white wine and large menus printed in italicized script.

Instead, in her good clothes, she had to walk four blocks to eat alone once again in a cheap slop house with paper napkins in empty water glasses and no one there even worthy of notice. Although some did notice her. Many always noticed her. Twenty-eight, though Hirum thinks twenty-six and once even thought eighteen. Flattering of him or simply stupid of him? Which? Well, perhaps they'll keep noticing for years to come. Hope so. That, at least, to look forward to. Men always looking is nice. Like that one there. Sitting alone. My, how bold. Must be from New York. Let's see, breaded veal cutlet. Pork chops with sauerkraut. Take a peek. New York all right. Pressed suit in the middle of the week. Buttoned down shirt. Twitching nose. Glasses. Bright, perhaps. Type who reads too much. Passing through, probably. Staring again. Let see, spaghetti with tomato sauce. Chopped steak with french fries. Still staring. Bold isn't the word. Getting up. Coming this way. Napkin on his ankle as he walks. Smiling boldly. Grilled cheese sandwich. Ham and cheese sandwich. Letuce and tomato sand ...

"Excuse me," he said, "but is your name, by any chance, Camilla Epps?"

When Colonel Nimols finally left after a dozen gracious good-byes and several exuberant compliments, Hirum ran up and burst into Lorrie's room. "Where the hell is she?" he yelled down from the top of the stairs.

Cathrine called back that their daughter had gone out.

"What?" He descended like a rockslide. "After I told her not to."

"She said she had an appointment to keep that was very important. Whatever you wished to speak to her about, she said, could probably wait."

"*Wait?*" His face turned faintly orange. "*Wait?*"

"Yes, I do believe that's what she said," Cathrine replied, secretly admiring her daughter's courage. "Why? Is there some problem?"

"Oh, just a small one. Hardly worth mentioning. Seems your daughter burned down the Selective Service Center, that's all."

He explained about the key found in Lorraine's bag which a certain army lieutenant admitted was stolen from him by one of Lorraine's friends, and that another soldier who should have been standing guard and wasn't was also one of her friends. Cathrine frowned.

"There's enough evidence right there to bring her to trial," shouted the orange-colored lawyer.

"Oh, I really find it hard to believe that our daughter ..."

"You might, but a jury won't. And I got news for ya. I think she did it. You heard her at lunch this afternoon. She's been spouting that radical crap for months now. I asked Adam to drop the investigation as a personal favor. I only hope to Christ he does instead of trying to make a hero of himself. Cathrine, I don't know what to do with that girl, I honest to God don't."

His wife was in deep thought. She brightened. "Hirum, I'm sorry but I really find it hard to believe that our daughter..."

Lorrie drove westward out of town along a sinking, rising two-lane road that took her beneath trees and between stone fences and then out across open country. At first she could only see the smoke. Then the four tall chimneys came into sight with their black rivers of filth. The factory was squat, grim, and ugly, fatiguingly ugly, as if it had been built in revenge by the blind. Around it was a wire fence and guards and, mercifully, silence.

She drove past to a graveyard of low round wooden tombs and grassless ground. She expected to be sickened with grief again at the sight of it. But all that happened was that she became angry once more. She parked the car and walked into the gaping pasture of tree stumps, touching a few lightly with her fingers and occasionally studying the circles of years in the wood. Rain clouds were moving toward her from the east. That's all she needed: a downpour. She sat on one of the stumps in the middle of the field and faced the rivers of smoke blowing away from her toward Port Madison. She drew up her legs, rested her chin on her knees and waited. Some Chopin from a record that Justin often played came back and she hummed it into life and grew sad.

Things became better when Briggs arrived with her string of small pearls, and her matching shoes and pocketbook plus her thick glasses that always made her look angrier than she was or somewhat angry when she wasn't at all. David Fenskie was doing some broken field running among the dead stumps, his long hair twisting and flapping, his beard bending, his Lord Byron shirt expanding with air. Lorrie had been delighted to see Briggs. But now she was overjoyed. She hugged and kissed David and Willoby Brown, too, who wandered up to them through the wooden graveyard, doing an occasional leapfrog over a stump, his bald head glistening in the sun. Of course, he called them all horses' asses for getting involved in something as utterly stupid as a vigil.

There will always be these small miracles like sitting at a table again with Camilla Epps. They studied the menu, ordered veal cutlets, and studied each other. Her face had cunningly turned the corner of youth. Its beauty had loosened slightly and become more penetrable to his gaze as though its owner was able now to give of herself in part or by degrees, unlike indented, one-piece Lorrie with whom, as always, it was all or nothing.

As they talked, the check in his pocket began to overheat. Or was it only his fear that he might have lost it? He reached in with a finger to feel its hard edge.

"This is very, very funny," she said. "Fifteen years almost. I don't know how you recognized me."

"You're part of my mythology, that's why."

"I'm …" she leaned forward "what did you say?"

"You're my Helen of Troy, to be exact."

She nodded, cautiously, her face full of nothing.

"But in the myths and legends of my beginnings, Paris had cold feet."

"Oh?"

"So all history was changed. No Trojan War. Or is it still to come?"

"You've been," she said, carefully, "to Paris?"

Adjusting his glasses without moving his hand, he exhaled and nodded sadly.

"I've always wanted to travel," she said, returning hopefully to firm ground.

"Well, you know what Helen of Troy said? Paris is a move-able feast."

This also got him nowhere.

"Did she now?"

"Look, Camilla, what I'm saying is that when I was in high school you were a great sexual temptation for me. That's why I didn't forget you."

She smiled at last. It was the old song and Camilla purred to show she knew the tune. She a temptation? Surely he was making it all up. Yet she waited for more. It's the truth, he said. He could still remember how struck he had been at the first sight of her legs. She snorted happily.

"Why is a man always interested in my legs?"

"Perhaps because he knows where they lead."

Her tawdry laugh turned all the dazed faces in her direction. It was as if a joyful obscenity had entered the room and, since it wasn't meant for them, they frowned. The rest of the meal was easy, except for his veal cutlet.

She had left New York, she said, after her marriage ended. He explained he was here for the summer to shoot a film. She was very impressed. He said he wasn't too sure what kind of a film it would be. She was still impressed. When he said he was searching for a subject, she nodded for she understood what searching meant. And what, he asked, did she do for a living? She worked for a lawyer. Did she like it? Sort of. Well, at least you can get free legal aid from your boss, he said. She surprised him with another tawdry laugh. More followed. He found he could provoke it as easily as touching a button. They exchanged addresses. There was no phone in his room, he explained, but there was one in the manager's office. He was given two phone numbers. One was her home in ugly Port Madison, she said, where she lived with her younger sister and their widowed mother in the very house in which Camilla had been born. As he copied it down, she tapped her cigarette, shifted it from one hand to the other, and tapped it again. The other number was her office. As he copied that down, she blew a thin stream of smoke at his face. He picked up her check. Oh, you really shouldn't. But I want to. She puckered seductively, drawing smoke deep into her body. Thank you, she purred, as two long streams descended from her nostrils. She blew him a kiss.

121

In the street, beneath a cloudy sky, he held the door for her while with his other hand he touched, in his pocket, the hard, sharp edge of the check. On a nearby telephone pole was a poster he was certain hadn't been there when he went in to eat. It said:

VIGIL TODAY

A SILENT VIGIL OUTSIDE THE EQUIPMENT PRODUCTS BUILDING IS BEING HELD TODAY IN PEACEFUL PROTEST AGAINST THE POLLUTION OF AIR AND WATER BY THIS FACTORY AND BY THE AID IT GIVES IN HELPING CONTINUE THE IMMORAL WAR IN VIETNAM. WE ARE ALSO PROTESTING THE PROPOSED EXPANSION OF THE FACTORY TO STOP IT FROM DOING MORE OF THE SAME.

WHY NOT DROP BY AND STAND WITH US FOR A MOMENT TO GIVE US YOUR SUPPORT?

Camilla overlooked this for she was busy noticing herself in the restaurant window. As she and Justin walked to the corner, several men noticed her. She noticed no one, or so it seemed. Justin asked how he could get to the factory. She pointed to a bus stop. Really there's nothing out there. He said there might be an idea for a film out there. She was sorry she couldn't drive him but she had to hurry back to the office. He said he'd forgive her if she'd let him use her car to take a certain girl he knew out on a date. Her face went blank as a wall. The certain girl is Camilla Epps, he said quickly. She suppressed a smile and asked what day exactly would he want the loan of the car? He suggested tonight. She drew smoke deep into her body and blew it back at his chest. I think it can be arranged, she said, but call first. About five. One other thing. When I walk away, please don't look at my legs. Where should I look? Between my shoulder blades, she said, because that's where my heart is. OK. I'll try. But if I fail? If you fail, she said, I'll forgive you.

"If she doesn't look out she'll get burned," Hirum said, standing beneath the threat of rain.

❧ ❧ ❧

"You mustn't worry," said his wife, kneeling beside her plants. "I do believe she'll be all right."

"Cathrine, I don't understand what's happening. Really, I don't. She has never disobeyed us before."

"She was never nineteen before."

"Hell, she's still a kid."

"To become a woman she must be allowed to disobey."

"And does she have to go to jail to become a woman?"

"I should hope not."

"And must she burn down a building to become a woman?"

"She did not burn down a building."

"I got news for ya. I'm fed up with you and with her, both. If you'll excuse me, I've got to go back to the office."

"I'm not holding you, dear."

"There's work to be done."

"Yes, I know."

"Real work. Not gardening or burning down buildings."

"I should hope so."

"Adios."

"Bye bye."

"I bet you never once disobeyed your father."

"But I did."

"How? I'd like to know how?"

"With you."

"That's nonsense. You weren't disobeying him, you were obeying me."

"I was obeying my heart. I was most certainly not obeying you." She glanced up at him, then went back to digging in her garden.

"But your heart didn't tell you to burn down a building, now did it? And if it had you certainly wouldn't have done it, would you?"

"If I had, who can say?"

"Oh, for crying out loud. I suppose everyone is supposed to go around listening only to their heart. Christ, it sounds like a god-damn country of cardiac patients.

When Justin saw them, he stopped walking. They were like hundreds of amputated arms reaching helplessly out of the earth. Slowly he began walking again. He was determined not to be distracted. He rehearsed his speech. Here, I'm giving you back your father's check. I don't want any part of the goddamn thing. I never did. Goodbye. He would throw it at her feet just as she had done to him.

He picked his way between the stumps as though it were a battle-field before the dead had been removed. A paper banner sagging between two bamboo poles announced JOIN THE VIGIL—TAKE TIME OUT TO SAVE THE EARTH. They were all there: Briggs, standing like a lost librarian, holding the strap of her purse with both hands; Fenskie, the mod Christ, in a yoga position on the ground; Willoby with his back to the others, his arms crossed; Viola in a white gown and a headband with only her toes and the murky outline of her bra and panties showing. Looking lovely again, Lorrie was sitting on one of the stumps.

And she was being roundly scolded by everyone. The vigil was a failure. Although posters had been tacked up all over town, no one had taken even five minutes from their lunch hour to drive out and show their support. This after all these months of trying to educate the people about the need for action. It was worse than depressing. They had maneuvered themselves into defeat.

Violence is the only answer, Willoby shouted, his back still turned. They should have held the vigil in Port Madison, Viola said, because that's where the wind blows the soot from the factory in the first place. When Lorrie pointed out that Port Madison was across the state line and has no authority in matters concerning the factory, Fenskie suggested that they organize Port Madison to march on Salemville. Willoby turned as though to throw a punch. You are all horses' asses, he shouted. The only answer is to bomb the factory because the people in this town understand nothing. As long as the factory is making them money while polluting someone else, they're happy. Even if the factory supports the war and the war increases inflation and inflation shrinks their paychecks every single day, they're happy. As long as they can strike to win a raise, though mounting prices dwindle the dollar so that they end up earning even less than they were getting before the strike, they're happy. As long as those supporting a war that is wrecking the country are called patriots and those opposing the war are called traitors, they're happy. They're horses' asses, he said, and we should simply bomb the factory. He spit at the earth.

"That's simplistic," Briggs said.

"You're simplistic," he snarled.

She turned to Lorrie: "I demand to know if you agree with this ruffian."

Viola, pointing at Lorrie, turned to Briggs. "Who is she all of a sudden, our guru?"

"She is a person my instincts tell me to trust," Briggs declared.

"Baby, I don't trust your instincts," Willoby told her.

"In point of fact, I don't trust you."

"In point of your ass," Willoby shouted.

"Hey, man, like leave her alone."

"She's a dried-out twat and I'll bother her if I feel like."

"I said like leave her alone, you bald-headed bastard." This from a tranquil Fenskie in a half-lotus position.

"Twat," said a starry-eyed Viola Testi. "I haven't heard that one since my uncle died."

"Who you callin' a bald-headed bastard, you mother?"

"Like how many bald-headed bastards we got around here?"

"You should call him a black bald-headed bastard," Viola explained, "so they'll be no confusion."

"Keep your fat ass out of this." Willoby told her.

"Fat? It's cute and sweet and you only wish you had it in the sack."

"Ain't you forgettin' somethin'? I already had it in the sack."

"Then you wish you had it in your sack again, big boy."

Briggs said that she failed to see what all this filth was gaining them.

"Man, it is like uncool of you to bad-mouth this chick," said Fenskie, pointing at the Indian. "How do you know I didn't sack out with her. But I don't rap about it in public."

Viola, hands on hips. "What is this, a fantasy gangbang? And me not even getting the benefit."

"You're getting the benefit of the doubt," Fenskie replied.

"*You* groove with *her?*" Willoby's laugh was like a sonic boom. "I heard that when you do that yoga shit, you spend the whole time floggin' your julius."

"Hey," said the alert Miss Testi, "that's a whole new concept in meditation."

"All right. Enough." It was Lorrie.

Viola held up her hand. "Shhhh. President Jefferson may wish to say something."

"Tell 'im he's a horse's ass."

"Cool it, will ya."

"Say something," Briggs pleaded.

Lorrie obliged. "We have a guest."

"Hi, everybody."

All but one was glad to see him.

"You've come to give back the check," she announced.

Justin was startled. "What makes you say that?"

"Don't give it back. You must cash it."

Angry again, he readied himself for his big speech. "Why, may I ask, should I cash it?"

"Cause I'll need that money to fight them."

He paused as though trying to understand a foreign language. "You want the money your father gave me to be given to you?"

A tilting grin.

"I am going to make a film with this money," he said indignantly.

"Oh, I didn't know." She blinked several times. "But isn't it unethical to take my father's money and then ... skip out?"

"I'm going to make the film right here."

"Oh, I see," she said, so calmly and precisely that he was reminded of her mother. "How wonderful."

"What's this check shit?" Willoby asked.

"Justin is going to make a film. Perhaps about us."

"I didn't say that."

"I know you didn't."

Viola pushed herself away from a tree stump and announced she was leaving. Willoby said, so was he. Standing up Fenskie slapped at the seat of his pants. Briggs was still dangling her purse from both hands, frowning painfully. Lorraine jumped down. She punched Willoby on the arm with all her might. She kicked Fenskie hard.

"Goddamn shitty fuck," she yelled.

Briggs covered her mouth. Willoby smiled, and Fenskie felt his rump. In the act of touching the edge of the check, Justin stopped. Lorrie calmed herself and gave a desperate speech on how much she needed them and why they mustn't leave. They must think of themselves as the only six people on earth who care enough to save it. Seven, if they considered Nick Columbo now in the brig in Fort Gilbert. They had to stick together and follow a leader. She didn't care who. But they had to stick together.

It didn't take. With no small degree of embarrassment and mumbled goodbyes, they wandered off. Briggs was the last to go. She promised to stay loyal but she had to baby-sit now for a member of the Women's Lib. So they all left, winding their way through the wooden gravestones until only Justin remained. Lorrie turned her back on the band of traitors and sat on a stump. He smiled encouragement. Trying her best, she produced a lopsided grimace, her eyes filling with tears. She rubbed the side of her face with her hand. She didn't cry. She was determined not to cry. Soon he had to fight back tears of his own.

"All lost," she whimpered.

"No, sweetheart."

"Everything."

"No."

"I'm a terrible failure."

"You're not."

"Am."

"We all have setbacks."

She shook her head and rubbed her face.

"You look lovely."

"What do. You know." She blinked and tears made sudden rivulets down her cheeks.

"A few things I know. And I know you're lovely."

"Big." She paused to regain control. "Man."

With pity added to love, he wanted her more than ever. But he couldn't look at her face for her distress burned him. Yet he had to look somewhere. Her breasts were like sensational secrets badly kept whose presence he was supposed to ignore. He failed as always, this time rather badly.

"You look great in that sweater."

"So much has gone wrong."

"You have lovely breasts, Lorrie."

"Do I?"

"You do." He touched and found them braless beneath the Orlon. It was a pleasant shock that seemed to comfort her. He reached for her face with his lips. She didn't turn away. He was almost there, his mouth harvesting hers.

The sonic boom of Willoby's voice bounced off the sky. "Hey, you mothers."

He jumped as if caught abusing a child.

"Look," screamed a manic Briggs Smith. "The wind, the wind."

For the first time anyone could remember it had changed. Now the rivers of filth were flowing over their heads, eastward, toward the hills. Everyone except Justin understood what this meant. Lorrie ran to kiss Briggs, and Willoby lifted them both in the air, turning around and around in place as Fenskie leaped on his back for the ride. Viola, skirt held high, jumped from tree stump to tree stump singing "The Battle Hymn of the Republic."

Afterward it was known as the day of the black rain. A silent sliver of lightning was seen through the filth. Then the sound of a mountain of children's blocks crashing in all its tonnage. Soon the town was hit by a deluge of diluted ink and afterward everything was covered with filth.

The river in the sky continued to flow directly overhead and no one in town could remember anything like it. The problem was where to fix the blame. On the first day it was simply bad weather. On the second, bad luck. Next it was the direct result of the Apollo moon program. On the fourth day it was the factory. Lorrie and the others saw to that. Posters demanding action had appeared all over town and pamphlets with this same message reached everyone through the mail. By the fifth day Lorrie's newly formed Committee To Bring Back Air, Water And Sanity organized a protest group to march in front of the factory. Half a dozen new people joined them. By the sixth day the number had doubled. This meant that since enough people now understood what had to be done, the rest were forced to do something to stop them. By the seventh day nobody rested.

Colonel Nimols paid a hurried visit to Hirum Benglesdorf and several hours later Hirum Benglesdorf paid a hurried visit to Sheriff Honeycutt. Nobody visited Mayor Kinch for they knew he hated to be bothered by civic problems and because he had arranged things so that even when people did get close enough to talk to him they found it impossible to discuss town business. Yet the problem was getting serious. There were growing demands for clean air now or for the factory to be shut down. At first no one took seriously the idea of a shutdown. A change in the furnaces appeared to be the real issue. Then Hirum learned that if the protest movement didn't go away, the factory would. This was because the expenditure necessary to rebuild the furnaces was said to be prohibitive. If pressured, Equipment Products would move to another state. Hirum grew desperate. Money was at stake. In fact, he went beyond desperation. He went into action.

At the barbershop, he allowed a striped sheet to be placed over him.

"Light trim. Easy on top," Hirum said.

"Razor cut's real nice. Only three dollars."

"Just a one-dollar trim please."

"Most women like a man with a razor cut."

"Just the one-dollar light trim, easy on top."

"You're the boss."

A few minutes of silence was all Hirum could stand. "Bill, something has got to be done," he blurted out.

An arm went up and a pair of scissors pointed at the sign on the wall that said: THERE WILL BE ABSOLUTELY NO DISCUSSION OF TOWN BUSINESS WHILE THE MAYOR IS CUTTING YOUR HAIR.

Hirum exploded. "For crying out loud, Bill, this is important. You're never at your office, your home has no phone, and you spend all day in this stinking shop with that goddamn sign on the wall. Well, I got news for ya, Mr. Mayor, I have something to say and you're going to listen."

William Kinch was the only mayor and barber they had. He saw to that. He had enacted a law that made it necessary for every plumber, electrician, and barber to pass a standard of excellence test before being allowed to work in town. Kinch didn't worry about plumbers and such. But people who wanted to open another barbershop found that passing the standard of excellence test was rather difficult. Even Hubert, the mayor's son, who had been taught to cut hair by the mayor himself, and who had worked in his father's shop for five years, didn't pass. Hubert finally decided to become a plumber instead and easily passed the standard of excellence test although later he flooded the basement of the town library. Hubert reapplied for permission to open his own barbershop. But again he failed the standard of excellence test. He decided to remain a plumber. Afterward, when everyone complained about the low standard of excellence of his service, Hubert would say that it was a damn sight better to work at something you were lousy at then be excellent at something that wasn't worth a bucket of spit.

The way Barber Kinch obtained a monopoly on his job as mayor was to hire for positions in public office only people he considered potential opponents. To these he offered lesser jobs demanding that they sign a document stating that they would not now or ever in the future run for any elective office in Salem Country. Mayor Kinch explained that such a declaration would see to it that city jobs were not acquired for reasons of personal gain and thus be made into stepping-stones for self-advancement. The people liked the sound of this document and eventually the city council, which included the mayor and two of his friends, passed it into law.

Bill Kinch was considered to be odd but harmless. Nevertheless half the men in town went to Port Madison for a haircut. But when they or anyone else passed Bill's Barbershop they waved and the mayor, if he was awake, waved back. He considered this an important part of electioneering and, during campaigns, he used the advantage of being a barber to plant propaganda in the minds of his customers. The sign on the wall prevented debate. But it didn't prevent a monologue. The propaganda consisted of sly suggestions of financial or sexual wrongdoings on the part of others. Then Mayor Kinch would add that he had long considered retiring from office except for the fact that he could not in good conscience leave the town in the hands of such a one as his worthy opponent. That Bill Kinch always won reelection was considered a remarkable track record. It was said that he had charisma.

"Careful, Hirum, 'cause agitation is bad for your heart," said the mayor who looked thin and wasted, like some diseased jinni who had popped out of a urine bottle.

Hirum whipped off the white and blue striped sheet to produce, as if by magic, a furious American businessman in all his double-breasted fury.

"We got a problem here, Bill, and you're not going to duck out of this one. By God you're not, because this town's in trouble and you've got to do something."

The arm went up and scissors pointed again at the sign which Hirum now yanked from the wall and sailed through the open back door where it bounced off the trash can with a clang of doom. The mayor backed away as the lawyer advanced with a thundering landslide of verbiage which came roaring down the custom-made, blue-silk mountain of the man until Kinch backed purposely into one of the barber chairs to try to regain some semblance of dignity. From there, he quickly spelled out the solution, spontaneously and without notes; proving, when he was forced to the wall, that he could still think, when he was forced to the wall.

"Careful, Hirum, 'cause anger is bad for the blood pressure. Now the thing is to make these here kids look like Commies. Make it seem like they is tryin' to screw up the whole war effort and betray our fighting boys while they are off in Asia defending our homeland. In short, they are Commie hippie queers and we must get the sheriff to beat the livin' tar out of each and every one of them. Also the thing is to convince our good and loyal townsfolk that as the factory goes so goes each and every one of their jobs. Thing is to remember that almost fifty percent of our loyal townsfolk directly or indirectly owe their well-being to this here factory. That's the thing to remember. And to get them to remember it, too. Now I believe you said a trim and light on top."

"Beat the tar out of them? I got news for ya. My daughter is one of them."

"If you can't handle your own daughter, Hirum, the City of Salemville will have to do it for you."

"No threats, please. I'll handle her. Somehow I'll handle her. But pollution. It's a popular subject."

"Sure. But we gotta snatch the clean air movement out of the hands of the wrong people. I hear there's money to be made from them pollution control systems. But only if the boys who pollute are left alone to continue to pollute. If the town gets too upset we'll hit Equipment Products with a small fine every year or two. But the thing is to keep the owners happy by passing along the cost of installing control systems to the taxpayer. What we really need is another factory in town to build pollution control systems. We can make this place a financial paradise if those boys are left alone to pollute. So what we got to do is convince the people that moving very slowly against pollution in a good conservative way is the only true American way."

Hirum stared at the mayor in silence.

"So the war comes first. And after that, building more missiles comes first. And 'cause we don't want the Commies to beat us out, getting to Mars and Jupiter comes first. Lots of things comes first. That is if we're good Americans."

"I got news for ya. I'm not convinced."

"You want the factory to leave town?"

"Hell, no."

"I got news for ya. You're convinced."

"Now slow down a minute, Bill. How do you convince *them?*" And he jabbed his thumb over his shoulder at the street beyond the window where a woman in a flowered hat drove past in an old Ford and waved. "You've got to do something to convince *them*. It's your job, damn it. You're the mayor."

Bill Kinch asked Hirum if he had enough money to pay to convert the furnaces. Hirum asked Kinch not to talk nonsense. The mayor then asked if he had enough money to pay for a full page ad in the local newspaper. Hirum looked suspicious.

"Why do you, er, ask, Bill?"

"'Cause that's what it's going to cost ya by way of a patriotic contribution to subsidize your poor mayor's splendidly written open letter that will appear in our town's only paper tellin' folks about the terrible crisis of these here Commie kids wantin' to sabotage our American way of life. Now aren't you sorry you chucked that sign out the door?"

"You know something," Hidum said as the mayor led him back to his chair and threw the white sheet with the blue stripes like a tablecloth over his bulk. "For a long time now, Mr. Mayor, I have seriously underestimated you."

"The three-dollar razor cut looks right nice on a man," Kinch suggested.

"Whatever you say, Bill, whatever you say."

"Well, you're the boss."

Hirum considered the mayor an astute political madman. But a helpful one. And you had to accept help in this crazy world from anyone who was rash enough to offer it. Especially if the country were ever to get back on the right track. Usually Hirum loved politics because it was so much like business. There were no holds barred and the sole object was advancement. Now, the fun was missing.

He drove toward his office at top speed because usually it made him feel young again and manly although this time all he felt was naked around the ears and behind the neck. Usually he looked forward to having people wave and waving back. Today he ignored everyone as though fleeing from a plague of friendship.

It was all the fault of his daughter. She, as the ringleader of this band of rotten, unwashed troublemakers, was personally responsible for putting him in a position of losing perhaps hundreds of thousands of dollars. But he would willingly lose all that and more, he told himself, if he could only keep from losing her. And worse yet, losing her to everything he had always despised including a snobbish, left-wing, ivy-leagued intellectual.

"I'll strangle her. I swear to God I'll strangle her."

For him the problem was a new one. He loved his daughter *and* his money *and* his country. He loved them all deeply and profoundly and he loved his daughter best of all. Yet he could no longer stand idly by while his daughter proceeded to lose him money and attack his country. He had begun to feel, of late, as if he just might possibly explode. His country was the greatest in the whole world. This they had taught him in school. And the freedom to go ahead and make all the money he wanted was the greatest freedom his or any other country could ever offer. This no one had to teach him.

But still he loved his daughter more. Lorraine-Louise wasn't just his grown up little girl who had her father's nose and her mother's eyes and God knows whose breasts. She wasn't just that smiling blonde whom everyone liked because she was bright as a whip and full of spunk and who dressed to expose more of herself than any other girl in Salem-ville of sound mind and body. She was in fact a dozen girls all in one and of varying sizes and he remembered them all when he looked at her, even that earliest of his daughters who toddled her very first steps, arms outstretched to kiss her father while friends watched amid beautiful trees at a once popular picnic site where Equipment Products now stands.

By the time he slammed shut the solid door of his plush Buick and chugged like a chubby track star up the stone stairs of his office, he knew he would have to stop Lorraine-Louise once and for all or have Sheriff Honeycutt shove her back into jail. Or send her to England to finish off her schooling. Or get her good and married to that left-wing fink and send the both of them to England to finish off someone else's schooling. Yes, that was what he would have to do and fast.

When he opened the front door of his office he was practically in tears for the love of his daughter, for the cherished, selfless, tender, concentrated, worrisome, flirtatious love of his daughter which, from time to time, made him burst out with:

"I'll strangle her. I swear to God I'll strangle her."

"Strangle who?" asked Camilla Epps without removing her eyes from the letter she was busy retyping for the fifth time because she kept making an error on the phrase " ... litigation due to child abandonment."

"Never mind," he grumbled which made her more curious.

"Strangle who?" she repeated, this time seductively, which only made him more angry.

"None of your business."

He marched into his office and slammed the door. Camilla placed her hands on her hips, leaned forward in her seat and stuck out her tongue. Then she opened her address book and did what she had been tempted to do all week, she found, with a long, red fingernail, the name Warmflash.

Justin spent the rest of the week trying to catch up with Lorraine the Elusive, while remaining unimpressed by the changing of the wind. "Look, big-shot historian, sheer coincidence is all it is. It has nothing to do with voices or the supernatural or hallucinatory drugs. It wasn't due to the moon shots or atomic testing or the Big Bertha of World War I. It was simply a case of incredible good luck." That's what he told himself. However, to play it safe, he carried with him his 16mm Bolex.

But as his resistance to her cause faded so did that flickering projection of them arriving at dusk in a damp and hollow woods, building a fire that snapped and crackled, and undressing in the chilly air to hurry and try out their strange new bed. Any bed would do now. But she had become a revolutionary fanatic and never seemed to sleep. She kissed him whenever she saw him and told him she loved him whenever she kissed him, yet they were never alone. And when she moved, her breasts nodded as though con-firming his worst fear, that he would never get his hands on them again. Then, kissing him goodbye, she would rush off to distribute leaflets or join the picketing or knock on doors to argue her case before the sluggish citizens of her hometown. His resistance faded because he decided he had been a selfish professional fink who was more interested in hoarding her body than continuing the growth of her mind, and also because he loved her and wanted to keep her and protect her and save her body and because, if the truth were known, the wind had changed.

Even Cathrine Benglesdorf was enlisted to carry a sign. With a lovely green valley sloping gradually away from them on one side and the factory rising stolidly above them on the other, she and doz-ens of others walked back and forth in front of the main entrance talking and picketing gaily. Hers said MOTHERS FOR CLEAN AIR. She didn't endorse the others, certainly not the one her daughter carried which proclaimed THIS FACTORY SUPPORTS THE WAR, POLLUTES THE AIR, EXCLUDES NEGROES, DESTROYS THE LAND, AND IS GROWING LIKE A CANCER. Cathrine didn't really see why everything had to be tied together this way. All she knew was that the foul air was making their swimming pool filthy and probably harming her plants as well. This was what spurred her into action.

Lack of clean air for children bothered her but it had only made her cluck her tongue. She didn't mind picketing for Negro rights; it was just that she didn't want to march with Negroes to do it. Actually, she couldn't help thinking when she saw a black man that he might all of a sudden take hold of her and do something terrible. She didn't know just what this terrible thing would be and she certainly didn't wish to find out. She disapproved of the war because she knew that somehow it was hurting her husband's business, that somehow it was hurting everyone's business, and this was bad because she still remembered her father quoting Herbert Hoover to the effect that what was good for business was moral and what was bad for business was immoral. She was certain now that the war was immoral although, once again, she didn't know exactly why or rather she did and she didn't according to what newspaper she had just finished reading. She loved doing things with her daughter. But she didn't like marching with hippies who needed a bath, disregarded conventions, and took drugs that damaged the mind. She assumed they needed baths although she had never gotten close enough to find out. The convention they most disregarded, according to her husband, was holding a job. Yet she was almost glad of this, for to her it meant there would be that many more jobs available for her daughter. Her husband obviously disagreed for he got livid when people didn't hold down a job just as he was forced to do. But she knew for a fact that hippies took drugs (although their minds didn't seem any more damaged than the sheriff's deputies who only drank beer) because the newspapers said they took drugs and that drugs were harmful and she always believed what she read in the papers provided they didn't confuse her as they did on the war.

Nonetheless life was a funny thing if you could keep your sense of humor. For example, her husband and daughter weren't speaking to each other as a result of their being unable to reverse each other's opinion on anything, yet here was Lorraine-Louise trying to reverse the opinion of the whole country. And here she was, Lorraine's mother, who never approved of all the shoddy-looking protest groups she had seen on television, now actually part of one marching up and down the sidewalk with her middle-of-the-road placard.

When she told Hiram of her intention to march, he said he wanted to strangle her as well, and then he slammed a few doors which was his ultimate form of social protest. But Cathrine knew she had done the right thing because that same afternoon Hirum reappeared to ask her to bring Lorraine-Louise and her young man to the house so they might have what Hirum called a showdown. Since things could hardly get worse she knew they must surely get better.

Leaving the picket line, she walked to where Mr. Warm-flash was crouched in the road aiming his camera at the line of march. This ruined the scene he was trying so hard to shoot and she suspected as much from the look on his face after the hum-grind of the camera ended with a click. Yes, yes, yes, he said, he would be delighted to come to her house whenever she wished and now would she please return to her place in line.

When Cathrine rejoined her daughter, to whom she had already extended her husband's invitation, she was introduced without warning to black, savage Willoby Brown who boldly encircled her shoulders with his iron arm and boomed how happy he was to finally meet Lorrie's mother and to have her here with them at last. Cathrine somehow managed to smile into his fierce, scorched face. The feeling was mutual, she mumbled, as she felt her knees grow weak.

The mayor's open letter appeared that afternoon in *The Home Bugle.* It said, in part: "Loyal Americans do not criticize their country. They don't want to weaken it at home while our brave boys are dying to save us from the Communist scourge. Equipment Products is in business to help win that war and anyone who tries to stop them is no better than the dirty Viet Cong.... They give jobs to almost half of the people in this town. Think about it.... Air pollution is an unfortunate thing. But our factories all over the nation polluted the air in World War II and nobody complained.... I give my word to every citizen of this town to do everything humanly possible to reduce pollution so long as it doesn't endanger the safety of our brave boys facing gunsmoke in Vietnam while we are asked only to face factory smoke here at home. That is until the glorious democratic forces of America conquer global Communism and there is finally liberty and justice for all."

The drugstore on Lindbergh Boulevard had a marked increase in the sales of American Flag Display Kits. Although it was too early for anyone to have written yet, the editor of *The Home Bugle* prepared a front-page headline announcing that letters were coming in at a rate of thirty to one in support of the mayor's stand. When David Fenskie entered a candy store to buy an ice cream cone, the usually pleasant young woman behind the counter said, "You're dirty and have long hair and we just don't want your kind around here anymore." Normally Old Glory appeared above the entrance of the American Legion Building on holidays only. Now it hung there all week without once being lowered; soon the white stripes were all gray. Lorrie gave Mrs. Durkee, whom she had last seen at the railroad station, a cheerful hello but the woman walked right by. It was the first time anything like this had ever happened to Lorrie, who stood in the street as if slapped.

At last he had found something to shoot. It would be a beautiful film about a bitter conflict in a small town. It would be a microcosm of the nation's agony. He could hear the critics praising him already. Unfortunately, he had missed capturing some of the earlier events, like the changing of the wind. Well, he could always restage that later. The best news was the mayor's letter. Now the conflict would not wither away or end in dull compromise. Political polarization made for exciting photography. From here on, it was up to him. The world would soon learn of that rarity among artists, the historian as filmmaker. He saw himself standing in bright lights accepting an Academy Award for the best documentary of the year. There would be a thunderous ovation while Lorrie, in her front-row seat, bounced and cheered.

As the heroine for the movie she was perfect. Her face was photogenic from any angle; her breasts, money in the bank. And by making her into something as public as an actress, perhaps he could keep her from doing something rash. As for the other actors, they couldn't have been better if Fellini had cast them himself.

Briggs resembled Jean-Paul Sartre in drag. With her almost bulletproof glasses and terrible swift frown, she had won Justin's affection and even respect. He, unfortunately, had also won hers for she kept coming to him for advice. Did he think her poster was worded properly? Would he proofread her latest flyer? Did he know how to spell intransigencies? (It turned out he didn't. Remember, said Lorrie, English is not his subject.)

Viola, of course, was a cameraman's dream. She was sex in the art of hippie protest offering refreshing vistas among the motley picketeers. How malleable she was as an actress was something else again. Missing was that ingredient which often encouraged an actress to perform at her best: sexual attraction for the director. But as far as Justin was concerned, Viola was immune. This seemed to hold true for all the men, all with a single exception.

He was the one man Justin expected to like least but who, it turned out, he liked best: Willoby Brown. His rage was a problem and Lorrie did her best to hold it in check. Occasionally, when his anger left him he might recite for them the Pledge of Allegiance while standing on his head, or he might take Lorrie by the waist and lift her straight up into the air where she would beat on his dome with her fists. But when he thought the enemy was present, he grew dignified again putting on sunglasses against the glaring hypocrisy of the white world and adopting his slow, smoldering

Black Panther walk, as though he were making his way to the final battleground and triumph.

On the other hand, Fenskie had no hostility at all. He became increasingly beatific with each passing day and when he parted their company, he presided over a spiritual orgy of farewell. "Love ya, Lorrie." "Love ya, David." "Viola, love ya." "Love ya, David." "Love ya." "Love." "Love ya." "Love, love." "Love ya." "Go, would you go," said Willoby. But when he returned, it was: "Peace." "Peace, David." "Peace all." "Peace." "Peace." "Peace to you too, fella." Fenskie saw only the best in people. He would share anything he had with anyone in need. He went to the aid of those in trouble. He never hurt a soul. He was free and happy and trying always to improve. He was a walking illustration of the modern. revised New Testament and the people of Salemville, in their secret heart, wanted only to beat him to death.

They were all of them perfect for the camera and so were some of the new recruits. Mrs. Swarthson, wearing as always her flowered hat and holding her sign as if carrying a cross to the Holy Land. Sally Ranslick, tall, sad, and wrinkled beyond further damage, with all the really heavy blows having, at forty-five, already fallen. They left her quiet, dazed, and hardly, if ever, concerned with fear.

The only real problem proved to be the off-screen Lorrie, the almost virgin warrior with her platonic camaraderie, her ever-present followers and her completely scheduled, long, manic day.

Then this too changed. The protest in front of the factory had ended at nightfall. Everyone said goodbye to everyone else and to the guards at the gate as well. Some took cars and others the bus and all went back to town. He and Lorrie became separated. He gave up looking for her and went back to his hotel to package his film for shipment to New York. Defreeze knocked on his door. He was wanted on the phone. Down in the vestibule, at the rolltop desk with Defreeze in the room, Justin said hello and heard:

"Where you been?"

"With you up at the factory."

"I mean afterward. I finally get some free time and poof, you're gone. Don't you want to sleep with me?"

He turned. Defreeze was adjusting a locomotive. "Yes, I would like that."

"You would like what?"

"What you said."

"He's still there, I take it."

"Affirmative."

"Well, true love must overcome obstacles."

"Ours has enough already."

"You were saying what you'd like to do with me."

"Put you over my knee."

"Ah, gallantry, there's nothing like it."

"Where shall we meet?"

"For what?"

"To take you to bed with me," he said, making sure that Defreeze was not only out of the room but out of the building as well, the screen door having slapped shut behind him.

"He's not still there?"

"Yes, he is, aren't you. Mr. Defreeze?"

"You said that in front of him? Right in front of him?"

"Yup."

"You're kidding. He's not there, is he?"

"Yes, he is. He fainted, the pictures all fell, and the desk rolled shut."

"Big man. When no one's around, you're a big man."

"Where do we meet?"

"I'll pick you up with the car in half an hour."

"Perfect."

"It will be if I can get the car."

Defreeze was speaking to someone on the porch. Justin didn't bother to look. Taking the stairs two at a time he burst into his room and threw off his clothes as if late for an orgy. Wrapped in a towel, he charged down the hall to shower among dozens of well-endowed

Benglesdorfs vamping playfully in his steaming head. Back in his room, he kicked and punched his way into his suit, wobbling on one leg and then the other to rub his shoes behind his knees. A car horn blared twice. He combed his hair as he dashed down the stairs. In the open convertible, with an elbow on the door, a hand high on the wheel, and a lopsided grin, was Lorrie, a feast for the observant, a victory for the bold, and a pain in the ass for the lucky winner. Which is me, he thought, and waving once he dashed up to his room to jab a handkerchief at his breast pocket, to check his wallet, his tie, his fly, his slightly suntanned and astonished face, and then, ready, hurried off to get undressed.

When he clattered down the stairs and burst onto the porch, she was gone. A car was receding down the street. A man in uniform was at the wheel. Beside him, turning to look back, convincing in her confusion, shouting at Justin, shouting at the driver, was Lorrie Benglesdorf, gesticulating and calamitous, and evidently abducted.

But not quite convincing enough. Justin had recognized the driver and decided there was no danger, not from someone in business with her father. So he sat on the porch waiting for the phone to stir or the car to return, yet somehow knowing they wouldn't. Anger rose in him as he smelled the absurdity of his after-shave lotion. A stranger waved and Justin nodded, agreeing with his fear that he wouldn't see her again.

An hour of waiting was long enough. He climbed the stairs to pack and leave. He had gotten just what he deserved for leaving Manhattan and going into the desert. He was finished with small blondes from small towns. They could damn well clean their own sky. He would go back to where the women were less warm though more reliable.

Cursing, he dumped his valise on his bed. He searched for his best tie and found it like a noose around his neck. Tearing it off, he threw it down. There was a knock at the door. He pulled it open, to follow Defreeze on the run to the phone. Camilla Epps stood in the way.

For weeks now Lorrie had pushed hard. She was tired. She had nailed up posters and rung doorbells begging and pleading for people to save their lives. But things move slowly and there is always something that threatens to explode. She had agreed to burn down the draft board because Willoby's impatience was becoming hard to contain. Now he was becoming restless again. For a while it seemed that progress had been made. Then everyone all over town stopped smiling. The mayor's letter wiped away nearly all they had done.

She simply went at it all over again. Now everything annoyed her although she tried not to show it. She was annoyed by the condescending stubbornness of those she was trying to convert, by the disputes among her friends, by Viola's midriff, Willoby's anger, David's benevolence and Justin's backlog of lust. Not to mention her father, her own father, who seemed able to understand nothing. Or her mother, wrapped in cellophane and living with the King's English on the moon.

As if this weren't enough, there was always Colonel Nimols who materialized at odd times and in strange ways. For example, on the phone: "I dreamed of your thighs last night, my dear. I think that's a fantastically good sign, don't you?" In the mail: "I take the liberty of sending you this charming *Playboy* foldout because it reminds me so much of your lovely self." If Jefferson hadn't warned her against it, she might very well have called the police.

And all this for just one factory. She hadn't started the rest. She wasn't sure even where to start. She had to tame the Pentagon, liberalize Congress, bring housing and fair employment at long last to the blacks, liberate women, reform the prisons, reform the zoos, halt insecticides, lower the noise level, feed starving children, stop inflation, end the war, save the seals, save the Indians, the air, the sea, the land, the earth. She was tired.

And in love. Sometimes she remembered. Sometimes not. Why did those damn voices have to come and ruin her life? She wasn't up to it. Not any of it. Maybe her first fear was correct: she was going mad. Surely she needed a rest. She phoned Justin and his voice was like lovely music forgotten and then remembered. He wasn't angry. Perhaps he loved her still. That settled it. For an hour or two the rest of the world would have to take care of itself.

She pampered her skin with powder and put on clothes he would want to take off. She stole, more than borrowed, the car and drove through the giant cobwebs humming along with Beethoven on his bicentennial. She pulled up, blew the horn and made a last check in the rearview mirror. A carefully casual pose with her arm on the door and her hand on the wheel. He came, he saw, he waved. And disappeared. She relaxed her smile and waited.

The uniform appeared from nowhere. She had to say something.

"How are you, Colonel?"

"Fantastically well. And yourself?"

Camilla Epps crossed her legs like a curator arranging two works of art. She leaned back on the bed, her hand palm down in his empty valise, toying with his favorite tie. She expressed surprise that he hadn't phoned her. He alluded to the burden of work film-directing entails. Her legs seemed to give off a pale glow. The heat in the room was rising. She tilted her head: yes, but why hadn't he phoned her? He reworded his answer. She chose to reject it. Drawn into a major battle, he deployed a major lie. He hadn't phoned for fear that once he had allowed her into his life he would be unable to think of anything else. This she was willing to accept. She grinned and lit a cigarette. How did she get past Mr. Defreeze? She was very pleased with herself. She had rented a room for the night across the hall. Her smile broadened. She rearranged her works of art. The temperature continued to climb. Justin, to change the subject of their silence, found himself humming "On Moonlight Bay." He stopped, clapped his hands together, and said, "So what else is new?"

She crossed the room and sat on his lap.

"I may possibly have guests at any moment," he said.

"Then we'll use my room."

"Isn't that dangerous, actually?"

"Only if I scream and I only scream when I'm bored."

"Ah!" he said, feeling something similar to arthritis overtaking him. He asked himself a question: Why not? The hell with Lorrie. The bitch deserted me, didn't she? And you always wanted Camilla and her legs, didn't you? Well? Answer me!

"My legs, did you look at them?"

"When? Now? No, no."

"When I walked away that time, I mean." She blew a stream of smoke across his bow.

"No," he lied. "Uh, uh."

"Good."

"Really, I didn't."

"You're a very good person."

"Thanks."

"And you deserve a reward."

"Oh?"

"You may touch my legs."

The arthritis was almost complete. She took his hand and placed it on her thigh. It seemed to fuse to her skin.

"I'm not a bad-looking girl, do you agree? Well, a girl gets sick of being hunted by men. It never stops. Anyway there's always more hunting going on than there are bullets in the gun. A girl gets fed up. She wants to do some hunting, too. Most girls don't have the courage, that's a known fact. Well, I need love. Everything is empty if I don't have love. I don't mean gifts. I mean love. Sometimes I get very, very angry. I do. At men. So many are worthless, really. Just bedroom politicians. But I need love. Everyone does. Even my boss is worthless. He's always busy making money. But he's worthless. If you knew him, you'd agree. I left a note on his desk today. It said, Hirum, you're always busy making money. But you're worthless."

"Hirum?"

"He's a lawyer." She blew smoke at the celling.

"Benglesdorf?"

She looked into his eyes. "You know him?"

"This is fantastic. Yes. Actually, he's, well, he's helping me with the film I'm making."

"In my opinion, he's worthless."

"Tell me more, I'm fascinated."

"Later."

"Now."

"Later."

"You're unbuttoning my shirt. I suppose you know that."

With Nimols at the wheel they sped down Lindbergh Boulevard to where the road swung over Creek Bridge past Colin P. Kelly High School and along Route 4 past the lumberyard and the turnoff that led to Tuckabunkwac Road and the old Willis Farm. All the while Lorrie kept saying, No, I don't want to go there. Did you hear me? I don't want to go. But the colonel kept driving and Lorrie, who could have reached for the ignition key, didn't.

She didn't because of what her voices had said, though she was no longer sure of the wording. Could this wild ride to Fort Gilbert be part of the grand design? Or was this latest Nimols maneuver just another ploy ending as always with a penultimate grab for her boobs? And what of her lover now lost to her, surely, forever? She could still see him receding repeatedly in her mind as he stood beneath the porch light with a stunned expression, not under-standing, and she not able to explain that she had to let it happen because, who knows, it just might possibly have been preordained.

He had placed both hands on the door of the car and smiled with his obscene teeth in that energetic way of his that made him look a graying thirty instead of a man older than her father.

"Miss Lorraine, would you care to learn how you can win your clean air battle here in town overnight and win the same fight throughout the country in a matter of months?"

"How?"

"I just heard from my cousin in Washington." He looked cau-tiously up and down the street. "The Pentagon is worried. There's a rumor which the government has killed in the bud. But it could bloom again at any time. If it does, almost all our national wealth will have to be poured at once into cleaning the air. The war will have to stop. The missiles will have to wait. Even Mars and Venus will have to wait."

"How?"

"Move over, my dear, and I'll tell you."

During the ride he droned on about a fabulous manuscript that had come into his possession through secret army channels. It was too sensational even to publish. She decided he was telling her more of the latest sexual news from around the world and she asked him to get to the point. He assured her he was. After a while she didn't listen. She looked for stars in the heavy night and, to discourage tears, evoked a little girl's dream of a great stone fort to which Mad Nimols was taking her and where the mystery, at last, might finally be dispelled.

But Fort Gilbert turned out to be dozens of dull rows of low buildings extending further than she could see. It also had a fence. The boy on guard duty snapped all together and gave his head a reverse karate chop. Lorrie grinned. It was rather late for the army to be up and they only met one other soldier as they drove across the compound and he, too, snapped all together and brought his right hand hard against his head.

The colonel parked between two parallel buildings near a dark drill field.

"They're asleep, but would you like to see them?"

"Whom?"

He led the way, and suddenly she understood. She pleaded for him not to; it was late, it was embarrassing, he mustn't, but he did. He left her, entered a doorway and bellowed so loudly that even Lorrie, backing off into the darkness of the drill field, flinched at the noise. Then the darkness exploded trapping her alone at the bottom of a sea of light. In less time than she had thought possible the door through which the colonel had disappeared burst open again and out into the glare of the klieg lights came a stream of boys as if a bomb in the building was about to explode. They were all in their underwear and it seemed the flow of them would never stop. They ran right at her until she considered sprinting for her life. Except they began snapping all together into a rigid line of undressed robots, three-deep, dead-faced and ready for her inspection. She nearly died. The colonel appeared and led her closer. She felt equally underdressed in her micro skirt and see-through blouse, yet no one looked. They all stared into the far distance as if transfixed by an unspeakable horror.

"How do you like them? They're good boys, these. Some of my best."

As she turned to the colonel to beg for their release, he screamed, "Companyabahhhhhhhh-*FACE!*" They whirled like a hundred doors slamming shut. When she tried to beg him again, he screamed, "Companyleaaaaa-*FACE!*" It was a nightmare that might never end. With each scream, something new and terrible happened. They marched this way and that, right at her and away again then finally, at last, they snapped all together and stopped.

"Send them away," she hissed softly, "send them away."

"Would you care to give them an order yourself, Miss Lorraine?"

She nearly screamed: "*No!*" Then whispering desperately, "Away. Just send them away."

He bellowed once more and off they went like frightened toys back into their box. With great relief, she allowed herself to be led through a different door, up a flight of stairs and into what the colonel called his little retreat. There was a sword on one wall and a framed photograph of General Douglas MacArthur on the other. The bookcase was jammed with papers and letters but no books. She saw a *TV Guide* but no TV. She saw a golfbag but no clubs. He ensconced her deep in a leather easy chair where she tried her best to put her skirt to use.

"I believe," she said, "that the articles of war as set down by the Geneva Convention allow abducted young ladies one free phone call and a scotch on the rocks."

When he went into the kitchen she phoned the hotel to ask slow Mr. Defreeze if she might please speak to Justin Warmflash. There was a painful wait. When someone said, "Hello," she said, "Hello, Justin," only to realize that it was Defreeze again telling her that no one had answered when he knocked. Instructing him to take down a message, she realized she didn't know what in hell to say. "Say I've been abducted to an important business meeting. No, that's silly. Say something very important came up that I couldn't avoid and that I look forward to seeing him tomorrow at my Dad's place and that I remain as always, his, so to speak, only more so."

"Who's Justin Warmflash?" Nimols asked, handing her a drink after she had hung up.

"Who's Justin Warmflash? Justin Warmflash is a motion picture director."

"Should film these boys on the drill field. A splendid sight." He sat down and lifted his glass. "To another splendid sight, your lovely thighs."

"Here's mud in your eye," she said.

He drew his chair closer, their knees almost touching. A train in the valley whistled sadly. Moths tapped the screen trying for the light. The colonel began a long story.

He told her that someone from Hitler's high command had gained a key position in the Pentagon. For ten years now this Nazi, masquerading as a U.S. general, was involved in a diabolical scheme to avenge his Führer. He had, however, made the mistake of writing a book about it. The FBI stole the manuscript from the general's home. The CIA stole it from the FBI's files and Nimols' cousin in Washington had stolen the manuscript from the CIA. Now Nimols had it. The text, he said, was dynamite. It would be the greatest blow to America since the Kennedy assassination. This Nazi, he said, was out to destroy our country. And what's more, he was succeeding.

Lorrie, from the look on her face, might well have been waiting for the bus to Nyack. The colonel fetched a ream of paper from a locked trunk and dumped it on her lap. It was all in German. Nimols translated the opening sentence. "Little did I dream as I ran for my life down a back alley in flaming Berlin that I would eventually get to the New World and, indeed, begin anew." Further into the book Nimols pounced on another quote. "The general was drunk. I offered to drive him home. I took the wrong turn deliberately, crossed the Delaware and stopped at a farmhouse. In the cellar was a fully equipped operating room. In a matter of months my face became his. With the appropriate papers in my possession and having trained myself to forge his signature, the dead general and I, Martin Bormann, became one." Nimols snatched up the manuscript and found a place he had marked with a pencil. "My plan was to steer the U.S. Army into a hopeless, unnecessary and endless war. Only this would sap America's strength. Then, as the Führer said, divide and conquer. But how was I to do this? I thought hard and long. Suddenly I saw the light at the end of the tunnel. Yes, yes, that was it. My job was to convince them that the Holy Grail lay somewhere in Southeast Asia. Heil Hitler! I convinced President Eisenhower. I convinced President Kennedy. I certainly had no trouble convincing President Johnson, God bless him. My only problem was President Nixon. He kept saying one thing and doing another. I never knew what the hell to expect. It made me nervous."

Nimols stopped reading. Lorrie reclaimed the top sheet to read the title. It said: *Martin Bormann Reisebuch. Touristenfüwrer Für Rache.* Again he translated. "*The Martin Bormann Travel Book.* The subtitle: *A Tourist Guide to Revenge.*" Lorrie stared at the page.

She looked up to find the colonel engrossed in her thighs. She tried to stretch her skirt. She wondered, on this muggy night, if she dare ask to borrow a blanket.

"Colonel." She held the tip of a finger between her eyes. "Here I am. Up here."

"Your legs destroy me."

"Colonel, please." She put the title page like a napkin on her lap.

"And your breasts are the horns of plenty."

She lifted the page like a shield. "Colonel, this book, it's phony, right?"

He seemed startled. "Miss Lorraine, this manuscript is a great historical find. Imagine one man, single-handedly, causing the fall of the Roman Empire. And then having the balls to write a book about it. I tell you we have here the very cause of America's decline."

"So why hasn't he been arrested?"

"We can't, my child. He's too big. You would shudder if I told you his real name. And this document, as you see for yourself, is unsigned. We have no proof, don't you see. That's why he's still a free man."

"Do you intend doing nothing?"

"What?"

"I say do you intend doing nothing?"

"I intend to persist until your legs are around my waist and your arms are around ... "

"Colonel, you're drifting."

He stood up and came closer. Would a scream bring help or more madmen?

"Guess what I'm going to do now, Miss Lorraine?"

"Is that an essay question and how much time do I have?"

He laughed, took her glass and went to refill her drink. Relieved, she sought a toilet. She found a room full of naked girls abducted from a magazine harem, their sensual lips barely able to hold back a giggle. *The Story of O* lay on a table. A stuffed brassiere dipped in bronze had been mounted on the door. Lorrie felt more at ease in the lion's den of the living room.

"You asked what I intended to do about this Nazi in the Pentagon?"

"Yes, I did," she said, sitting down and wondering how she could get him and his knees further away.

"That's exactly why I brought you here tonight, my child."

"I was about to ask you that, too."

"I'm an army man, Miss Lorraine. My whole life is army. I love it. But we have to get the hell out of Asia. That's our only hope of regaining our military glory. And how do we do that? We do that by ceasing financial support."

"Cutting off funds, you mean?"

"No, the Senate is too cowardly for that. We must divert the funds instead."

"How?"

"Miss Lorraine," he said, as if talking to a child, "what's the one thing that will convince America to pull its army and its money out of Asia?"

"I give up."

"A greater threat somewhere else."

"Such as?"

"Such as convincing America that pollution is a Communist plot. Then, buddy boy, you will see such a flow of funds as will make your hair stand on end. Get me?"

She stared at him. "You're mad."

"I am angry, yes. I grew up believing in the army. In its great days of glory. Ah, the invasion of Mexico. The War of 1812. The Battle of the Bulge. God, those were the days. Wars we could be proud of. So our course is clear. Pollution is a plot. Pass it on. I swear to you, that's the answer."

"Colonel," said Lorrie, after a bracing swallow of scotch, "Colonel, I don't know how to break this to you but pollution is a problem in all countries even, repeat, even Russia."

"That's just it," he shouted, slapping her knee and making her drink jump in her hand. "It's a trick, see? They pretend to have the same problem. But they don't, really. It's a trick. Do you read me? It's a trick to keep us complacent so we won't do enough to stop it and so it'll grow and grow and kill us."

Her spine was ice. "Then you really, truly believe it's a plot?"

"It's not important what I believe. Look, we've had so many. One more Communist plot won't hurt anyone. As long as it's real this time. That's the point. It's got to be real this time."

Hirum knew that this was the day he was set to explode. He need only wait as he was waiting now for them to appear, as he was waiting now because they were late. The fuse was lit. But what he really wanted was for calm to prevail, for today he had to reason and be convincing. This is what he had to do to save his daughter's life and he hoped to God no one would see how frightened he was.

She was still in her room. Printing posters probably or making her daily dozen phone calls. Her future husband was God knows where. Making his film, perhaps, or corrupting some other young girl with his left-wing shit. Let us hope so, he thought, for then perhaps he might leave my little girl alone.

Cathrine, as usual, was out by the pool fussing with her plants. Did nothing ever bother her? And did this make her more or less of a woman? It was a question he often tried to answer during those rare moments when he had time to think and when she wasn't driving him crazy with her calm.

The truth was he was ready to kill. And he felt better for it and as free of confusion as in those days years ago when he could cheer for his college team and not have to concern himself with the problem of whether his university should extend its boundaries into a 99 percent Negro slum to build dormitories for a student body that was 99 percent white. Now he simply wanted to kill. The trouble was he didn't know who, exactly, or how.

He was ready to explode because Sheriff Honeycutt had phoned him to explain that he could no longer give soft treatment to Hirum's daughter. The word had gone out. From whom, he wouldn't say. But the people were demanding action. The troublemakers would have to be stopped no matter whose daughter was among them. Did Hirum understand? He did.

And when he sat down for dinner he couldn't eat. That night sleep stayed away like someone withholding love. He went down in his bathrobe to sit in the den and rotate a palmful of cognac at the bottom of a glass the size of a cannonball. What's-his-face had called it that. May he drop his camera and break his foot. Hirum filled his glass several more times before the family car slipped into the driveway and his baby came into the house. He wanted to scold her for the lateness of the hour. But, since they weren't speaking, he had to stay where he was, secret and lonely, listening as she mounted the stairs two at a time, her shoes in her hand. He listened to the water running, the toilet flushing, her bedroom window rolling open, a train in the valley crying in pain.

154

In the morning he came down again and waited for their arrival while cool Cathrine puttered in back. Finally What's-his-face arrived with his glasses and ivy league suit looking as if he had spent a poor night himself and carrying a three-eyed camera by its strap. Lorraine-Louise descended the stairs in a floor-length dress holding one end in her hand, her hair up, and thoroughly a lady. She even walked like a lady as though, if she weren't careful, she might slip. But Justin (he remembered his name now) hadn't entered the house after all. He reappeared out in back talking to Mrs. Benglesdorf who took him across the yard to admire a geranium. Lorraine met them beside the pool and Hirum, opening the kitchen window, heard her say that she had phoned his hotel last night and again this morning to explain. But he wasn't there. Had he gone out? I don't remember, he said, and that was all he said like a well-coached witness under oath. She seemed contrite. He seemed not to notice. Hirum, who noticed, was delighted. Then all three entered the house to do battle.

Cathrine washed her hands. Justin offered one of his in cold greeting. Hardly $10,000 worth, the ungrateful bastard. Lorrie took her young man's arm like a grand lady with her bored lover. She nodded in her father's direction with her smooth mask of defiance and Hirum—he couldn't help himself—wanted to slap her face.

While they were each seated with a plate of cold cuts in their lap and Justin's camera on the floor, Hirum rose like a lawyer on his most important day in court. His task, as he saw it, was to defend his daughter against herself. He began by conceding that all was not well in the world. But stability depended on the acceptance of authority. Man must adhere to a moral consensus, a willingness to sublimate one's ego to the mainstream of social values. He deplored the country's growing inability to unite in community membership. He castigated violence, loose sex, contempt for government, the erosion of controls, the rise of self-interest, the unwillingness to sacrifice. He was getting carried away.

Justin interrupted. What sacrifice of self-interest was Mr. Benglesdorf prepared to make? With her little finger pointed at the ceiling, Cathrine sipped her tea. Lorrie, who had been resting her jaw in her hand, looked at their guest in surprise. Hirum said he was prepared to make the same sacrifice as anyone else. In fact, he had news for them. He had already sacrificed plenty. He had gone to war against Hitler and not once did he complain or protest. He had always given his daughter the best even when it meant depriving himself. He supported his government. He upheld the law. And he didn't bitch. Not once. Not even once.

Justin spoke with the patience of an opposing attorney who was waiting for the best moment to present the most damaging evidence. "I mean what sacrifices of self-interest are you prepared to make in reference to the factory?"

"I don't get you?"

"We want to clean the air and stop the war. You want us to end protests which so far have been our only voice. What are you willing to give up? Are you willing to work with us to prevent contamination?"

"Don't worry, young man. The air will be cleaned. I guarantee it. It's a matter of ... "

Justin broke in. "I ask again. Will you work with us to stop them from doing more harm?"

Hirum shifted smoothly into the comfortable position of outraged indignation. This, he would have them know, was a free country. And industry also has a right to be free. He would not join in with childish people who demanded all problems be solved at once.

Justin lifted a napkin to his mouth before he spoke. "Sir, isn't it a fact that when you learned that Equipment Products had decided to expand, you bought much of the land they wanted to use because you knew that with the colonel's connections you could sell it back to the government for three times your original investment? And isn't it true that if our protest succeeds the deal will fall through? Isn't it also a fact that you ordered the trees cut down and the money you made selling the lumber went to pay for the mayor's letter? And that you ... "

"A lie," he shouted, lurching in his seat. "Who told you that? It's a lie. I want to know who told you that?"

A hot, dry wind swept through the room and he struggled for air even as he shouted. Lorraine stared and said nothing. Her mother closed her eyes. He continued shouting but no one heard him, splashed as they were by the caldron of his rage. You will get yourself killed, he screamed at his daughter. If you continue with this stupid lawlessness, you will get yourself killed. She didn't speak. She had the calm of one who knew she could conjure multitudes to their feet. Who taught you such lawless ideas? he wanted to know. He taught me, she whispered, pointing at her fiancé. A wounded animal could not have bellowed louder. I gave you good money. It was to make a movie. Not to overthrow the goddamn government. Justin plucked a folded paper from his shirt pocket and dropped it on the table. You have ruined my daughter, Hirum raged. You are a traitor to your country. Cathrine expressed a desire for all present to lower their voices. Mr. Warmflash was most certainly not a traitor to his country. Now, would Mr. Warmflash like a second helping of caviar? He would, thank you. Lorrie sat dazed by the loss of an innocence she had proudly believed she had lost long ago. Hirum caught his breath and screamed again. You're playing with fire. Listen to me. I'm telling you something. You are playing with fire and you're going to get burned. But her eyes had nothing in them as if she hadn't heard a word. It's not true, he shouted at Justin. Who told you? I want to know who told you?

The sun's breath began to calm them. They walked along idyllic streets, the camera hitting occasionally against his leg. The boy with the foxtails said, "Found her, finally, huh?" then pedaled away standing up. People who would have waved at them two weeks ago, didn't. She looked miserable.

Justin took her arm and said: "I thought the only stranger here was me."

"It's catching."

A man in his undershirt, watering his lawn, glanced at her and frowned. Lorrie lifted her skirt in mock refinement and stepped daintily over his garden hose.

"I have a headache from all the screaming," she said after they had walked for a while. "But what really gets me is how on earth can that man be my father?"

"More puzzling is how you could be his daughter."

"Wasn't easy. Like I said, I got this headache."

"At least you're not sick to your stomach. I hate caviar."

She grinned. "Then why'd you keep eating it?"

"I felt sorry for your mother, I guess. I kept seeing her as the hostess on the *Titanic*. Not wanting anyone to be upset."

"I felt sorry for her, too."

"I felt sorry for everyone."

"Me first 'cause I have this headache."

"OK, you first."

"You're a good guy, you know that?"

Then she asked the question he knew was coming. How on earth had he learned so much about her father's business? He told of tutoring Miss Epps in American History and amazingly of meeting her years later in a restaurant in town and then discovering to his further amazement who, exactly, her employer was. He censored only a few details. The half-naked dash across the hall; the obligatory love scene as they sculptured each other in hushed irreverence; her several times fast, then slow, then fast again teasing motion that, for all of its surprise and delight and regrettable tendency to expedite matters, was unable finally to make him forget the ever-present dozen or so Benglesdorfs who sat quietly watching and disapproving; or lying in bed afterward with this modern Mata Hari who compulsively gave rather than sought information. Anyway it was she, Camilla, who told him.

"I only met her once," said Lorrie. "I remember she smokes too much."

He had been told that violence breeds violence. He knew that apathy breeds apathy. But now it was driven home to him ever so clearly and happily that sensuality breeds sensuality. Or was it only that true love like a pigeon always finds its way home? At any rate, he was delighted to discover that suddenly yesterday didn't exist and that today he wanted Lorrie as much as ever.

"Oh, you do, do you?"

"Yes," he said, "and this time *I'm* doing the abducting."

"Big man, big man."

"And I'm doing the abducting *now*. OK?"

"Well, if you put it that way, fine."

"OK."

"And can we get nice?"

"What?"

"With your golden pocketwatch."

"Well ... "

"Please."

"Well, OK."

"See? You're really a good guy. What did I tell ya? First, though, I promised Briggs I'd deliver some signs."

"What?"

"To the factory."

"Wait a minute."

"We're picketing again and ... "

"Oh, no."

"Not stay. Just deliver. My turn's tonight with Fenskie and a few others."

"You're picketing?"

"But that's tonight. Now I'm free."

"OK. Where?"

"What do you mean where? I'm free all over."

"Where do we go to make love, you clown?"

"Your hotel?"

"No, no, that's not good. For you, I mean. How about your top-less church?"

"My who?"

"You know, your Latter-Day Subcellar of Underground Saints."

She bent forward in soundless laughter. "For shame. It's not a topless church."

"After I take you there it will be."

"Well, after you take me there, perhaps."

Then he asked the question she knew was coming. About her visit with Nimols at the fort. She told the story in detail even leaving in the colonel's running comments on her thighs (hell, self-advertisement never hurt) and also of his drunken pseudogallant seduction attempt: *Voulez-vous coucher avec moi?* No thanks, she said, but she didn't wish to coucher avec him at the moment. Perhaps next time. Ah, bon, the colonel said and fell off his chair. But she did censor unessential details like letting him kiss her on the stairway, keeping in mind the colonel's importance in the grand design, and because she felt sorry for him, since the more he drank the more he became like a little boy, and because he was, let's face it, gorgeous. Since she censored out this first unessential detail, she did so to the second, which was when he kissed her again as she stood beside her car, squirming away only when he squeezed her rump. You know what I do when I get sexually excited? he asked her. Goodbye, she said, starting the car. I give my boys a workout on the drill field, and he giggled like a tipsy lady. Please don't, she begged. But he was already bellowing like an insane football coach and staggering toward the barracks.

She sped from the fort as if she had planted a bomb. On the open road, however, she drove slowly and sadly while vivid ideas for furthering the revolution and bettering the nation bubbled about in her head along with too much straight scotch and the sweet memory of her voices, silent now as were the woods. Her headlights revealed a dead raccoon and she felt the immense tragedy of life lost for no reason and of young love stranded alive.

She led her abductor up the driveway of an ungainly wooden house that needed painting badly, not to mention the replacement of several missing balusters in the porch railing. In back was a crumbling garage; inside was Miss Swarthson's old Ford. Lorrie gave a lopsided grin and produced the car key from inside her bra. Justin noticed that the backseat of the car was filled with placards.

They jiggled up the street in rampant raucousness with Miss Benglesdorf clutching the wheel as if it were trying to get away and, at a corner, turning the thing mightily as though trying to unscrew it from its shaft. When they passed the hotel, Justin looked up at its windows. All was safe if not sound.

This time the sinking, rising, two-lane road that took them beneath trees and beside stone fences seemed to go on forever and the comic, semi-internal combustion of the engine made their every gesture exaggerated as in a silent film.

Viola appeared trying to hitch a ride in black hip-huggers and a halter cut from a faded American flag. She lifted her pant's leg to display an off-white tennis shoe and a bony ankle while she jabbed at the future with her thumb. When she realized who they were, she ran toward them faster than they came toward her, shouting did they have room in the car for an Indian? Justin knelt where she had stood and, with his Bolex purring, shot a sequence of the two girls jiggling in the front seat as the Ford came jogging up the road again. But Viola waved at the camera and they had to do it again. Then he placed her between himself and the approaching car and restaged her hitchhiking charade to capture it on film. Lorrie kept coming, Justin leaped on the running board, and Viola, left behind, shouted, "Hey, you jerk-offs, wait for me." When they finally stopped to let her climb in, she said, "Damn, we Indians always get fucked."

Again they assembled in front of the factory with their small band of faithful, or those who were only friends of the faithful, or even those who were somewhat unfaithful but useful, who came because they wanted to assuage their social conscience and then not have to exert themselves again for another year, or frankly because they hoped to meet girls.

Yet to the faithful it was boring because they had done it all so many times before, because polite protest produces such meager results and includes such endless drudgery not to mention how those who give of their time must neglect the other activities of life in an often endless attempt to catch the attention of that great bulk of people too absorbed in the daily money race to even notice those who are trying to save them, and because even the most important of causes becomes, after years of exhaustion and frustration, finally boring.

But for now, at least, the problem was not hers. Lorrie had only come to make a delivery. She was not due to appear until that evening, for having decided that they should picket around the clock, she had, as always, assigned to herself the worst of the hours.

When they saw the familiar faces they postponed, for a moment, their rush to make love. Justin grabbed Briggs as Lorrie hugged Willoby. Lorrie hugged Briggs as Justin shook Willoby's hand. Sally Ranslick hugged Justin while Viola grabbed Briggs. Willoby pinched Viola's rump and made her yelp and she grabbed his groin and made him bow. Greetings took time. It would have taken even longer if David "Love ya" Fenskie had been there.

Then one of the guards said something. He said it right to Viola's face or more specifically at her firm, upreared, and abutting rump, which she was no less proud of than her sensual lips and large brown eyes but whose ethnic message the guard misread, not realizing she was an Indian whose ancestors had lived in America long before his had arrived to make their money and ruin the land and would probably still be here long after his had died out in decadence or gone away rich. In short, he had called her a nigger.

The trouble was, Willoby heard. No one, afterward, could give more than a sketchy account of what had happened. He broke from the line of march to shout at the guards protecting the gate. That day their number had been increased for some reason to six from the usual two. Among them, this time, was Honeycutt's club-carrying, crew-cut deputy named Moe Mullen. It was he who had gone into the church with the sheriff to search for the key. It was he, after receiving a number of Willoby's counterslurs as to his sub-intelligence and his God-fearing hedonism, who proved unable to take what he had dished out. And it was he, with all of his officially deputized un-Christian rage, who stepped forward and swung his club.

Viola ran and knelt at Willoby's side. But he had fallen less from the blow than from tripping over a crack in the side-walk. Lorrie, who hadn't seen him fall and who was on her way to the Ford, stopped when she heard the screams and ran back. Others hurried to his side as well and suddenly in the confusion, the frightened guards began swinging madly with their clubs. Now the screams were terrible. Briggs elbowed her way through and found Viola unconscious on the ground. Somehow a handful of chopped meat had been pushed into the girl's face. Then Briggs realized that this *was* her face. Or what was left of it. Willoby, on his feet again, stood crouched at Viola's side as if debating how to pick her up. He was so stupefied at what he saw that he seemed moronic as if the problem of lifting a girl in his arms was too complex for him to solve. Lorrie shouted, Look out, Mullen struck, and down he went again. Briggs tried to kill the assailant with her fists and Lorrie tried to hold her back. Sally Ranslick shouted elaborate obscenities as Briggs was struck on the head with a glancing blow and Lorrie tripped in her long dress and fell. Briggs remained upright. She was almost certain she remained upright. But the ground tilted treacherously until she was forced to lean against it as someone would against a wall. Except the wall was the floor and she was on her back with hot flames slowly melting one side of her skull. Blood was on her pocketbook. It made her sad.

Lorrie screamed for everyone to retreat. At that moment she saw Moe Mullen being held aloft, fixed in space, though swimming wildly in the air. Justin also saw him: through the viewfinder. He had hoped to shoot some additional footage of Viola's midriff and star-spangled top knowing that a little sex in the film wouldn't hurt. But he was in the middle of changing film when the trouble began. Finally ready, the screams made him lower the camera and run forward. Then remembering his life's purpose, he set the camera purring. Concerned for Lorrie's safety, he stopped and again ran forward. But the frightening beauty of the mad scramble stopped him and once more he started shooting just in time to see a flailing Moe Mullen being offered to the sky by two black arms. Lorrie shouted, No, sprang up, and tripped once more in her long dress. Mullen was lowered then suddenly lobbed high over the heads of the mob to land hard on the roof of the old Ford where he bounced out of sight into the street.

Briggs sat up, remembered, and bit with all her might into someone's leg. The leg belonged to Willoby Brown, who had finally succeeded in lifting Viola in his arms. But not before Lorrie, on her hands and knees, noticed for the first time an unconscious girl, dressed much like someone she knew, and whose face was a swamp of blood. With both hands to her mouth, Lorrie was unable to think or speak or turn away.

Justin had recorded all this on film when he heard someone yell, *Get that camera!* Two guards were coming at him. Down the sloping valley of dry grass he ran, with the club-carrying madmen right behind him. One fell. Justin leaped a wooden fence with the remaining madman gaining. Since no safety was to be found in the open pasture, Justin swung back to the road, knowing what had to be done to gain speed but discovering sadly that he was unable to jettison valuable equipment even though his life was at stake. When he reached the road again, realizing he must soon turn and do battle, the ancient Ford came blustering into view with Lorrie at the wheel and Sally Ranslick beside her, waving. Justin leaped onto the running board and Lorrie poured on the gas which only meant that the enemy wasn't gaining any longer or losing ground either. The man simply kept running beside the left fender, club in hand, like someone utterly insane and thoroughly convinced that he could cure the world's ills with a skull-cracking blow.

Not wishing to wait and see how things would turn out, Justin climbed in through a window with the help of several rude hands that pulled at his tie, his hair, his left ear, until he was yanked through and dumped onto the floor in back. It took him a while to arrange himself so as not to be sitting on his neck with his feet on the roof. It took him a while longer to actually climb into the seat so that most of him was facing forward while the rest of him looked through the rear window to watch the club-carrying madman slowly lose ground, then throw his stick, then stop and just stand there breathing hard and growing smaller in the triangular road.

The back seat was crowded. To his right was Briggs Smith, her glasses gone, her eyes like those of a desperate sea creature stranded on shore. The cut in her scalp had painted her cheek. She tugged on Justin's sleeve like an impatient grande dame summoning a servant by repeatedly yanking on the bellcord. "My glasses they. Stepped on them." Justin tried to calm her. He seemed to be succeeding. Then she leaned out of the moving window and threw up into the street. Turning to ask if someone had a handkerchief, Justin noticed the stars and stripes and then the sodden facelessness of the unconscious girl. He thought he might have to join Briggs at the window. His part in all this now seemed as nothing.

Willoby, in whose lap she lay and into whose clothes was seeping her blood, sat breathing heavily, not from pain or lack of breath, but due to fear that she was dying. He was trying to encourage what life in her was left by exaggerating his own.

They drove into the parking field of the Southboro Hospital. Viola was awake now though dazed and in shock. Whichever one of them went in with her he, too, would be arrested, of that they were certain. Yet each insisted on being the one to go. Willoby shouted that he was her boyfriend, that they shouldn't try to stop him. Lorrie, who hadn't spoken during the ride and who seemed to be in shock herself, insisted that the job was hers. But Justin had the best argument. He had not engaged in violence; Willoby had, and the result would be a prison term for assaulting an officer. Lorrie had been arrested once already and, as the organizer of the movement, should remain free. Justin, however, was a college professor. Surely that would carry some weight in court or more important now, in the hospital, when help was needed.

It was all done in a hurry. Briggs's scalp wound they would take care of themselves. Lorrie asked Justin to leave his camera behind, certain that now on film was proof that the police had attacked first. And he hadn't the heart to tell her that he had missed the moment they needed. Sally Ran-slick kept saying, hurry, hurry. Justin got out and took the girl in his arms.

"Where are we going?" she mumbled. They told her. "No, I hate hospitals."

"They'll make your face all pretty again," Willoby said.

"What's wrong with my face?"

"Take her in," Lorrie whispered.

"What's wrong with my face?"

Feeble old men in bathrobes made sliding sounds with their slippers and there was the stink of everything kept thoroughly clean. Justin tried to get her to a doctor at once. But protocol could not be rushed. Viola was placed in a wheelchair and asked questions while she bled. A nurse printed the answers to these questions in the proper places left blank on a large manila card. Justin asked that Viola be taken to a doctor at once. The nurse stopped printing on the manila card to explain that all pertinent information must first be placed on a manila card. She smiled. She returned her attention to her manila card. She asked the girl her name. The reply sounded like an old woman speaking without teeth. She spelled her last name. The nurse asked if it was pronounced, Test-e. No. it was pronounced, Test-eye, said the girl. Born? Here. Southboro? No, Salemville. Age? Twenty-one. American citizen? Sure. Place of residence? No preference. But you must live somewhere. No place special. Occupation? Waitress. Place of employment? Howard Johnson, Route 4, near the Salemville Drive-In. Estimated monthly income? Three hundred twenty dollars. Married or single? Single. Who do we notify as to your injury? Richard Nixon. Who else? Lyndon Johnson. Do you belong to a medical plan? What's that? How did the accident occur? Justin demanded that she be taken to a doctor at once. Instead, the nurse asked Justin how the accident occurred. She was beaten repeatedly with a nightstick by a sadistic officer of the law. Where did this happen, please? In front of Equipment

Products building. What time did this happen? I don't know what time it happened, Justin said. Approximately, asked the nurse, smiling. Look, can't she see a doctor while I devote the rest of the day to answering your questions? Sir, the card must be filled out before I can enter her as a patient. Again she smiled, but less so. Did Miss Testi sustain any injuries beside those on her face? I don't know, Justin shouted. That's why I brought her here, to find out. What's wrong with my face? Viola asked. Printing the answer very neatly in nicely formed letters in all the empty boxes on her large manila card, the nurse asked Justin what was the nature of his relationship with Miss Testi. The nurse jumped up and said, Sir, you cannot take this patient into the emergency room until all the questions on this card have been answered. She ran and blocked the moving wheelchair with her body. Listen to me, you bitch, Justin said in a controlled, guttural rage, either she gets to a doctor now or there'll soon be two ladies needing emergency treatment. He was astonished at how easy, even pleasant, it would be to hit her. Wait here, she whispered, as if they had just become joined in a magnificent conspiracy. In her soundless white shoes she scurried through two soundless white doors that swung in and out and in and stopped. What's wrong with my face? Viola asked.

A state trooper, chewing a toothpick and wearing a gun, stood blocking the exit to the street. He had appeared from nowhere to inform Mr. Warmflash that Sheriff Honeycutt had phoned from Salemville requesting that any and all persons who appeared at the hospital from the scene of the violence be detained. The sheriff himself was on his way over. The prisoner was told to sit on the bench and wait. The prisoner had an urge to return a sense of balance to things by grinding up the officer's face. But he sat down and kept busy biting his nails.

Nurses in soundless shoes came and went like corrupted saints, eyeing his good health with secret displeasure. Occasionally, he asked about Viola. She had been rolled away an hour ago after Justin patted her on the shoulder and was patted on the shoulder himself by the man with the gun and the toothpick. No one had further news about the girl. Everyone he asked was profoundly calm. What would they do, he wondered, if he danced? Or imitated his loud mother's popular rendition of "The Battle Hymn of the Republic"? A car slammed to a halt. The revolving door whooshed into movement and Hirum Benglesdorf emerged. His face sagged when he saw who was sitting on the bench.

"How bad is she hurt?" Hirum asked, lifting his hand as if to ward off the answer.

"It's not good."

Hirum sat down and gripped the other man's arm. "How bad, exactly?"

"The face. The face is all ... well, it's not good."

Hirum stood up and, finding himself standing, sat down. He shifted suddenly and awkwardly on the bench like a man suffering a nervous spasm of pain.

"What room is. My baby. In? What room?"

"*Your* baby? It wasn't Lorrie who was hurt. It was another girl. Is that what you thought? No, Lorrie is fine. She's perfectly OK."

Hirum rubbed his face. He went to the water fountain and drank from a paper cup. He leaned with both hands on the wall and stared at one of his shoes. When he returned and sat down, he patted the young man on the knee. It was a while, however, before he could speak.

Then the big man in the silk suit took the younger man by the sleeve. "We've got to stop her. I'll send the both of you to England. Anywhere. You must marry her. She'll obey you. You marry her and take her away. To England. Anywhere. And don't tell me differrent. Do you want her killed? Do you? She's playing with fire. You've got to be crazy if you don't take her away. It'll be your fault if something happens. I've got news for you. She's gone wild. She's gone completely wild. Get a job in England. I'm sure you can. I'll support you for a year. Make a film. Anything. We've got to stop her. Because her mother. Her mother is upset."

"Isn't Lorrie old enough to decide her own life?"

"Are you mad?"

"You can help her."

"I'm trying to."

"By supporting her fight."

"You are mad."

"You can help her win."

"Win?"

"Then everyone will be saved."

"I've got news for ya."

"I know what it is."

"You're mad."

Sheriff Honeycutt was now standing beside them. Justin Warmflash, he said, you are under arrest.

The father rose to become the lawyer. He was outraged. How dare you detain a distinguished professor of a famous university? It is a clear infringement of his civil rights. What is the charge against my client? I demand it be put in writing. A girl has been seriously hurt. The sheriff is subject to litigation amounting to a quarter of a million dollars in damages. The girl might even die. There would be criminal charges and national headlines. Calamity was around the corner. The sheriff stood listening with his mouth partly open. Hirum allowed for a dramatic pause. He gave a significant look at his innocent client. He led Honeycutt to the water fountain. They spoke in huddled animation for a full minute. They returned to where Justin was sitting. Honeycutt scratched his knee, then held out his hand and said, "Son, I'd sure like to extend congratulations on your up-and-coming wedding. You're a lucky man, sure-nough. And me and the missus wishes you and Lorraine all the luck in the world in England."

Hirum took Justin by the arm and led him past the state trooper, through the revolving doors, patted him formally on the back, tousled his hair, said he was counting on him, really counting on him, and then went back alone into the building.

As the warm sun breathed on his face, Justin wriggled his nose to adjust his glasses. He wanted to run. But he didn't know from whom.

He bought *The Home Bugle* and read it on the bus. Militants had attacked the factory, screamed the headlines. The authorities had successfully beaten back a group of hippie agitators and left-wing revolutionaries from completing their carefully planned assault. Deputy Moe Mullen had been hit by a car and suffered a dislocated shoulder. Several revolutionaries had been injured. It all started when certain Communists in the movement saw their chance and launched their attack.

Justin sat with his eyes closed for a few moments. Then he turned to the sports page. Nothing seemed real. He turned to the editorial column which deplored violence at home and applauded the President's escalation of the war abroad. Nothing here seemed real either. There was a James Bond film and a Disney revival. A letter to the editor attacked, with indignant outrage, the growing movement in America to eliminate the mini skirt. A column entitled "Kitchen Frolics" explained how to make Beef Stroganoff. There was a marriage in Port Madison and a dented fender on Route 4. The cartoons weren't funny. The forecast was for rain.

He folded the paper into a hat and wore it when he got off. He dialed Lorrie's number. No one was home. He opened the pamphlet-sized phone book and looked up the numbers of his Communist revolutionary friends. But those who were listed weren't at home. How typical of Communist revolutionaries. He gave his paper hat to a kid. He ate a dead sandwich and drank some weak coffee. From where he sat at the counter he could see raw hamburger sizzling sickeningly on the grill. He decided he needed a joint.

In his hotel he tiptoed past Camilla's room to wistful safety. An envelope had been slipped under his door. Inside, in Lorrie's handwriting, was this: "The Old Willis farm. Tuckabuckwack Road. Bus to the lumberyard. Get off and walk. Make sure no one follows." How did they know he hadn't been jailed? He ran down the stairs. He ran through the street. He lifted the paper hat from his little friend's head and placed it on a fireplug where it could easily be retrieved. And he kept running because he found it a pleasant substitute for his persistent urge to deface an officer of the law.

He followed a dirt road through trees filled with birds and saw a cherished glimpse of a deer. The farmhouse looked abandoned. The adjoining field that sloped down from the road to the woods contained a rusty hot-water tank, a set of tangled bedsprings, several loads of dumped rocks, an old Chevy that was now scrap metal, and a faded sign announcing that the property was for sale. Outside, the farmhouse seemed beyond repair. He realized his error when he saw how beyond repair the inside was. In the kitchen he traversed a modest mountain range of unnameable junk and empty tin cans to reach the stripped ruin that had once been the parlor. He called her name and heard only birds in reply. Taking his life in his hands, he climbed the barricade of the stairs and found more ruins and, amazingly, a door still on hinges. Beyond it was a room whose wallpaper had been ripped loose. There were sleeping bags on the floor and, hanging from a nail, the long dress she had worn that morning. The window screen had a hole the size of a cannonball through which he saw a view of the road, the junk in the field, some birds in flight, and Briggs emerging from the woods hugging a watermelon. Behind her came Willoby Brown carrying two tall bags of groceries like a Congolese chieftain home from sacking the A&P. Then Lorrie, in Levis, swinging a gallon of wine and carrying a rifle.

There was the usual mass ceremony of hugging and kissing though now the mood had changed. Briggs, with her head in bandages and feeling sick again, went upstairs to sleep. A sullen Willoby sat on the floor of the porch drinking wine from a paper cup while Lorrie produced bandages from the pockets of her work shirt, knelt, and treated the teeth marks in his leg.

They assumed Justin had been released when there was no news about him in *The Home Bugle.* The news about Viola, however, was all bad. The hospital had her on the critical list. Willoby wanted a bloodbath. Lorrie wanted her country's salvation. They came to a compromise. They would burn down the factory.

Here was a Lorrie different from before. Her voices were now her only counsel and her high spirits were those of a woman who had made up her mind to do something dangerous and romantic.

Justin asked what the plan was. They weren't certain yet. They would gather in force, she said. David Fenskie would join them with guns. So would Nick Columbo who had recently escaped from Fort Gilbert. (He had borrowed some pot from a fellow prisoner and bribed a guard.) Briggs would be fit in a few days. Willoby, who had been hiding out in the farmhouse to avoid arrest, was ready for action now. That he was wanted for assaulting an officer seemed only to increase his determination. And the others? Where were they? Lorrie admitted there were no others. Sally Ran-slick and Mrs. Swarthson had more or less deserted them.

"Five against a factory," said Justin. "That isn't much."

"Six," said Lorrie.

"Who's the sixth?"

"You are," Willoby said.

Justin helped himself to some wine. He had always been for political action. Now all he could think of was that he was trapped in madness. How to get out was the question, and how to pull her out with him. He explained the dangers. There were too few of them. They would be killed outright or imprisoned for years. Or hunted down like diseased dogs. Their careers, he added, would be at an end.

"What career?" asked Willoby. "I can't get a job."

"My career is to save my country," she said. "At the moment the field is wide open."

"Well, *my* career *will* be ended," Justin blurted out, "I'll tell you that."

Her voice was terribly calm. "You can leave us, you know. Others did. And we'll understand. Perhaps you should leave. You have a career. Teaching is important. Right? Look, what do I know?"

"Do you want me to leave?"

"No, I want you to stay. But some can't. It's not in them."

"If I go we'll probably never see each other ever again."

"I know."

"Do you really and truly want me to stay?"

"Really and truly I want you to stay."

"Shit, this is breaking my heart," Willoby said, rubbing his smooth dome.

Lorrie waved at him to be silent. "I love you, Justin. But if you must leave, I'll understand."

Sitting beside her on the floor, Justin recalled all the things her voices had asked her to do and which even a total national effort might never get done. He listed them all from war to peace, from pollution to health, from bigotry to love. It took a while.

"Now, they did ask you to do all that, didn't they?"

She looked very tired. Willoby poured her some wine. "Yes," she said, "they did."

"Well," said Justin, driving it home, "get arrested now and none of that will ever get done."

"Listen, you mother, what do you want her to do instead? Go back on that fuckin' picket line? They'll beat the shit out of them anyway. Go back to her daddy's house and write more letters to Nixon? Go back and vote again for Lyndon Johnson, the great peace candidate? Go back to college and listen to you con her about the need for political action because the U.S. of A. is piling up with shit? Well, what do you recommend, Professor?"

Justin stared in silence at the dirt road and the junk in the field. Lorrie squeezed his arm. Their bed in Vermont, long since gone, reappeared in the distance, empty. Would he ever be able to face another class again? Now it was he who felt tired. He couldn't leave and he couldn't stay. The helplessness he felt was that of a child. So it was not ordained that he would triumph, that he who meant so well and worked so hard would ever achieve the happiness needed. Millions of people with hopes like his had ended, eyes shut, in early graves, or were condemned to live on alone in busy emptiness. And self-pity warms no heart except one's own. She let go of his arm.

"Well, what do you recommend, Professor?"

"Justin, if you have to go back, I'll understand. I will."

"You should call a doctor for that wound," he said to Willoby.

The Negro finished his wine and said: "These days only the cops make house calls."

A firm wind pushed through the trees. Far off they heard the lament of yet another train bringing perhaps still more lovers to grief.

"Six isn't enough," Justin insisted. No one spoke. "Well, if I'm to be the sixth, I want a say in what's done."

"Just what we need. Another mother who wants to be a leader."

"Let him speak, please."

"Guys with ties always get to speak." Willoby crushed his cup and tossed it at the trees.

"You just can't do it with six," warned the professor of history. "You need, you need an army."

Lorrie picked cork out of her wine. "Big man. Where do I get an army?"

"He wants an army so he can film one of those horse operas for horses' asses."

"I don't think so," said the blonde.

"Don't be so sure," said Justin. "Do you still have my camera?"

Lorrie said she did.

"If I help you do this, this thing, will you go with me to Vermont?"

"Yes," she said loudly, "oh, yes."

"Then I'll get you an army," he said.

He was received with great formality and Lorrie felt what it was like to have her hand kissed. They sat in their chairs sipping scotch with MacArthur holding his pose upon the wall.

"Mr. Warmflash. So you're the film director I've heard so much about."

"Colonel, I have been talking with Miss Benglesdorf and I am convinced that we must do something to awaken America to this plot to poison the air."

"Hear, hear," said Lorrie.

"Amen," said Nimols.

Justin learned forward. "Lend us an army and we'll finish the job."

"An army?"

"A division."

"A division?"

"Enough men to fill a playground," said Lorrie quickly.

Justin sat back and jabbed at the ice in his glass. "Colonel, I have decided to make a film about an army officer who courageously, and on his own initiative, leads his men into battle to save his country." Justin licked the tip of his finger. "Sir, I want you and your men to be in that film."

"Me?"

"Yes, Colonel, you, in full-dress uniform, front center."

"Me, eh?"

"You, Colonel. With your help I hope to make it the most important film in years."

"I see."

"But I must warn you that the project might make you famous."

"God knows he's handsome enough," said Lorrie.

"I hope to make it a stirring epic like *Alexander Nevsky*."

"That was a very great film," Lorrie explained.

"I must have missed it," said Nimols, as if trying to recall what movies he had seen that month.

"It's about a great man who saved his country when all seemed lost."

Nimols dried the bottom of his glass on his knee. "And is that the same theme, sir, of your own film?"

"Exactly, Colonel."

"Tell me about it, Mr. Warmflash, in your own words. Briefly, that is." Waiting, he lifted his drink in an unspoken toast to Miss Lorraine's multiple warheads. With a smile of sweet innocence she took a deep breath and lifted her glass in return.

"All right," said Justin, leaning forward, "here we go. It's a heart-warming story that asks the question can a handsome colonel in the U.S. Army, listening to the deep and profound dictates of his own conscience, save his country single-handedly or ..."

Willoby was right; he wanted to lead. He had to lead. How else would she be led to safety? And if his plan blew up he hoped it would do so in his face—not hers. The problem was that to succeed he needed the cooperation of all, even that of her father.

Sleep didn't come; not that night or the next. He perspired now even while sitting still. Once, without warning, he threw up in the street. He had a persistent urge to shout at people. He bit his nails until they bled. He began to understand her father better.

Camilla Epps also felt she understood him better. She decided to begin a diary and these were the opening words: "Men ruin love because it isn't very important to them. Other things are more important. To women there is nothing in the world more important than love." But that was as far as she ever got, except for one more entry. "He was so sweet and nice. Why doesn't he phone me? I could tell he was a very good person by how nervous he got when I went to see him. I could scream, I really could. He hurried to my room and then he walked out of my life. Why do the ones who want me always have something they want even more? It's men who always ruin things. I hate them. They give me gifts and say nice things. Then they break off. They always break off." And there her diary ended.

It was the dirt in the air that confused them. Some said this cost money because now they had to clean their clothes more often, wearing them out faster, having to buy new ones sooner. This they learned from reading posters in the street. These same people—who read the posters—were also saying that everyone's lungs were turning black. You had only to ask a doctor over at Southboro Hospital what the inside of a lung of a city person looked like after they opened him up to see why he died. These same people said that the air in Salem-ville was getting as bad as city air and they told stories of terrible diseases that this would cause. Everyone agreed this was very bad. The mayor should act. Even the mayor agreed. But change takes time, he said. Industry keeps America strong. Industry keeps America healthy. How else could it resist the Viet Cong and all of those? Free enterprise was the American way. To interfere was clearly subversive. Besides, no one liked to lose money. It weakened America. It was dangerous to freedom. And everyone agreed that freedom was a wonderful thing. It was all very confusing.

Her Lady Aurelia was beginning to wilt. This made her feel sad as if her own daughter had become sick. Actually, as the plant grew weaker her daughter grew stronger. She was very proud of her daughter because she dared to defy You-know-who. That was a courage Cathrine never had. She even dared defy the entire town. This gave her mother a secret, tingling joy. Sometimes her daughter frightened her and she worried. Yet she was glad that years ago she had allowed her daughter to read only the children's books that talked of courage and bravery. Cathrine had told her many times that a real woman had more on her mind than just motherhood. A real woman was the equal to any man. She gave a sigh and watered her plant.

Sally Ranslick hushed the children with what she knew had become an old-maid's voice. This was a public library and they simply must hush. She stamped some take-out cards with a series of hard blows. Each time she pounded the desk she was reminded of what the club had done. Because she was frightened of this happening to her, she was convinced she was a coward. Where was a man's dignity, Malraux had said, if he was never willing to endanger his life? She decided she had no dignity either. At noon she bought a get-well card with dancing teddy bears on the front. She mailed it off and felt worse than ever.

Hirum drove past where the mayor sat asleep in his chair. He was looking in vain for his daughter who hadn't been home in two days. He knew she was well for she had sneaked in one night to change her clothes and pocket her checkbook. That she was well made him even more angry. He turned at the corner and waved at old John Banks who purposely failed to wave back. Oh, so the father was guilty of the daughter's crimes, was he? The hell with you, Mr. Banks, and Hirum punched the wheel and blew the horn by mistake. He sped off in a wailing screech of rubber, hunched with embarrassment.

At the office he gave Camilla Epps another gift of jewelry. It barely stirred a smile.

Earlier that day in the inner office having a lonely lunch at the big desk opposite the leather couch she had grown to hate, Camilla sat waiting for her boss to return as promised, to share with her a little of his private time. He had been far too distracted lately by his truant daughter to show concern even for his clients. Camilla Epps, disgusted with life, swung in his swivel chair to watch, through the window, the boring procession of nobodies going nowhere. She was startled by a troop of soldiers marching up the street behind a snappy, gray-haired, ramrod officer and preceded by an ugly girl, head bandaged, driving a jeep in which, seated in back, lo and behold, was Justin Warmfiash aiming some kind of camera steadily at the parade.

The sheriff had been watching them all week without knowing what to make of it. They were shooting a film, or so he was told, but he was suspicious all the same. When he stopped them to ask where a certain Willoby Brown might be hiding, Hirum's daughter shrugged her shoulders. She said she was looking for him herself. She asked a favor. If he should stumble across Mr. Brown, would he please let her know? She smiled, thanked him, and went back in front of the camera.

And none of the places in which they chose to shoot their scenes made any sense to him. They wanted to use Lindbergh Boulevard, then the Creek Bridge, finally the football field of Colin P. Kelly

High School. Since he was glad to see Hirum's daughter apply herself to activities somewhat different from inciting to riot or committing arson, the sheriff granted permission. Colonel Nimols thanked him each time in person as if to dignify the agreement with his newly pressed uniform. But Adam Honeycutt was still suspicious.

He was particularly suspicious of officers, especially after losing an arm in the Pacific in 1943, when some show-off lieutenant decided that a certain hill had to be taken when anyone could see that going around it was a far wiser move. Adam Honeycutt would not have been suspicious of officers if he had succeeded in his plan to become one himself. But he kept getting busted for being drunk and thus became more suspicious than ever. When he returned to the States he made up for this exclusion from the officers' club by becoming an officer of the law. Now the only people he wasn't suspicious of were other officers of the law. On everyone else he kept a most careful eye.

Especially Colonel Nimols, who strutted about as pleased as punch just to be filmed with a blonde on his arm. And he had his men do all kinds of crazy things while that slick-looking city boy with the glasses and narrow tie directed everyone, actors and soldiers, as if he were God himself and they nothing but toys from the Five and Ten.

To make matters worse, the sheriff was also suspicious of blondes. This held true for all pretty women but blondes were the first to catch his eye and so they were the first to be suspect. He reasoned that if a pretty woman excited him, she excited all men. And men in a constant state of excitement were like a massive, life-long landing party rushing her beach-head wave after wave, year after year, until surely like that hill in the Pacific, she is taken. And taken once means taken many times. She becomes, in fact, quite skilled at having her fortifications breeched while, of course, managing always to appear properly impregnable. In other words, she becomes a tramp. However, if she, unlike that awful hill where he had lost his arm, cannot be captured, this means she is good and pure with breasts and thighs all the more challenging due to her strict and snobbish virtue. And it means she looks down on him, just as the officers in the army looked down on him, for being unworthy.

He was also suspicious of Mr. Four-Eyes, the wise-ass intellectual from New York. He would like nothing better than to throw that one in the clink. His wise-ass accusation that Adam had accepted bribery was a brazen bluff. But Honeycutt, a cautious card player, decided not to call it. Twice he had Four-Eyes as good as jailed and twice her father talked him out of it. So the boy was supposed to marry her, was he? To take her off to England, was he? Well he packs up real slow and that's a fact.

He kept a careful eye on them, indeed. But it wasn't easy. If the places they chose were puzzling enough, the scenes they were shooting made no sense at all. To be doubly safe he kept a heavy guard at the factory, though to his surprise they no longer showed an interest in the place. The fight to close it down had given way to the spectacle of Wise-Ass forming a square with his fingers and peering through it at the conceited colonel in his well-pressed uniform as he marched Miss Lorrie up and down a line of rigid soldiers standing in the playing field of Kelly High School. It was a scene they shot again and again until boredom overcame suspicion and the sheriff went home. He was back the next day to watch a scene involving the well-pressed colonel carrying a mini-skirted Miss Lorraine across Old Creek Bridge, stepping over the bodies of supposedly dead soldiers while a long-haired hippie Christ in beads waited for them on the other side holding two uplifted fingers for victory. Then there was a scene one Sunday morning with Miss Lorraine sashaying down a deserted Lindbergh Boulevard with a pair of toy pistols low and swaying on her hips while the fool colonel came prancing up from the other direction like some flaming army queer, letting it all be put on film for the whole world to see. They even drew their guns, fired caps, fell into each other's arms and, yes, kissed as Four-Eyes yelled cut. The sheriff, disgusted, went home.

Secretly he had hoped to take part but was never asked. This began his disgust. Watching her kiss a man she couldn't possibly care for added to it. The boredom of watching the same, slow, fool-ish scenes filmed time and again completed it. And worse even than causing disgust, it didn't make sense.

A few townspeople came but it didn't make sense to them either. And their attention span was short. Usually, only the sheriff was present sitting alone in his police car with the small American flag glued to the windshield, he and a young Negro boy on a bicycle. A few weeks of this and the sheriff stopped coming. After that, no one came.

As if he didn't have enough troubles, Hirum caught a cold. He knew his life had become absurd, but this was the finishing touch. Camilla was sent to the drugstore for two pills of acromycin which he washed down with a glass of Canadian Club. He became groggy and lightheaded. Soon nothing whatever seemed real.

What exactly was a Camilla Epps? She was an unofficial second wife who appeared in his official second home to write down his words and return with them in triplicate plus errors. Pure farce, he decided.

Cathrine wasn't real, either. She was only someone he lived with and tried to put out of his mind. His unofficial second wife helped him with this. But the trouble was each wife constantly reminded him of the other. If he had any courage, he would fire them both. It was surreal.

So was his daughter. She infuriated him and he loved her. He wished jointly to kiss and slap her face. How odd that he, the town's most prominent attorney, who saw himself, at best, defending law against order, at worst, representing the iron conformity of civiliza-tion, which was more than he could say for the one-armed sheriff who will do nothing unless bribed or threatened, how odd that he, Hirum Benglesdorf, giver of delicate legalities, should have a daughter who was the epitome of anarchy.

And what could be more unreal than for Lorrie to phone him while he was at that very moment thinking lovingly and furiously of no one but her? The girl's cheerful voice was like a sudden windfall of counterfeit money. Cathrine probably asked her to call; he guessed this when she assured him that she was healthy and well. Silence. He said he had a cold. She was sorry. He asked her to come for dinner. She said she would one day soon. He didn't believe her and didn't get angry and it was all unreal. He asked about the marriage. She said she hadn't fixed a date. Why hadn't she? She wasn't sure. Why not? She didn't know. Why didn't she know? She wasn't sure. It was all unreal.

Suddenly she was gone. Something about having to rush to work. What work? Goodbye, Dad. Was it the film? See you soon, Dad. Did that mean no more trouble with the law? She was gone and nothing had really been said. It was always like that. He played back bits and pieces of conversation from the past. "Daddy, Daddy, be happy for me, I'm going to overthrow the government." This at the dinner table. Some days later at the same table he threatened to cut off her support. She was infuriatingly magnanimous and triumphantly condescending. "I know you can't go on supporting me while I attack the corrupt establishment that you are paid to represent. But please don't feel bad about it, Daddy, because I still love you and always will." How dare she play the saint? It wasn't right. It was disrespectful. He wanted to slap her face.

Instead he phoned the hotel to try once more to activate her fiancé. Defreeze knew nothing of his whereabouts. Neither did Honeycutt. Feeling worse, Hirum sent Camilla out for aspirin. The phone rang. It was Justin. All very unreal. His future son-in-law explained he needed Hirum's help in marrying Lorrie. He had put her in his film to distract her from rebellion. It was a way of defusing her social consciousness. When the film was over he would take her away. Marriage would follow. But the Committee to Bring Back Air, Water and Sanity was planning a serious conflagration. His daughter, of course, would take part. She would surely get hurt if she did. Justin's request was this: Could Hirum get the sheriff to put her in jail overnight? The charge could be the withholding of incriminating evidence. The key that was found in her purse would do. The next day they could drop the charges and let her go free. After all, only the police could kidnap someone and not be brought to task. And that one night in jail would make her innocent. Her presence would be accounted for when the big crime was committed.

It was unreal. Hirum coughed and blew his nose. Yes, he had a cold. Yes, he would try to take care of himself. He blew his nose again and confessed over the phone that Justin's plan had problems. Lorrie had to be found first to be arrested. And could Justin tell him where the conflagration would take place? His future son-in-law didn't answer. Hirum explained that he could probably get the sheriff's cooperation provided he could bribe him with the truth. It would be a feather in Adam's cap if these radicals could be caught. That was why Hirum had to know where the crime would take place. Justin hemmed and hawed. He said: She must never learn that we spoke together. The lawyer agreed completely. Finally the information was given. They were going to attack Southboro Hospital to free Miss Testi who was being held there under guard. Clearly, unreal.

Although the day was unseasonably cool, Justin was drenched as he climbed off the bus at the lumberyard. He stopped in the almost chilly forest, waiting in its dusk and silence to dry off. Yet he continued to perspire. The hell with it, and he marched off to the farm that dated back, he was told, to the time of the Revolution. Plenty of history around here, Defreeze had said. What he hadn't said was that it was all in the future and coming fast. He loosened his tie and massaged his neck.

The old French Dauphine that Lorrie had borrowed from the colonel was parked in the rear of the building. He negotiated without incident the mountain range of junk in the kitchen to find Lorraine and Willoby seated like children working on a sandcastle. This time the twin doom of her bosom had a black pin with white letters that said: GIVE A DAMN.

She jumped up and hugged him. "Wow, you've been running."

"Sort of."

Willoby frowned. "From the pigs?"

"Not yet."

"Best to save yourself for tomorrow."

"Did you bring some?" she asked.

He held up his pocket watch. She smiled as women once did when given perfume. Willoby warned him to get rid of it by tomorrow.

"Will do."

"Sweet man, there'll be no more left by tomorrow."

But Justin's faith had weakened. Perhaps he had been sold inferior stuff, for he had sampled it earlier and all it had done was slow down his terror and make things worse. Nor had it relieved the sweating or the nausea or that relentless tremor as if America were a machine that no one could stop.

She slapped his back and he nearly yelped. She kissed him, said, "Join us," and sat down. He did, wondering how he had remained standing this long. As he rolled the joint, he asked what they were doing.

"Making dynamite," said the man with threads where his sleeves should have been.

"Eight percent ammonium nitrate with twenty percent nitroglycerin," Lorrie volunteered as though back in class.

"We put it in these pipes," Willoby explained, helpfully, "then we add a fuse and blasting cap."

Justin paused, the match in one hand, the matchbook in the other, the cigarette dangling from his mouth. He saw the house blasting apart with everything in it spinning and landing in bits and pieces far away in different places in the woods, the violent belch of flame and timber causing people in front of Howard Johnson or huddled in convertibles at the drive-in theatre to turn and look in the same direction. And the first to arrive at the smoking rubble would find perhaps a battered pocket watch or the limbless torso of a headless girl.

"Scary, isn't it?" Lorrie asked, sitting cross-legged on the floor.

"Don't worry," Willoby said, "you can light up."

Justin leaned back, lit the tip with circumspection, put out the match with dedication, inhaled more deeply than he ever had in his life, and handed it away as he would a loaded gun to a reckless child.

"Those are Molotov cocktails," the blonde explained, pointing at a collection of bottles. "Two-thirds gasoline and one-third oil."

"A guy could get killed here."

"Nobody's goin' a get killed, you mother. Not now or tomorrow."

"Jailed maybe, not killed," she added. "That's the point of the plan, isn't it?" And she looked at the man who had invented the plan.

"That's the point of it, yes." He adjusted his glasses with a wiggle of his nose.

Lorrie, cross-eyed as she watched the tip flame up, inhaled.

Willoby was filling one of the lead pipes. "Ever been this scared before?" he asked, looking at Justin.

"I get the definite feeling you don't like me."

"Can't say that I do."

Lorrie looked hurt. "Why don't you like him?"

"The mother's not with us."

"I'm here. What the hell do you want?"

"He is so with us."

"And I'll be with you tomorrow, friend."

"We'll see," Willoby said.

She inhaled, handed away the cigarette, held her breath, then exhaled: "And if he comes tomorrow, will you like him then?"

Now Willoby held it to his lips, his chest almost doubling in size. Then, in a smokeless flood: "He's scared shit, I kid you not."

"That's silly," she said, "we're all scared."

"But his fear scares me. I saw the mother faint. Cat didn't fall down or stop talkin'. But when the cat came in here and seen the action, he clean fainted away. First time brave whitey's got to put something on the line and like he's got instant arthritis."

Lorrie slapped her knee. "Big man. Big fierce, tough talking, sleeveless type. With a pound of steel wool you'll knit us a stove.

Well, just you get your black ass out there tomorrow and we'll take care of ours. Whatever their color."

"We'll see."

Justin scratched his swamp of a scalp. "Take it easy. He's right. I'm probably the most scared guy here."

"You're scared?" she said. "With me it's diarrhea and beautiful red rashes all over. How's that for calm? The trouble with him is no one can tell how pale he's getting."

Willoby smiled and rammed more dynamite into a length of pipe.

"Yes, but I mean this is, to say the least, a bit dangerous." Justin eyed the pile of explosives. "One wrong move ... "

"Give me liberty or give me what's-his-face?" she said sweetly.

"Sure, and you know which of the two he got."

"So what are you trying to say, big man?"

"The time is out of joint; O cursed spite, that ever I was born to set it right."

"*Hamlet?*"

"Correct."

"Would you two scholars pass me some blasting caps?"

Lorrie did so while Justin stood up and walked around the room. It looked as if an explosion had already taken place. Ribs of wood could be seen behind punctured plaster. The window was simply a gaping hole. Something had been written in crayon across a colorless piece of wall.

Napalm sticks to kids, napalm sticks to kids,
When'll those damn gooks ever learn?
We shoot the sick, the young, the lame,
We do our best to kill and maim,
Because the "kills" all count the same,
Napalm sticks to kids.

Napalm sticks to kids, napalm sticks to kids,
Blues out on a road recon,

See some children with their mom,
What the hell, let's drop the bomb,
Napalm sticks to kids.

"What's that?" Justin asked.

"A helicopter pilot song," she said.

"Who put it there?"

"This one. He was a skytrooper in you-know-where."

Justin glanced at Willoby who sat fixing a blasting cap in one of the pipes.

"He doesn't like to talk about it," she whispered.

"Who says I don't?"

"Correction. He likes to talk about it."

"I'd love to hear what he has to say," Justin told her.

"Maybe he met your mother over there."

"She's entertaining the troops," Justin explained to him.

Willoby held out his arm. Lorrie leaned over to take the cigarette. He worked as he spoke, unwinding the fuse and cutting it into lengths.

"I followed orders. Wanted to be a good boy. Not get spanked. Well, I paid the price. No, the people I burned alive paid the price. Now I intend to balance the budget."

Dusk had removed the detail in their faces. The birds were silent. There was no wind.

"Once we hung Charlie by a rope from a chopper. Wanted info about the V.C. forty-eighth. He wouldn't talk. Screamed but wouldn't talk. If he had famous last words like Patrick Henry, no one heard them. Cat just wouldn't talk. Wasn't reasonable. Someone let the rope go. We heard him scream all the way to the ground. Real good screamer. When we napalm a village we don't hear the screams." He paused. "Here at home they make me live in shit. Then they make me go over there and do that. I am finished being a good boy."

The whites of his eyes glowed with light.

"Yes, well, it's no Garden of Eden this country," said Justin.

187

LEON ARDEN

For the first time that evening Willoby laughed. "There were these two cats once called Adam and Eve. They had this real shit pad. The housing was just not good, dig? And the landlord said, you can eat any old thing you want 'cept this here apple. Point being that all the other apples was rotten. This fact is not generally known."

Now it was Lorrie's turn to laugh. In doing so she let some smoke escape. She took another drag and held it. When she exhaled, she said, "Wow, wait a minute. It's here again." She stood up.

"What is?" Justin asked.

She didn't answer. She seemed transfixed by something in the dim woods.

"The mother voices," said Willoby, "that's what."

Justin nearly wrenched his neck looking first at him and then back at her. She sat down against the far wall, hugging her knees, her head tilted back, breathing deeply. Justin went and knelt beside her. Willoby signaled to him for quiet. They looked like three sculptures in a dim museum. For a while there was only the eerie, audible silence of the forest.

"I was hoping you'd drop around," she said.

"What?"

"She's not speaking to you," Willoby explained.

Lorrie nodded. "Yes, it's tomorrow."

"Holy Christ," Justin whispered, "she really does talk to them."

"We're ready to go," she said, her eyes still closed.

Justin took hold of her knee. "Tell 'em it's dangerous. Explain that it's very dangerous."

"Don't touch her now, you mother."

"Shut up," Justin hissed.

"Who you tellin' to shut up?"

"Shut up, I said. Lorrie, tell 'em it's dangerous. I want to hear what he has to say."

She remained calm. "He heard you. He says it's always been dangerous."

188

"We don't have a chance," he insisted, his voice rising.

"Neither did General Washington," she said, repeating to him words that only she could hear.

"Violence breeds violence."

"Apathy breeds apathy. Indifference breeds indifference. Chauvinism breeds chauvinism. Blind obedience breeds blind obedience."

"We're committing violence, damn it."

"He says yes we are, in Asia."

"I mean we're committing violence *here*."

"Yes, against the blacks, against the students, against protestors, against…"

"I mean we, *we* are committing violence."

"He says we are committing *counter*-Violence."

"Who am I speaking with, please?" Justin demanded. "I want to know."

"Samuel Adams."

"Oh, hell, that bastard always was a troublemaker. Let me talk to Jefferson. No, make it John Adams. President John Adams."

She shook her head.

"What's wrong?"

"Only Sam is here." She closed her eyes again.

Justin stood up. He turned to Willoby. "Incredible. She's off on some crazy trip and here I am trying to climb aboard."

The other man laughed. Lorrie, her head on her knees, was mumbling privately with her invisible guest. Justin circled the room and stopped.

"Amazing. She talks to them like on the phone."

"What'd ya expect?" Willoby asked.

"I don't know."

"You don't know."

"This is absurd."

"You're absurd."

"OK. OK. You want to step outside and fight or what?"

"Me?" Willoby grinned. "I don't have enough ego problems for that. Besides, I got work to do." And he unwound another length of fuse.

Justin suggested that this might very well be their last night together. She agreed.

"Then have dinner with me," he said. "The two of us, alone."

She nodded with that imbalanced wistful smile of hers that ran him through whenever he saw it.

"But first... " and he pointed upstairs toward the only room that had meaning for him now.

"Better later, no?"

He explained that if they waited they would just be rushing through dinner to get back to that room. He didn't want that. He wanted her now.

"Don't mind me," Willoby said. "I'm just the bombardier." And he stuck another blasting cap into a pipe.

"Poor bombardier." And she hugged him. "You'll be OK, no? I mean Briggs and Fenskie are coming soon."

"I'll be OK either way."

She turned to Justin. "Oh, did we tell you? Viola is off the critical list."

"Thank God."

"All that means," Willoby said, "is she won't die."

"She'll be all right, you'll see."

"Yeah, she'll be OK I guess."

"She'll be as good as new," Justin put in.

There was a long silence in dim light.

"So what do you think?" she asked, touching his black bulging arm.

He looked at her. "Now easy does it. Too much bouncing around up there and this whole damn house could collapse."

How typical that when he had all but given up, it happened. For the first week of filming they had spent each night apart because the sheriff kept following them home and so they didn't dare go to the farmhouse. Lorrie slept with Briggs, and Justin went back to his room. And there was also Colonel Nimols. He had to be kept blind to the fact that there was anything going on between "his girl" and their young director. In fact, once during that week he insisted that she come back to the fort with him to have dinner and it was all she could do to get the colonel to allow Justin to come along. Nimols was unhappy with this arrangement but he considered himself to be a sophisticated man and sophistication to him was the art of wearing a smile when in truth you wanted nothing better than to beat the living shit out of someone. Afterward he insisted on driving them back in his Dauphine, Justin to his hotel and Lorrie to Briggs's place. Soon this chaperone system had put everyone on edge.

After a week of shooting, Lorrie was more eager to get into bed with him than the semiparalyzed and profusely sweating Justin was eager to get into bed with anyone. But she persisted. She waited until no one was looking and then borrowed an open jeep from one of the colonel's men and drove against a fine drizzle to the Southboro Motor Court only to hear a knock on the door before Justin could undo a single button in her dress. There stood Sheriff Honeycutt with three deputies, certain that he had found at last where the nigger was hiding. They searched all twelve cabins and all they uncovered was Mr. Defreeze sharing a room with Sally Ranslick, a fact that the sheriff discreetly covered up by letting no one else in, closing the door himself and saying to his deputies that there were sure as hell no niggers in there. When Adam threatened Lorrie with telling her father of her secret rendezvous, she became indignant, reminding him that the man she was with was her fiancé and offered to call her father and tell him herself. Honeycutt let the subject drop, hoping they would see this as an act of benevolence. Lorrie asked him not to do her any favors and to kindly get the fuck out of their room. Justin leaped fully dressed on the bed and threatened to scream. Lorrie joined him, wobbled a bit, took his arm and offered to help with the screaming. Together they shouted mock announcements of police brutality, denial of civil rights, entering without a warrant, and finally exiting without a warrant, which is what the sheriff did, slamming the door after him. "Only crazy people in there," he said, and drove off with his men.

But the owner of the motel insisted they leave. They had caused a disturbance in a respectable place of business and if they didn't go quietly he would most certainly summon the Southboro police. They got back into the jeep and with the rain falling hard, drove off, became drenched, and stopped for coffee hoping the torrent would let up. It didn't. Lorrie started to cry. Justin soothed her as best he could from across the table while people watched as if they had purchased tickets. He grew to suspect that he had failed in life at everything that possibly mattered, that even the weather had turned against him, that her tears would never stop and would finally kill them both.

He closed the door, propped up a candle in the empty room, and watched her getting undressed. A slim finger of yellow light played over the subtle indentations and bulbous possessions until, free of her clothes, she crossed her legs at the ankles, pressed one palm against the wall, the other against her hip, tapped with her fingers and waited, humming. He hung his clothes on a nail, turned away and heard everything fall. Lorrie beckoned to him with a toss of her head. He took hold of her warm hips; she took hold of his glasses. Detaching them from his face, she placed them on the floor by the candle. When she stood up she was fuzzy. He explored her slowly like a blind man unsure of what he had found.

He wanted, in a single sexual act, to place her forever under his control. Then she would do only what he said and always be safe. But her smooth-skinned tenderness encircled him like a sensual homecoming. Her devotion to his needs threatened to melt him into someone helplessly hers. He resisted. What he was doing must be nothing less than a bold appropriation. And it must last as long as possible. To stress how fully she had come under his control, he kept bending and turning her body into various postures of supplication. When she finally burst with her special gift of inner explosions, he swelled with triumph. This dissolved when he slowly realized that, finished with the task of giving her joy, he was now, himself, having trouble ending. He strove with unceremonious fanaticism down a long, repetitive length of time, easing up as he decided to enjoy his plight, then on again, almost alone, almost a prisoner, as though finally in man's mad millennium of copulation, need had become instinct and instinct, farce.

He had found the Holy Grail only to discover a note inside sending him somewhere else. Meanwhile, she hugged and praised him for being the sexual athlete he wasn't. In the agitated candlelight, he waited for his desire to cool down.

"Sweet man."

"Speaking."

"We must do that again real soon."

"We may have to."

"Well, don't stand on ceremony."

"Don't worry."

The dark, flickering room did delightful things to the surface of her body.

"Tell me something," she said.

"Anything."

"If the President makes a promise to the people which he can't keep because the power to fulfill that promise is in the hands of Congress, then that's not a balance of power, that's powerlessness. Am I right?"

"What brought this on?"

"Just thinking."

"Not when your clothes are off, please."

"It's really complicated."

"You have beautiful nipples, you know?"

"And this impotence is built right into the Constitution."

"Very good, Miss Benglesdorf."

"Well, how does one change all that?" She drew up her knees to support her chin. Her eyes studied him.

"How? By changimg the Constitution, pretty girl."

"Will that ever happen?"

"I strongly doubt it."

"Wow, there's so much to do."

"Leave a little for the other people, would you?"

"A change in the Constitution has to be ratified by what? Three-fourths of the States?"

"Come on, what started this?"

"Sam."

"Adams?"

She nodded, sadly.

"Goddamn it, Lorraine. You cannot do it all by yourself."

His outburst seemed to weaken her. "I know," she said in a voice as soulful as any train whistle he had ever heard. She shook her head. "It's too much. I told them that. I can't go on. Really, I don't think I can."

"Then don't. OK? Don't."

"I'm so frightened, sometimes."

"Then stop. It's crazy to expect a young girl to do it."

"Who then?"

"All Americans together. All countries combined."

"How does that start?"

"People start it."

"I'm people."

"There you go getting yourself killed again."

She bent her toes up and down. "It has to start with someone. There's so little time. You said so yourself."

"Do you want people to get killed tomorrow?"

"In Vietnam? No."

"I'm talking about that damn factory."

"Stop one and you stop the other."

"I see I'm going about things the wrong way."

"Who isn't these days?"

"Look, do me a favor and tell me something."

"What's that?"

"Do you love me?"

She smiled.

"Come on. Do you? Yes or no."

"Yes I love you."

"Very much?"

"Very very much."

"Good."

She shrugged. "But what do I know."

"Cut it out. Now listen. Question number two. Will you marry me?"

"Wow." Her toes curled up and down again.

"Well?"

"I wish you had asked me a little sooner. Not just hours before I'm going to get killed."

"Lorrie, you are not going to get killed."

"Good. I like long engagements."

"Be serious."

"OK. I like long marriages too."

"Will you marry me?"

"Of course I'll marry you."

"Phew." He kissed her rather lightly on the lips.

"Hey, I'm engaged."

"Now for that favor I wanted to ask you."

Her grin widened. "I thought that *was* the favor."

"No, that part comes now."

"OK. Shoot."

"Call off tomorrow."

"No."

"Why not?"

"No."

"Please."

"No."

"You're frightened."

"Very."

"So am I."

"Poor baby."

"Call it off."

"No. Stop asking me. No." The candle splashed her with a golden fire.

He stretched out face down on the sleeping bag. "Well, I tried."

In the room below, Willoby was singing. Justin didn't speak or move. After a while she touched his shoulder.

"Are we still engaged?" she asked.

On the wall was the enormous fluttering shadow of a moth. Lorraine lay back so she could see his face and he could see hers with its smooth beauty and the tiny flame dancing in each eye.

"We're still engaged," he said.

The only restaurant still open was Howard Johnson's. The steak was bulletproof, the carrots cremated, the salad heavy in specific gravity. She complimented him for being a smooth date and for taking her only to the very best places. He pointed out that if Christ had eaten his last supper in such a dive as this, the police would never have found him for he would have been flat on his back for a week. She drank to his rather oddball grasp of history but assured him that she would be well enough for tomorrow. He was about to reply with some deft remark when one of the waitresses came to their booth to ask for news of Viola. Only then did he remember that the girl had worked here. Lorrie fell into a depression that lasted the meal. Smooth date, indeed, he thought. However, the dessert was so bad, it cheered her up. After sipping the coffee she gave a look of critical, cross-eyed horror. Soon she was herself again.

He noticed with sad pleasure the number of people who made a quick study of her as she passed the cash register and the gift shop and went out into the night. They kissed in the jeep under the 28 flavors and he drove her to his hotel explaining that he had to get some more money. Then he would take her to a charming bar in Port Madison.

"Oh, I'm wise to that one," she said about going back to his hotel.

"Then stay here." And he kissed her one last time. "I'll be right back."

"You're a good guy."

"Don't go way."

"No such luck."

He made himself step out of the jeep. He made himself climb the stairs to the second floor. At the end of the hallway, he stopped and pressed his head against the door. The hotel was silent, cadaverous. He knew he was a fool. But how, exactly? That he didn't know.

There were harsh noises in the street. He hurried along the hall, opened the balcony door and stepped out. Lorrie was shouting. Several men were talking. Justin reached the railing and peeked into the street. Honeycutt and a deputy were trying to pull her from the jeep. She pushed and scratched. Honeycutt lost his cap and then his temper.

"You're wanted for questioning, is all."

"Go fuck yourself."

"Step out of there, miss. That's an order."

"Screw off."

"Get her out of there."

"Take your stupid hands off me."

She was dumped into the road. She screamed Justin's name. When they tried to stand her up she went limp. When the deputy pulled her hair, she bit his leg. He jumped back with a yelp, stepped forward and kicked her in the stomach. She writhed in silence on the ground as if trying to get herself as dirty as possible.

"You bastards. Touch her again and I'll kill you."

Two dull faces tipped upward. But Justin was gone. He charged through the hall, made a turn, slipped to one knee, grunted with pain, reared to his feet, clamored down the stairs, toppled the umbrella stand, banged open the door, burst across the downstairs porch and leaped into the street. Doors to the police car were thumped shut. Justin shouted for them to wait. He ran. They gained speed. He kept up with them for a while. Then they screeched around a corner and out of sight. But not before he heard, or thought he heard, a familiar voice spewing a goddamn shitty fuck.

Justin ran back to the jeep and kept it roaring and sliding until it bucked to a halt four blocks away in front of the sheriff's office. The once grocery store window was painted gray so no one could see in. Black lettering said OFFICE OF THE SHERIFF, SALEMVILLE, NEW YORK and below that, in smaller letters, was AMERICA LOVE IT OR LEAVE IT.

Justin barged in on a young man who was seated behind a card table. Where had they put the prisoner Lorrie Benglesdorf? The boy, wearing his underwear top, lifted a gray uniformed shirt off the back of his chair and put it on to display the badge.

"Prisoners ain't kept here, Mister. They're kept over in Southboro 'cause that's where the jailhouse is at."

Without shutting the door, Justin sprinted for the jeep and twice nearly wrecked it on the road to the other town. Surrounded by a wooden fence, the desk sergeant, body fat oozing up through his collar to form a multiplicity of chins and a bloated face, sat like a judge on high, angry and fearless. Justin demanded to speak with the prisoner Lorrie Benglesdorf. The sergeant took his time emptying a container of coffee. When was she booked? Ten minutes ago. The sergeant checked the list slowly, shook his head slowly, and said, No such prisoner. Justin insisted. The sergeant insisted. Justin leaned over the railing and called him a liar. Like an absolute monarch, the sergeant rose in a luxury of wrath to point down from his throne at his victim and demand that he be ...

Adam Honeycutt entered from the street on the run. He saw Justin and stopped. Justin saw him and ran across the creaking floor to put his hand on the sheriff's armless shoulder. "Where is she?" The sheriff winced like a little boy. "Where is she, damn it?" The sheriff winced again and said, "She got away."

At first he felt joy. One girl against two men, her two arms against their three, plus guns and clubs, and she got away. Safely, too, for he could tell by the sheriff's embarrassed face. Then it hit him.

"You fool," Justin said, "you clumsy, clumsy fool."

The first thing to do was to find her. Then stop her. How, he didn't know. At the farmhouse, Willoby was asleep. Briggs and Fenskie hadn't come yet or they had already left. There was no sign of anyone else. Justin drove to a phone booth, called Briggs and got no answer. Fenskie wasn't listed. As usual Cathrine Benglesdorf was no help at all. She didn't know where her daughter was or her husband either. She had been reading another Simenon. He went to the basement church. No luck. He drove back to Howard Johnson's. No luck. Only then, for some reason, did he think of his hotel. As he drove up, it looked as dead as ever. Her black pin with white letters was lying in the road. GIVE A DAMN. He picked it up and put it in his pocket. Someone else had picked up the umbrella stand. He climbed the stairs and saw light under his door. He opened it quickly and there she was, stretched out with a magazine on his neatly made bed, Camilla Epps.

When dawn came through the gutted windows, Willoby Brown awoke. Again he was delighted to find himself in a totally empty house and he wandered through like a wealthy landowner observing his mansion. For someone who had spent most of his life in rooms crowded with others, he was learning, in ruins, the pleasures of privacy. He walked barefoot and shirtless down the slope of the damp meadow, gathered twigs, said hello to a squirrel, and returned to build a fire near the back door. He cooked eggs and made coffee, and the food he had left he opened and dumped on the ground for the animals in the woods.

He put on the uniform Lorrie had secured from Nimols and he smiled at his promise never to touch such a death suit again. With his box of explosives balanced on his shoulder, he walked Tuckabunkwack Road to Route 4, put down the box and waited. He was a man in an army uniform but he was also black so no one offered him a lift. When the Dauphine came sailing along with Fenskie at the wheel, Nimols, sitting next to him, said, "Who is this?" As Private Brown climbed into the back, Private Fenskie said, "Another one of us," and sped way. "What's in the box?" the Colonel asked, over his shoulder. "Film," Willoby answered, and gave it a pat.

Willoby Brown had been born in Africa many times. He, his wife and children were sold and forced to sail off together on an endless ocean. When one of his children became sick, the lad was taken from his family and thrown overboard into the sea while Willoby wrestled with his wife to keep her from trying to save him. Willoby was sold to a plantation owner in Georgia while his wife, whom he never saw again, went to a rich Virginia landowner who demanded that she be stripped naked before he bought her. Willoby never did find out where his children went.

He was whipped, put to work, schooled in Christianity and talked to like a child all his life, even when he had grown older than any of the white men who owned him. He was so continually humiliated that he finally came to believe there was something inferior about the black man, or else why would God have let this happen? He existed and grew old until even the obsequious bow he had learned became difficult to execute. One day he heard tell of a rebellion some miles off. A few days later, in retaliation, he and ten other slaves were hanged.

This happened to Willoby just as if he had been there. It happened to him many times under different names until the rage and sorrow burned steadily like an eternal flame. And the only way to lessen the pain was to spread the fire.

Willoby no longer felt shame because of his skin or his past. It took his latest reincarnation to teach him that. He was placed in a flying boat and sent across the ocean to follow the white man's orders which were to kill and count the bodies of as many brown men as he could. Willoby dropped his weapons from the air and watched as they splash-roared a lake of fire that stuck against and burned to death all living things so efficiently that afterward, when one or two brown men were found barely alive and brought into hospitals, they were often still burning from the fire of these bombs which even in the operating room could not be put out.

Finally he and his crewmen agreed on a plan. Whenever possible they would drop their bombs on empty hillsides or open areas and, when they couldn't get away with this, they would give the enemy as much time as possible to run or dig in. But the guilt and rage that grew with the body count was getting worse than he could stand and when a blond corporal from Detroit referred to him one day as "Boy," he and several other blacks tore into a line of white men in the mess hall and in three minutes everyone was covered with gravy and mashed potatoes and in some cases blood.

He was sent home. Three days after he arrived at the slum building where his mother lived it was burned down in a riot following a local incident of police brutality. He sent his mother to live with a cousin and went to UCAL to finish his education. But a month later riots in Berkeley closed down the school. He enrolled in CCNY in New York and soon this college, too, was closed by riots. He applied to several other schools and was finally taken by a serene little place called Kent State University. When the National Guard fired, massacring four innocent students, Willoby left in disgust.

All this time he was trying to be a pacifist for he felt he had done enough killing in his life. When he saw that he might have to start killing again to get an education, he simply decided it wasn't worth it. When he realized that to get decent housing and a decent job with a decent salary he might also have to kill, he frankly didn't know what to do. And that eternal flame inside him began to burn even brighter.

He fell in with a number of blacks who said they wanted to smash everything and stomp on the pieces. Now it made a lot of sense and he was good and ready. When he joined them, however, he spent most of his time with three other blacks in an automobile keeping the law in order by following a police car during its prowls through the ghetto. Also he helped feed poor children and set up unofficial schools for them. Willoby enjoyed his new life and although the violence was only talk and the deeds all peaceful, it allowed him to put his flame to use instead of trying to put it out. And this time whitey had a name to call him which he was proud of. He was a Black Panther.

Then he ruined it by falling in love. The girl had trouble deciding whether it was love or not and she, whom he thought of as a dream, became a recurrent nightmare. Her beauty was a bullet lodged near the heart, too painful to ignore, too dangerous to remove. In bed, she gave of herself as if he were the only man on earth. But when they left her room other men appeared and she noticed them. To Willoby, it was much the way a moth noticed a flame. When he finally discovered she was also going out with someone else, he came to her like a little boy and asked what it was about him she didn't like. He was stunned that what bothered her was the one thing that had freed him. "It's this way," she said. "You're just all the time too damn angry."

When the school year ended, she left Detroit to spend the summer at home. He suspected she was using the trip as a way of ending it with him. One week alone was all he could stand. With borrowed money he took off across country in a Greyhound bus. A black man following a brown girl across white America. It was absurd.

When he arrived he found no one who knew her or had even heard of her family. Two days in town (the nights were spent in a sleeping bag in the woods) got him nowhere. On the morning of the third day he bought a newspaper to wrap food in for the trip back. Instead, he sat down on the curb to read how three Black Panthers had been killed when their headquarters were broken into by the police. He knew personally each of the dead; one of them had lent him money for the trip. The story said other Panthers were being sought for questioning. The name Willoby T. Brown was listed among them.

In America that morning no white man hated him more than he hated himself. He had helped the white man kill colored people in Asia and now the white man was back at work killing colored people in America. Stopping on the outskirts of town to get a solid breakfast before heading for Detroit he spotted, behind the ice cream counter and beneath a sign that said 28 delicious flavors, the girl he had been looking for.

No one in town knew of Viola's family because their home was one of a series of squatters' shacks near the road that led to Fort Gilbert. Last year she had moved back in with them for the summer but this time she preferred instead a hippie commune located some miles away in an abandoned church. Her family refused to speak to her because of this. They disapproved of her friends and they considered such housing an act of sacrilege.

Viola softened toward him when she heard of the massacre in Detroit, though when he asked her to go back there with him, she said no, hoping she could keep him from returning as well. He left in a fury, got as far as Pennsylvania, and returned. Among the conditions she imposed on him for a trial period neo-courtship was that they join a small citizens' group who were fighting, of all things, the proposed destruction of (he could hardly believe it) some trees. To him the issue was a waste of time. But he had no choice. He was now the only black man in a group of white, bourgeois activists. He anticipated a long, boring summer. Worse yet, their blonde leader was a cutesy, well-dressed, social-protest playgirl who played at being color-blind as well. Even Viola didn't seem to care for her that much; the blonde had bigger breasts. Then Willoby learned about the voices. That settled it. Either she was in serious need of medical treatment, or an utter horse's ass.

Time, however, fucks up all such early fond impressions because growth, he decided, takes place in the most unlikely people. And anger: not his this time, but theirs. Anger began to show such signs of life in this town that his did not seem nearly so out of place. Not to Viola, at least. And her opinion, and the year-round sunburned body that came with it, was all that really mattered now. Yes, many strange things began to happen in this jovial, white man's playpen. Temperatures were rising toward an explosion. When it would go off, he didn't know. But it heartened him that others were beginning to learn what constant anger was like, others besides those whose flames burned like a multitude of pilot lights in all the dark and hidden ghettos. Also strange to relate was the fact that the blonde with the fashionable skin, clothes, and family connections, who should have been much more at home grazing in the blue grass beside green swimming pools, was actually working herself into exhaustion as she beat harder than the others against the strong white wall of nonthought. Many strange things were happening, indeed, when the skin of a blonde became not a symbol of all he hated but a pale glow of light. Or was air pollution getting to him quicker than he thought?

Mrs. Benglesdorf, still throbbing with sleep, shifted the phone from one ear to the other.

"She did what?"

"Escaped. Clean as a whistle."

"Who did?"

"Your daughter. Plumb escaped and that's a fact."

"Escaped from what?"

"Where's Hirum at? Got to speak to him real quick."

"My daughter, you say?"

"Had to upchuck. Leastways, that's what she said. We stopped to let her get out and soon as we did she jumped on the back of a motorcycle of this goddamned, long-haired hippie who just happened to be stopping for a red light. Help, she screams, the pigs are trying to arrest me. And damn if they both don't tear ass off like two bats outta hell."

"Who may I ask is speaking?"

There was something sinister about Camilla's smile as she rearranged herself carefully on his bed, recrossing one long priceless art work over the other. She closed her magazine. She wanted to share with him a marvelous discovery: that the key to one door in the hotel fit all the other doors in the hotel. That was wonderful, he said, adding that he had just stopped by to pick up something. She lit a cigarette and asked if it wasn't perhaps his camera he had come by to pick up. Yes, that was it, he said, willing now to say any-thing just so he could get back out of there and continue his hunt. Because if it is his camera, she continued as if not hearing him, if it is his camera he had come for, she had taken it.

He ransacked the room with nervous dedication. She watched as she shifted her cigarette from one hand to the other and tapped free some nonexisting ash. If he wished the camera back he would have to be, as she put it, real nice. Well, did he want his camera back or not? Yes, that was it, he said as though dazed, he wanted his cam-era back. Well, his camera would be returned if he found a good part for her in his film. She was enjoying herself as cats do with captured mice. An agreement was arrived at. He would include her in tomorrow's shooting. She smiled: and where might that be? In front of the Southboro Hospital. "Now can I have my camera back?" he asked as nicely as he could.

"Ah, hah!" She sat up like a jack-in-the-box. "Just as I thought. You and your subversive friends are out to attack the hospital, aren't you? My God, how very terrible."

By listening in on Hirum's telephone conversations she had learned of the plan. And Justin, shameful Justin, was going to pho-tograph the whole thing. He tried to calm her down. They weren't going to attack anything. Hirum was misinformed.

"Ruffian. You and your kind are planning to attack innocent people lying in their hospital beds. Oh, yes. Oh, yes. Or why else did you arrange to have your rich Miss Sweetie-Pie, your Secret *Fiancée*, kept out of it? Huh?"

The air was filled with her venom. It froze his mind as he tried to think.

"And you expect to get your little camera back by being nice to me, do you?"

Her cigarette changed hands and she smiled savagely as though the idea of going to bed with him again was so absurd it was amusing.

Justin took his key, crossed the hall, opened her door and ran-sacked her room. There were some frail French underthings, a jar of sourballs and, echoing from the sink, a single, sluggish splat. He went back. She hadn't moved. He was in a terrible state of panic. Visions of facing them without a camera tomorrow—the key to his whole plan—was as unthinkable as not appearing at all. How would it be to say sorry, fellas, but this chick I was making it with on the side stole my Bolex last night and so it looks like we just won't be able to strike that great blow for world peace and sanity after all.

She moved. She rearranged one vanilla masterpiece in relation to the other and explained in detail why it was, exactly, that she hated him. It was the way Justin had slimed around behind her back to get himself engaged to that wealthy subversive with the big tits. And she hated Hirum, too, for cheating on her behind her back. He had a wife and a mistress and he was cheating on them both, the pompous, big-bellied s.o.b.

Justin asked how she knew. She told this story: she had been sitting right where she is now when she heard Justin come up the stairs and stop by the door. Quickly she took off her dress and lay down on the bed. But he didn't enter the room. She heard noise in the street and Justin running in the hall. By the time she had stepped back into her dress and out onto the balcony, he was driving off like a madman in an army jeep. She went back to his room and waited some more. She even fell asleep.

The next thing she knew, Mr. Defreeze was knocking on her door across the hall. She waited until he had gone away, then followed downstairs to ask what he wanted. There was a phone call for her, Defreeze explained. She snatched it up to hear Mrs. Benglesdorf demanding to know where Hirum was. But Hirum had told his secretary that he had to spend the evening home with his wife. He had also told his wife that he had to spend the evening working with his secretary. He had lied to them both. Camilla said she would find out where Hirum was and call her back.

Camilla telephoned a motel in Nyack and asked for a certain Mr. John Henry. This was the name Hirum used whenever he had gone there with her. Sure enough the bastard was registered. She hung up in a cold fury and made a list of all the women who had come into the office in the past couple of months. There were only five. It was fairly late at night when she began phoning them. Only one wasn't home.

"And who was that?" Justin asked.

"Never you mind," was her haughty reply, as if ashamed to admit who had stolen him away. "But she's ugly." And the disgusted girl looked sad.

Justin asked if she had returned the call to Mrs. Benglesdorf. From behind a stream of smoke came a thin, cool yes. He asked what had happened.

"Mrs. Iceberg asked me again where Hirum was. Real snotty. Well I said I did not know where her Hirum was. She said I did so know. I said I did not know. She said I did so know. Finally I said, OK I know. I told her what motel to call. Ask for John Henry, I said, and when you get your husband tell him his secretary has quit. I pressed down the receiver with my little finger and felt very, very good."

"That was cruel, wasn't it?"

"Look who's talking, Mr. Sneak-Attack-on-Hospitals. Well, I got news for you. You're not going to get your finky camera back unless you agree to call it off tomorrow."

There was no harm in agreeing and so he did. She was right. The plan was ill advised. He would call it off. He asked for his camera back.

"Since you've called it off," she said with unctuous hatred, "there's no rush, is there?"

He saw now that her meddling could bring about a disaster. If his plan proved unworkable they would simply proceed with their own. The edges of his world began to curl again with panic. He marshaled his forces—what was left of them—to ask if she really and truly hated her boss. Boy, did she. Would she like to get back at him? She said she had already gotten back at him. Would she like to get back at him even more? The idea appealed to her. Well, then, he was going to tell her a little secret. They weren't going to attack the hospital at all. That had never been the plan. They were going to launch a surprise attack someplace else. She wanted to know where. Well, where did Hirum have the most to lose? Where had he invested the most money hoping to make the most gain? She sat upright. The factory? Yes, he said, exactly. We'll stop them from expanding. We'll stop them from existing. It would be a blow against war and pollution. It would be an attack against the selfishness of business and the blindness of government. And it would screw Hirum good.

Camilla jumped up, dropping ashes all over her dress. "You beast. Hirum invested good money buying up valuable land that will soon become even more valuable 'cause they need it to build on. That's a known fact. It was such a good deal he even told me to put money in it too. Oh, no. I'm not going to allow you or anyone else to lose innocent people their hard-earned money. Oh, I remember you, all right. I remember you very well, Mr. War of 1812. And you will never get your camera back. Never."

He took hold of her shoulders and shook her back and forth with all his rage, her hair like a gentle whip snapping repeatedly into his face. He stopped exhausted.

"And if you don't let go," whispered the disheveled, hateful girl, "I mean if I have to scream, I'll see to it that you get put away for twenty very long years. Oh, yes I will, Mr. War of 1812."

Hirum came home at three in the morning, closed the door and felt safe at last. But puzzled. The two framed photographs of Lorraine-Louise were missing in the living room. In his leather chair in the den lay an empty bottle of Remy Martin. On the carpet, like a frail cannonball, was a smashed cognac glass. Upstairs on the wall of the hallway was scotch-taped a typewritten note:

IMPORTANT ** REQUEST IMMEDIATE LEGAL DIVORCE DUE NOT ONLY TO YOUR ADULTERY OF THIS EVENING BUT FOR PLAYING GOD WITH OUR DAUGHTER AND FOR LETTING HER GET MANHANDLED AND PERHAPS EVEN INJURED SERIOUSLY BY THE POLICE AND BECAUSE I HAVE ASKED YOU TO TREAT HER LIKE A GROWN WOMAN WHICH SHE IS AND LET HER LIVE HER OWN LIFE WHICH YOU WON'T AND FOR NEVER DOING THINGS I HAVE BEGGED YOU TO DO LIKE NOT MAKE ALL THE DECISIONS ABOUT OUR

DAUGHTER YOURSELF AND IN SECRET AND EVEN DOWN TO LITTLE REQUESTS LIKE
THE NUMBER OF TIMES I'VE ASKED YOU TO GET THIS DAMN TYPEWRITER FIXED SO IT
DOESN'T WRITE ONLY IN CAPITALS!

    I HAVE BEEN MADE VERY PROUD, FINALLY, TO DISCOVER THAT I AM FREE ENOUGH
TO HATE YOU. IF THIS NOTE IS A BIT MUDDLED IT IS UNDERSTANDABLE BECAUSE I
AM SERIOUS DRUNK.

CATHRINE B

The bedroom was empty. Their joint photograph, taken during their honeymoon cruise to Bermuda, had been thrown into the corner. The bathroom door was locked. Inside was the raucous sound of his wife snoring.

Colonel Nimols, dressed to perfection, his hair newly dyed, his uniform newly pressed, assembled his men at Orleans Creek for what he was told would be the most important scene in the film. Dawn had spread into early morning, giving him yet another chance to inspect his troops who were also dressed to perfection, their fixed bayonets luminescent. The bend of the creek and the small clearing it semicircled was like a stage of an amphitheatre surrounded by hills and trees. Colonel Nimols saw himself as a modern colossus on that stage striding toward a new glory just as he had seen the great Douglas MacArthur on a newsreel screen striding out of the Pacific to reclaim the Philippines.

From where Justin stood high up on one of the hills, Nimols, knee-jerking his way across the clearing, resembled a man hurrying through waist-deep water. The lines of the soldiers standing at ease, legs apart, were like so many men urinating into the dirt. This absurdity didn't change the fact that he had to go down there and tell them it was all off. They must postpone things for a few days, not only because his Bolex was gone but because Camilla knew. They must. But would they? They wouldn't. They would think he was a coward and making it all up. Now came the big decision: either go down and break the news to them, or run. He didn't run. He was saved from that disgrace by masochism, which he often confused with pride.

He descended the hill ducking his way through a maze of trees when he heard, "Hey, you horse's ass, over here."

Corporal Willoby Brown was chinning himself on a low branch. Nearby was Fenskie, a smiling and preposterous Jesus Christ conscripted into the U.S. Army. He even had a gun to go with the uniform but nothing had been done to hide his long hair. Far more successful in trying to look the part of the stern American fighting man was Private First Class Briggs Smith now practicing a number of original and menacing postures with her long rifle. Lorrie, who had been sitting cross-legged on the pine-needle floor, eating a banana, saw Justin and climbed to her feet. She, too, had become, or had almost become, a soldier. Yet he never wanted to kiss her more than now. Also he could see something was wrong. She approached him with a frown.

"How are you?" he asked, quickly. "Are you OK? I tried to stop them. I saw them kick you. I understand you got away. Are you all right?"

She pulled him over to the privacy of an oak tree where no one could see them. Like a panic-stricken computer, he checked at lightning speed his programmed explanation for having led her into the trap. But how would he explain his affair with Camilla Epps? No, no, that one she couldn't possibly know about. Or explain why he was a coward. No, that one she already knew about and, strangely, didn't care. Well, OK, he was ready.

"Is this yours?" she asked, bending over to flip open the top of a cardboard box. Inside lay his Bolex. It was like being handed back a live grenade which he was certain he had gotten well rid of.

"Is that yours?" she insisted.

"Well, I'll be goddamned."

"How did it get into my father's office?"

"Wow, well I'll be damned."

"I accept that. But how did it get there?"

He could tell her the truth or lie. He told her the truth, and lied. Remember that girl he knew, the one who worked for her father? Well, recently she went into heat. Happened about the time Lorrie had become part nun, part Che Guevara. Well, Camilla saw Justin and tried to seduce him. And she tried and she tried and she tried. But he resisted due to his great love for Lorrie. However, the bait he could not resist, and which finally was dangled temptingly before him, was Camilla's knowledge of Hirum's business. Yes, his lust for knowledge had made him suc- cumb, knowledge which, as Lorrie knew, he had put to use with stunning effect.

It was the truth, dressed up in its Sunday best, trying hard to be better than it was. Her somber face absorbed his very best truth as he waited intently for hers to erupt.

"Then what happened?" she asked calmly.

He realized he had stopped before the end. Quickly he explained that he had dropped her. That he would have anyway even if Lorrie hadn't come back to him. But Camilla insisted on having her revenge. She hid the camera and nothing would per- suade her to tell him where. Trying to win her over to their cause, he had foolishly told her of their plan to assault the factory. This, too, was in vain. He didn't think there was any danger from this dis- closure for he doubted her word would carry any weight, especially when it was Hirum who had assured the sheriff that the target was the hospital.

"Hirum told the sheriff what?" she asked.

He was in it again up to his neck. Quickly he explained this other part of the story, making it very clear that it was his love for her and his fear that she might get hurt that had made him do it.

"I really wish you'd stop treating me like a child," Lorrie said.

She seemed in a forgiving mood. He relaxed. Then she added:

"You slept with her, huh?"

He was up to his neck again.

"Yes, that is correct."

"And never called her back?"

"Absolutely, not. Never called her back. Not once."

"Kind of cruel, no?"

"What would you have me do?"

"Treat her a little more gently, I guess. I mean the way you say goodbye to a girl yesterday might be the way you'll say goodbye to me tomorrow."

"Goodbye? You talk of goodbye? Here I am following you around at the expense of my job, maybe my whole future, following you and your craziness because I goddamn well can't break away though I want to, because I'm so stuck on you I'm probably by now a walking disease that should be put away like a mad dog, and you talk to me about saying goodbye? Holy jumping shit."

She gave him her tilted smile. "That's all I want to hear." She kissed him on the cheek. "You're a good guy and I will love you always and no one else ever, OK? Oh, and I didn't tell the others that I found your camera. Which is why I brought it in a box. Lucky thing I made a duplicate key to my father's office. Figured it might be a good place to hide Muscles Brown if the farmhouse didn't work out. I even offered it to him for late-night sleeping but he said, baby, I don't want no part of no fuckin' law office. Oh, listen, talk to Nimols. I don't want him to exhaust himself with pomposity before the action starts. Say do you like my uniform? Had to take it in a little. Columbo says it looks like I'm hiding a pair of helmets. So, you ready for the big day, big man? I'm so excited I can't stand still. It's going to be great. What's up? You're sweating again?"

"What's up? Listen to me." He took hold of her shoulders. "I want you to stay in the background, you understand? This isn't a game, Miss Benglesdorf. And I mean way in the background. In fact, if it's all the same to you, I'd like you to go home right now."

"You really must love me, you know. You worry so magnificently. Like my father. He doesn't even want me to take an aspirin for fear I'll choke to death."

"I'm not joking, damn it."

"Who's joking, damn it?" And she brought her smile closer and kissed him.

The colonel saluted when Justin entered the clearing. Out of sheer high spirits, he had his men snap to attention and salute

as well. Once again Justin asked the wrong question and the answer was:

"Fantastically well. And yourself?"

"Couldn't be better. Or if so I prefer not to think about it."

"Well, you're on time and ready as per usual." He indicated Justin's 16mm Bolex with its attached shoulder brace which always reminded the colonel of some newly designed secret weapon.

"And you, Colonel—soon to be General—are you ready?"

"Ah, you flatter me, my good man. But, yes, I can safely say that my troops and I are ready to go. Incidentally, have you been running?"

"Somewhat. Look, I'm going on ahead as planned. You start five minutes after I've left, OK?"

"Let's synchronize our watches."

"Why? Just leave five minutes after I do, that's all."

"I have 7:15. What do you have?"

"Seven twenty."

"I'm correct to the second."

"Fine. Then five minutes after I leave you, you leave, OK?"

"Affirmative."

"Swell."

"And where may I ask is lovely Lorraine? Ah, *très jolie, très formidable.*"

"She's très hidden in the woods avec the others."

"Ah, mais non, she should join us."

"As you surely remember, Colonel, we agreed her too-obvious presence might spoil the desired realism."

"Ah, yes, exactly."

"Also I want to shoot this in one take so please keep the scene going no matter what."

"Affirmative."

"Well, that's about it."

"Bet she's beguiling in her army uniform."

"Very."

"You know, I've grown quite fond of her these last few weeks. She's so sweet and gentle."

Justin yanked his hand from his pocket. He examined a finger. Carefully he reached in again to withdraw Lorrie's black pin with white lettering.

"Here," he said to get rid of it, "a little present she asked me to give you."

"Ah, how *très bien*. And how succinct it is in its emotional, i.e., sexual, message."

"What?"

"That I should give a damn and keep trying to win her."

"Colonel, just don't put it in your pocket, OK?"

"Affirmative."

Adam Honeycutt considered himself the best in a noble line of the town's great guardians. First, there had been Sheriff Bundy who, it was said, helped pave Lindbergh Boulevard and whose most noted arrest was that of Mike Woodrow for attacking a local mechanic with his bare hands because the man had tried to assault Mike's daughter. Mike Woodrow was later made sheriff himself because the town thought that any man who could so admirably take the law into his own hands should be allowed to keep it. And they hoped he would defend their women equally well. They also liked the public statement he issued to the effect that if elected he would stay sheriff as long as they wanted him and would never try to become, for example, mayor.

It was almost twenty years ago that Sheriff Woodrow made headlines by arresting a group of big-city perverts in the act of photographing naked women on the old Willis Farm. D.A. Keith, who staged the arrest, went on to become a U.S. Congressman while Ezra Willis, one of the only living descendants in a family that dated back to the Revolutionary War and who pleaded guilty to allowing his farm to be used for immoral purposes, came to grief soon afterward while still out on bail. He went to the Salemville Railroad Station to meet his twin brother, Noah, home from a three-year

prison term for selling stolen goods. Noah, who had read the head-lines telling of naked women cavorting on his farm, became so enraged over what he considered to be the blackening of his family name, that before the train had even rolled to a halt, he leaned out of his window and shot Ezra dead.

Honeycutt considered himself the best in this noble line. But he was pissed off that he had never had an opportunity of catching nude ladies cavorting illegally in an open field. If he had, his name would have been made and maybe afterward he could have run for a seat in the Albany State Legislature where, he heard tell, a man could be both corrupt and honored at the very same time. After all, how else could a person put away a little something for his ultimate retirement, be it voluntary or otherwise. Yet the cases that had come his way of late had propelled his name about as far, he said, as a man could lob turd from the roof of an outhouse. The burning down of the Selective Service Office was a crime he had to leave unsolved because he needed Lawyer Benglesdorf's friendship more than he needed a risky court action against his daughter. His swift action against those who wanted to save the trees earned him a few nods of approval and little else. The riot at the factory gate took place when he wasn't there. John Dillinger spent a night in town when Honeycutt was still a boy and as far as anyone knew that was the last time a public enemy had come anywhere near Salemville. Trouble. He wanted it so badly he was almost willing to start it himself. Then just when he was beginning to feel that nothing bad would come his way, Lawyer Benglesdorf told him about the hospital plot.

But early on the morning of the big day when he arrived at the once grocery store, now OFFICE OF THE SHERIFF, SALEMVILLE, NEW YORK, to collect his men, he saw pretty Camilla Epps sitting at the card table pointing a gun right at him. She was being fussed over by a few of his stupid deputies who had emptied a .38 of ammu-nition and were taking turns looking down Camilla's dress as they showed her how to aim. He bawled them out, took her into his office and sat her far enough away from his desk so at one and the same time he could hear her complaint and study her legs.

He had really expected Lawyer Benglesdorf to appear in a rage over his daughter's escape and to demand that the hospital arrests be called off, a request that Adam had no intention of granting. But he had not anticipated the secretary in his place, and on her own. Well, the view was a consolation, anyway, even if he did suspect the lawyer arranged it.

In a moment her legs were forgotten. He couldn't believe her, refused to believe her. He wanted to check with Hirum but she said he didn't know, only she knew. The sheriff suspected a trick. Maybe the lawyer was cleverer than Adam had thought. She begged the sheriff to believe her, pleaded with him with her wide eyes and soft lips, but he refused. Why did she have to appear like this and complicate things? She was misinformed or lying. Yes, probably lying. She was suspect, as every pretty woman was suspect, pretending not to know how infuriatingly desirable she was, pretending to be friendly, flirting slightly, trying to use him for God knows what purpose, yet all the while keeping him exiled from her pampered life because she worked for a lawyer and Adam was a cop.

No, he would station his men where Hirum had suggested. Southboro, an hour from now, at the hospital steps. His information had been furnished by a reliable source. He was not fool enough to change his plan. Precious time was being lost as it was. And he had no more explained this to her when Moe Mullen barged in. He had just arrived from his home, had been told by the other deputies that the girl inside was a real looker and with any luck he might just catch old Adam in some one-armed hanky-panky. Moe's excuse for entering without knocking was that he thought the sheriff was off keeping an eye on those leftists who were making a movie in the woods. Moe knew, of course, that Adam had given that up days ago, but since he had seen them himself from a distance that very morning on his way to work, a fact which he now mentioned, he added that he thought it was rather an odd place they had chosen this time which is what made him so positive that the sheriff would be there.

"Where were they at?" Honeycutt asked quickly.

"Oh, up at Orleans Creek," the deputy answered looking down at Camilla's legs. "You know, near the factory." And he smiled at her and said: "Hi."

Justin climbed away from the sound of rushing water. He listened to his shoes cracking twigs and, though the climb was an easy one through the trees, he felt a fierce hammering in his chest. Perspiration streaked his glasses and burned his eyes. At the top of the hill was the pasture, beyond that, the factory. A cluster of workers were waiting at the gate which hadn't yet opened. Others were joining them from the direction of the bus stop. He counted six guards. He had hoped for less. And the hammering didn't stop.

The moist grass was invaded by fidgety butterflies, reminding him of moths and flames. They and all the other creatures on this earth seemed placidly unconcerned with the trouble into which he was sinking. If he went to prison he wouldn't see her for years. It was better that he go than she. Yet he wouldn't see her for years. He tried not to think of this. But the thought kept coming as his sweat kept coming. If he went to prison he would not see her for years. She would fall in love and give herself to someone else and share her bed with someone else and he would be in prison, alone. Perhaps he would never see her again, ever. Now the loss of her was real, as if it had already happened and he stopped, closed his eyes, and stood still. How would he get through the terrible length of a single day if he couldn't phone to hear her voice or see her waving as she came to meet him. Time would keep stopping like a broken clock and he would be trapped inside his own hollowness, anchored to a single moment in time, unable to move. How idiotic to allow someone else's idiosyncrasies to become the crutch of his life. How astonishing that two people could so blend together that to be parted was to be cut asunder. How ironic that she whom he had begun by protecting would render him helpless when she left. And it was as if it had already happened. There was nowhere to escape but into self-pity, and warm tears blurred his sight. They

came as a great relief for now, at last, others would see the pain and show concern.

But there were no others. The sun had begun to dry the grass and moisten the air. In the cricket-punctured silence he reminded himself that if he really loved her all that much he would damn well have to get on with it. Taking a deep breath, yanking a reed from the earth, he once again set forth, sweating.

In the beginning all went as planned. The colonel's empty Dauphine was parked in the road some three dozen yards from the gate. Justin knelt beside it so the guards couldn't see him. He studied the rolling grass of the pasture through which he had come and waited impatiently for signs of life. Signs of life that would surely destroy him. "Don't be morbid," he whispered, "you're a big-time historian. Think of the article this will make for the *Yale Review*." "Or the San Quentin *Press*," she replied from inside his head. "Up yours," he advised. "Such eloquence," she countered. "Look, kid, I taught you everything you know." "Big man, big man." "And I know now I should have kept my mouth shut." "Too late, Professor." "You and your goddamn voices." "Sir, my voices are my nation's heritage." "Your voices are a load of... " She interrupted: "Hey, look who's talking about voices?" Jesus, she was right!

Then in the distance all at once out of the grass rose a fierce army with steel bayonets and horrible insect faces. Someone blew a glorious bugle and they charged. Leading the way was Colonel Nimols, the only one not wearing a gas mask because he didn't want his face hidden from the camera. Before Justin could focus through the viewfinder, there to the left from out of a screen of trees came Lorrie's own private battalion bumbling along to join in with the others. They, too, were wearing gas masks but it was ridiculously easy to tell them apart. Willoby was carrying two heavy suitcases like a suspicious soldier who, rather than leave all his belongings behind, preferred to bring them even into battle. Briggs, holding her rifle like a pole vaulter approaching a jump, had cut both eye pieces out of her mask to make room for her glasses. Fenskie's hair, tucked up

under his helmet, was beginning to fall loose and, for some reason, he was holding his rifle high over his head like a screaming
Apache. The only real soldier among them was Nick Columbo who
was carrying a long ladder like an army house painter late for work.
And, of course, leading the way with her bulging khaki shirt striv-
ing in vain to hide her gender, was Miss Benglesdorf, his Cross of
Lorraine, disregarding her own safety despite everything he had
said, and yelling "Straight on," as she sprinted forward to save the
world. Justin waved for her to get back. She waved a cheerful hello
and kept going.

What happened next was a sustained and well-paced blur. The
group of factory workers at the gate reacted to the attack as would
any other sober collection of men: they ran for their lives. The
guards, of course, had other commitments. They stood transfixed
by this sudden assault by North Vietnam (who else could it be?),
drew their guns, crouched, and looked fierce and determined. And
did nothing. They were outnumbered as the British were in India,
and this was clearly not a case of nonviolence. They could hardly
believe what they saw and what they saw was cold steel and a well-
trained army with horrible grasshopper heads coming on fast to
run them through. One guard clutched his pistol so tightly it fired.
Part of Columbo's ladder splintered away. The army kept coming
because no one except Columbo saw what had happened and the
rest, though they had heard the shot, had been told that the guards
in this make-believe movie scene would, of course, be using blanks.
Justin, as planned, jumped up on the Dauphine, faced the gate,
yelled, "Run, run," and, to his utter amazement, wasn't shot. The
guards, having finally been given an order, ran. Justin's relief was so
great that he collapsed into a sitting position on the roof of the car.

When he saw Lorrie waving frantically at him as she ran, he
understood immediately and nearly toppled off as he sprang up
and aimed the Bolex just in time for Colonel Nimols who, checking
first to see if he was on camera, quickly performed, for the edification of his troops, some impressive generalissimo-type gesturing in
handsome profile.

Lorrie missed all this for she was busy leading her gallant battalion full tilt into the factory whose gate had just been opened by someone from the inside who saw what was coming and fled. "You're supposed to stay with the colonel," Justin shouted too late to stop her. He jumped down to the road nearly landing on a bayonet because Nimols had ordered his men to take defensive positions in a wide semicircle around the entrance, each man on one knee, which of course left their commander beautifully exposed so that Justin could get a clean shot at him with his marvelous mobile camera. But Justin's only interest now was getting Lorrie the hell out of there and it was to this aim that he tripped over someone's foot, landed against another soldier and together the two of them knocked over still a third. One of them made a muffled and presumably unfriendly remark from behind his grasshopper mask but Justin was off again and running. He ignored Nimols, who called out to him, and ran toward the gate and the wide-open double doors of the building only to be stopped by several frightened factory employees who were exiting quickly with their hands above their heads, Briggs and Lorrie marching behind them, their guns pointed at their backs.

Suddenly everyone heard it. Police cars, hysterically screaming and coming fast. Justin looked at Lorrie whose hazel eyes blinked back at him helplessly inside her mask.

"Looks like the law," said a puzzled Nimols approaching him.

"So I see."

"You mean this wasn't planned?"

"Oh, planned? Yes, completely planned."

"Then why didn't you tell me ahead of time?"

"Wanted it to be a surprise, Colonel."

"So my men would react authentically, you mean?"

"Exactly," Justin said, signaling Lorrie to run for it.

Nimols took his eyes from the rapidly advancing police cars and smiled with new respect at this young creative film director. "You're all right, buddy. But how did you get the sheriff to ... "

"Told him he would get into the film if he put on an angry law and order bit."

"I understand perfectly," said the colonel as the angry cars rocked to a stop, doors swinging wide as crouched policemen, with guns drawn, emerged.

Justin glared at Lorrie, "Tell them to run, will you," then said, "Yes, certainly, sir," when the colonel asked if he was getting all this, meaning the splendid way he was about to stride off to meet the puzzled sheriff and his nervous men. Lorrie had dashed into the factory again. Also the six guards who had run away were now running back to reclaim their jobs.

Despite his fear, Justin experienced a quiver of triumph. Surely it was what Napoleon must have known standing on his hilltop above yet another memorable battle scene of history, his brilliant plans working to perfection. Perhaps the constant sweating had made him lightheaded but he felt that even General Honeycutt's counterattack could be handled.

"What the hell is all this?" asked the big-bellied, open-vested sheriff, who scratched his knee by sticking his revolver for a moment under the short stump of his lost arm.

"We," the colonel announced, "are occupying this building to call attention to the Communistic plot to pollute our country. By this action we hope to demonstrate to the American people their need to pull our troops out of the swamp of Asia and send them against the real enemy, this terribly devious industrial contamination."

"Is that a fact?"

"It is, sir."

"Well, don't you and your boys go hurt yourself none 'cause you're all under arrest as of now."

"Is that a fact?" Nimols said.

"Surenough."

"Well," said the colonel, with surprising stage assurance, "I must remind you that you're outnumbered. I insist that you lay down your arms." He faltered at this point because the sheriff had, in fact, only one. "I mean, lay down your guns and immediately surrender."

"Son," replied Honeycutt, pointing his gun at the colonel, "you're liable to get your pretty head shot right off if you don't tell your boys there to put away their toys."

Nimols made a signal with his hand. His troops moved up, knelt, and pointed their rifles at the sheriff, while another row of men moved up and stood just behind them pointing their rifles at the same target. Justin was reminded of the British at Bunker Hill. The sheriff and his men, with nothing to hide behind, made a subtle effort to hide behind each other. To his chagrin, Honeycutt found that the spot on which he stood had become front center.

The colonel raised his arm and shouted, "Ready!"

"*Ready!*" the sheriff bellowed at his own somewhat undisciplined group.

"*Aim!*" yelled Nimols.

"*Aim!*" the sheriff screamed as if voice level, not fire power, was the true test of strength.

"Sheriff, you're outgunned," Justin shouted inadvertently, "don't be a fool."

Nervous Moe Mullen blurted out: "We have God on our side."

Wyatt Nimols, who had been too self-involved to notice his film director's unaccountable entrance as an actor into the scene, insinuated a smile and asked, "May I ask which one of you is God?"

No answer. Beginning to dissolve in terror, Justin kept his camera grinding without looking where it was pointing. Instead he was fixated on the gate where Lorrie and the others should have already emerged if disaster, as he had planned, was to be avoided.

Too late.

"Fire!" the colonel thundered, in his four-star general's voice.

"*No!*" Justin screeched.

"Fire," announced a bereaved Honeycutt.

As the earth trembled and everyone jumped, a fearsome concussion of sound blew a large section of the factory wall into the road. Another horrible explosion knocked out the rest of the wall which, as it fell, flattened a frail police car.

"What the fuck?" Nimols asked.

"Shit, that's damaging private property," said Honeycutt coughing from the dust that was covering them like a tidal wave.

"Listen, buddy boy, that wasn't part of no goddamn movie," Nimols growled in Justin's direction before he, too, doubled over coughing.

A hot howling wind swept through Justin's life as he struggled for air and sanity. He screamed her name and no one heard him, for still another explosion split brick and steel, its effect unseen. You'll get yourself killed, he raged at the girl who, for all he knew, might now be dead. A frightened animal could not have bellowed louder. And he ran. Hugging his heavy camera, he ran right into a soldier who was sprinting through dust in the opposite direction yelling, "Fire, fire." Justin lay on the ground watching Vietnamese graffiti being written in chalk on the inside of his skull. He was up on his feet too soon after the knockdown and did a few mambo steps, hugging his camera. He tried to wave away the dust which in his scrambled mind he took to be just so much more goddamn air pollution. Again he hurried toward the factory entrance to try to save the girl he loved, but Honeycutt's hand closed like a vise on his arm. As a legal member of the Salemville Citizens Volunteers, Justin was required to join in and save the building from fire. "OK," he said and for the third time started for the entrance. The sheriff hung on, swung him around and sent him stumbling in the opposite direction across the street. Puzzled as to how he was supposed to put out a fire by running from it, he was about to turn and charge back again when he saw, looming out of the dust, a soldier at a fire hydrant busily pouring water into army helmets. With his tie conducting moisture, Justin carried a brimming helmet and a heavy camera as fast as he could into the smoke-clogged building. He called her name, heard distant shouts, and soon was completely enveloped by rolling waves of night. He used the braille system to climb a metal stairway. He heard coughing. He kicked a lunch box. He tiptoed onward. A hellish geyser of flame leaped up beside him and he threw his collection of water, helmet and all, out over the railing and down onto some blazing machinery. He saw a

long-haired gas mask, yelled Fenskie, saw the apparition wave him on and disappear. Justin followed and bounced off a wall. He tried another direction, at last saw Lorrie and they embraced. She was so happy she kept jumping up and down on his shoes. Justin, who had been holding his breath all this time, began showing signs of distress. He knew if he didn't make the street in one minute flat he would explode. But Lorrie hung on tight. He was on the verge of hitting her to get free when he saw that she was offering him her mask. He took a few deep breaths and became human again.

"We go. Run," he grunted like some half-assed Tarzan with eyeglasses and a half-wet tie.

"Isn't it wonderful," she laughed. "We did it, we did it."

"Must escape," he wheezed and dove into the oxygen again.

"This way." And she headed deeper into the smoke and heat. He was about to refuse when he realized she had taken the mask. He followed so closely he stepped on her feet.

The inferno into which they were descending was a fusion of night and flame with an occasional pop-flash of fire like napalm on a distant hill. When they had descended yet another steel stairway, Justin caught a glimpse of Corporal Brown tossing Molotov cocktails into the void. The three of them crouched and ran down a long corridor between mountains of ugly metal. Lorrie took hold of Justin's hand and pulled it up a spiral stairway to a broken window that revealed a heavenly wire fence, a splendid asphalt sidewalk, a sunwashed tar-black road.

"Go first," she said.

"You go first," he shouted.

"Hurry," Willoby yelled up to them. "They're coming."

Lorrie handed Justin her gas mask, kissed him quick and jumped out. Before following her, he paused to take one last look around at all that he and his plan had wrought. Something he saw transfixed him. A great chunk of the back wall was gone and as the smoke lifted for a moment there, clearly, were the one hundred or so amputated arms reaching helplessly out of the earth. Despite his fear and the heat of the furnace in which he stood, he felt such a

sense of exhilaration at the sight of these dead trees and the joint action that their destruction had led to, that he clung to the vista as, once in Italy, he had clung to his first sight of the Roman ruins.

"Get that black bastard."

Justin looked down from the railing and saw Moe Mullen and two army men attacking Willoby. So the army and the police had joined together. Look out! One of the soldiers, lifting his bayonet-mounted rifle, was about to use it. Justin had only one weapon. He threw it, shoulder brace and all, and watched the thing fall and land on the man's neck. The soldier hurried away as if he had suddenly decided to bayonet the wall. He bounced off, knelt to pray, changed his mind, and fell over. Justin clattered down the circular stairway. He dropped his mask and jumped one of the men who had jumped Willoby. Never having thrown a punch before, he emulated innumerable Western screen heroes and tossed a hard, conclusive right cross that missed. In return, the soldier threw one of his own that caught Justin on the shoulder and spun him around in time to see Willoby holding Moe Mullen aloft and, for the second time, tossing him away. Justin's cheek was grazed by a fist. He ducked, adjusted his glasses with a wiggle of his nose, aimed at the man's chin and hit his throat. The soldier gagged, clutched, and wrestled himself to his knees. "Run," Willoby shouted. They made for the spiral stairway and lost valuable seconds each trying to make the other ascend first. Then Justin heard, "Now, now, son," spoken softly and distinctly from behind. He turned and saw Honeycutt up on his toes reaching as high as he could with his only arm and bringing the nightstick down as hard as he could while Justin tried to avoid the... and everything was fixed in a searing lake of light. There was the graffiti again. Then a warm swift sense of...

At first the bandaged face was a reflection of his own pain. It receded and a man and a woman came and touched him. A great bonfire was blazing in his head and later the bandaged face reappeared. Day came and night and day again. More people touched him and left. The bandaged face always returned. When he tried to

lift his head the fire roared. It took hours to die down. One morn-ing the bandaged face said something. It said, "Hi, this is Viola. Remember me?"

The explosion had even awakened the mayor in his barber chair. As soon as the area was pacified, he had himself driven out by police car to inspect the damage, deplore the violence, and pledge himself to punish the guilty. And he skillfully stole the headlines from Sheriff Honeycutt.

The town's people were shocked that violence could strike so close to home. Many wrote angry letters demanding greater police protection. When it was learned that the board of trustees of the factory had voted to rebuild in Minnesota, there was a great out-cry for the sheriff's resignation. Knowing something like this was coming sooner or later, and not wanting the target of the public's displeasure to be himself, the mayor was the first to attack his own sheriff.

A few people did notice that for the first time in months they were able to smell fresh air again. But their greatest concern was for their personal safety.

"And Lorrie?" he asked the ceiling.

"Oh, didn't I tell you?" Viola replied from behind her bandages. But then a doctor came in and asked Justin's only contact with the outside world to leave. Later that afternoon she came back again to sit on his bed. "And Lorrie?" he asked. The bandaged face said that Lorrie had escaped. The only witness who might have implicated her was Colonel Nimols who purposely left her name out of the statement he made to the police. Evidently he still had plans of his own for her.

"She phones me every few hours to find out how you are," explained the girl behind the white mask. "She's terribly worried about you. She said it was a good thing they didn't bruise your mag-nificent body. You can't see it but I'm smiling."

He also smiled. "She's the last of the great insurrectionists."

"I'll tell her."

"And tell her to stay out of sight."

"I'll tell her that too."

"Say I love her very much."

"Oops, too late. I already told her. I even told her—are you ready?—I even told her that in your delirium you called for her."

"Did I?"

"Naw, but what she don't know won't hurt her or you either."

"Keep up the good work."

"Yar vold."

Then he asked about Willoby. She shook her head. "The bastards grabbed him. Seems he knocked the sheriff down and he knocked a few other guys down and he was climbing some kind of stairway or something when the pigs waiting on top grabbed him. He didn't fight cause he was carrying you in both arms. At least that's what the paper said. God, I miss him so much." She said nothing for a while and she pinched the sheet covering his bed. "One good thing about this mask. You can cry in private. Oh, and I sent clippings back to his friends in Detroit. I want them to be proud of him."

"He's one hell of a good man."

She said nothing. He tried to pat her hand but missed. He lifted his head and his brain caught fire. He lay back and closed his eyes.

"Are you still there?" he asked, later on.

"You jerk-off, where'd you think I'd be?"

"Pretty girl, talk to me. How's your face coming along?"

She shrugged. "Fine. The doctors say just fine."

"I'm very glad."

"You want some water?"

"Please."

Later when she took the tube out of his mouth he asked if anyone had been killed. She told him no. Thank God, he said. Yeah, she said. Then he asked about his banged-up head. He was listed as being in fair condition. They had taken X rays. They planned to perform a spinal tap. He asked if she knew what the police were charging him with.

"You really want to know?"

"Uh, huh."

"There are more charges against you than the entire Third Reich."

"I'm ready."

"OK here goes. Inciting to riot. Damaging private property. Endangering the lives of others. Organizing a rebellion. Assault and battery. Fraud. I think it was fraud. And one crazy one the wording of I don't remember exactly. Something like using the army for evil purposes. Something like that. I didn't know you could use the army for anything but. Hey, Professor, don't look so sad."

"Sounds like I'll get fifty years in the electric chair."

"Cheer up, OK? Hell, Colonel What's-his-name is going to get court-martialed, they say. And then there's Willoby. God knows what they'll do to him because of his black ass. And there's my— you know—face. But we did it. That's the point. Really it is. We really and truly did it."

"Yes, we did it. But I'm still not sure yet what."

That evening Hirum Benglesdorf appeared in his hospital room looking like a million shares of plunging stock. Justin's bed had been cranked up so he could face his guest somewhat equally. The lawyer, ill at ease, silently slipped a box of candy on the night table. He paced the room, then stopped to adjust a pocket flap on his silk suit. He blurted out that he had some truly bad news. Justin thought of Lorrie. He made two fists under the sheet and asked what the bad news was.

"I'm sorry, lad," the lawyer said, squeezing the patient's knee, "but your mother, your dear mother, was killed in Vietnam."

Hirum was as humorless as a rockslide. So it was true, then: his poor, driven, love-hungry mother had been swallowed up in that obscene war. He couldn't remember when he had last truly needed her. Now that she was dead he suspected he needed her again and felt weak and foolish because of it.

"The telegram arrived at your hotel," Hirum explained ever so gently. "Defreeze sent it on. I called your father right away. A wonderful man. He's out of the hospital, you know. He said he received a letter from some army bigwig telling him how it happened. Seems your mother is a great hero. Heroine, actually. She had given a superb concert for our boys. Those were the general's own words. A really superb concert. Sang all the old favorites. Was a real smash, lad. Very big. Well, they were driving her back to the airfield when she suddenly had to do duty. They stopped the jeep and she walked no more than a few yards into the jungle when she stepped ... well, she stepped on a booby trap. Died instantly. Without pain. I can assure you of that, lad. Direct quote from the general. Absolutely without pain. Seems they're going to hush the whole thing up. They feel it's bad publicity when someone entertaining our boys gets killed. But I got news for ya. Your Mom is a very, very great lady. Even your father is proud. He's very sad, of course, yes. But damn proud."

Justin said nothing. Hirum announced that he would step outside for a while so the young man could be alone. When he returned ten minutes later, Justin hadn't moved. The music to the line "We were sailing along on Moonlight Bay" had kept repeating itself absurdly in his head.

Hirum thanked Justin for keeping Lorraine out of the "whole ugly mess." Several times over he repeated how thankful he was and again, fondly, he squeezed the patient's knee. To do something for Justin he had pulled strings and thrown his weight around. He had succeeded, too, he said. Because of his mother's supreme sacrifice, Hirum had been able to get Justin freed on bail to attend the funeral. He hadn't told his father about—Hirum waved his hand in the general direction of the bed—all of this. He left it to Justin to break the news as he thought best.

"And for what you did for Lorraine-Louise, again, really..." He struggled to keep his feelings civilized. "Thanks."

It seemed odd to Justin that he should feel sorry for such a large, wealthy man. "And I'm sorry I screwed you up with all that land you bought because ..."

"Forget it. I got news for ya. It suddenly doesn't matter anymore. I let a lot of really important things slip through my fingers this week. It was one hell of a lousy week, I can tell you. The goddamn money is the least of it."

"I see."

"My daughter is what's important."

"I understand."

"A man has got to be crazy if he doesn't love a girl like that."

"I know."

"He's really got to be crazy."

"Tell me, in your opinion, honestly, how many years do you think, would you say, I'll get?"

"Honestly?"

"Honestly."

"With luck, ten maybe, fifteen. With luck."

"S'what I thought."

Hirum leaned closer, determined, desperate. "I got news for ya. I'm putting up the bail. Me, yes. So forget it. I mean, take her and jump bail. OK? Get the hell out of here. I can always visit her in England or Sweden. I mean she'll get herself smashed up if she stays in this damn country. The stupid broad won't stop until she ... When you get out, run, OK?" Tears flickered in his eyes. "After the funeral, run. Is that a promise?"

When Justin had climbed out of bed and into his clothes, he felt he had used up all the excess strength he had. He hugged Viola and told her he loved her. She loved him, too, she said, through the thin slit in her mummy wrappings. She wanted to go down to the lobby with him but a police officer refused to let her leave the floor. He stood alone, waiting for the elevator. Feeble old men in bathrobes made sliding sounds in their slippers and there was that smell again. He went down and walked out alone into the sun. With every

step along the path his whole body seemed to be growing weaker and coming apart. In the cab he said, "Rail. Stay. Shun." "What?" "Train. Station." The cab leaped forward and his head caught fire. It was still burning when he hauled himself with both hands (remembering waddling Mrs. Durkee) up the flying buttress of stairs to fall into a seat by the window. He was drenched again and felt so ill that he knew now, as the train pulled out, that he should never have left his bed. Hirum had agreed to visit his prehistoric hotel and send on his suitcase which Justin, with vivid premonitions, had packed in advance. Today he couldn't have moved it three feet. His Bolex had been impounded by the police.

America rolled past for his exhausted inspection. A telephone pole, a telephone pole, a telephone pole, a road and a fence darting away, a bobbing fence running alongside, a telephone pole, a telephone pole, a gas station, a junkyard, a brown house, a clothesline, an ax stuck in a tree stump, a road and a fence darting away, a telephone pole, a telephone pole, an ESSO sign and a telephone pole. He closed his eyes. The pain was spreading. He waited for it to die down. It grew instead and threw off heat like flames he had watched in a fireplace once on a cold night in Vermont.

He had to. There was no other way. Across the aisle were two hands and *The Wall Street Journal.* Up ahead a woman was bending forward and blinking loose a contact lens. The golden pocket watch snapped open. Soon the pain became a warm tropical sun.

He thought of his mother lying in a box at the edge of an airstrip with the fluttering props of a big bird settling down to lift her off. But she wasn't dead. Not yet. She sang one last song while he listened, as he once did in a dark theatre long ago, marveling at her voice bouncing off the balcony wall begging the people to join in. He felt even more sorry for his sick father now left sitting alone. He had been a kind and understanding father without really understanding anything at all. He had a lousy job, a son dead in battle long ago, a wife away from home half the year and now killed singing for our boys. He even hung out the flag each and every holiday. What could possibly be said to such a man to make him

understand why the side of a factory had to be blown away or why his only living son must ruin his life in an antiwar rebellion? Poor men make few requests and the only request he ever made of his only son was that he work hard, obey his mother, and love his country. Indeed the real victory would be to make this man understand what his son had done and be proud. But Justin knew that such a task was greater than knocking down a building wall or making the Republic live up to its promise. Father, rejoice, your son is a half-assed man of action at last. Hell, it's a start. Sing along with me, Dad. The words aren't hard. Hey, Dad, we did it. But no one understands. If only you, Father, if only you would understand.

A lunar landscape was passing before him. The train rattled onward almost recklessly. The sun grew larger as it came closer. He shut his eyes. There was a great heat as at the edge of the sea. Smooth, indented Lorrie lay broiling herself under the sky's wide furnace. Brown and naked afterward in bed with bikini ghosts on her burning skin, she made soundless laughter and boisterous love. Her tongue was stoking his feverish brain, her long electric nails feathering the length of his spine. And still the sun grew closer, hurrying him on. They became lovers again, fused and frenzied. She called his name in dismay like a delirious child who can see the future. He is set ablaze by her maddening skin. She asks him never to leave her, to be near her, now and always. Out of control, spinning and climbing, he splashes into the sun.

Would she run away with him? Lorrie had foolishly said, Oh, yes. Now in the angry anthill of Manhattan, she knew better and grew depressed. Earlier she had been appalled by the thought of friends hurt or left to rot in prison. New York forced her to think of all the work there was yet to do. To leave was impossible. She would live only in her own country, attacking it until it improved, frightening, whenever she could, cautious bank presidents and pompous politicians and all the other men who sit and do very little slowly. Justin would live in Canada and help her. She would travel to see him twice a month and occasionally, perhaps, he would slip across the

border to visit her. Their private happiness was less important, after all, than the job at hand. Yes, that was the trouble with America. It was filled with junkies too hooked on wealth to give much attention to the job at hand.

She hardly slept. She collared friends, wrote letters, made phone calls. She explained it again and again. The plan was this: on a given night every auto display window in New York City would be mysteriously smashed. Messages would arrive at newspapers explaining the reasons for the protest. A week later, on a given street every parked car would have its tires slashed and again that morning letters would arrive at all the newspapers calling for a crash program against all pollution to replace the polite national policy of chipping away at the growing problem. Perhaps this kind of protest would become contagious. Other cities might try the same approach. It might spread across the country. It might triumph.

Her friends listened with respect and complimented her on the grandeur of the project. But they had house cleaning to do or a term paper to write or a job to hold down. They were really sorry that they couldn't help. Perhaps some other time.

Well, she never expected it to be easy. Often she had to remind herself to remember this. Nevertheless she kept after people, explaining the need for action as she grew hoarse in the throat, trying not to argue if she could possibly help it, and allowing herself only one indulgence, phoning all the way to Viola's voice in the hospital. Today Lorrie was told that a spinal tap had produced no blood. She accepted this as good news although the surgical mystery of it all made her queasy. It was then that she was given that other bit of news. He had decided to jump bail and go to Canada. He wanted to know if Lorrie would go with him? Swamped by a flash flood of love, she answered first and thought later.

The next morning Viola informed her that the coffin had arrived. The funeral was scheduled for the following day, and guess who was to meet Justin at Grand Central Station at 10:00 A.M.? This sent her sailing through a tall blue sky of joy. He'll be safe now, she thought. He'll have me to take care of him.

On the day of the burial, Lorrie rose fully rested at eight in the morning. She bathed, sipped coffee, sheathed herself in basic black and quickly checked the time. No rush at all; it was just 8:00 A.M. She did her eyes in basic blue, opened a yogurt and cracked her way through a piece of toast. And it was still only 8:00 A.M. She snatched up the clock and pressed it to her head. She almost screamed. A quick phone call told her that the ti-um was tey-un twenty-nie-un. She screamed. A quick call to have him paged produced a busy signal. She clattered down the stairs, found a cab and helped rush it into Manhattan by sitting well forward in her seat. But there was no sweet wounded good guy among the healthy multitudes in Grand Central. And the train from Salem-ville had come and gone.

Screaming now would have done no good. Her vision of helping him to her apartment so he could rest before the ordeal, of undressing and putting him to bed so she could be nurse, cook, concubine, and left-wing compatriot all rolled into one, this delicious daydream of love and romantic selflessness died on the wing among the heartless troop-movements of commuters who passed her on all sides as she turned in all directions finding only strangers.

She dialed his empty Manhattan apartment in a guilty panic. She dialed his father and got only busy signals. Even the door to the phone booth conspired against her and she broke out only after much cursing, rattling and shoulder-ramming. She took a cab to South Ozone Park agonizing secret messages in her head which she hoped might somehow reach him: Don't be angry, please. I'm so sorry I missed you. I really am sorry. I want to be with you and help you and hold you so when bad times come we'll be so in love it won't even matter. Darling, do you hear me? I'm alone in the back of a checkered cab on the Brooklyn Bridge and I love you. The guilt meter is up to a dollar seventy-five and ticking like crazy and I'm so very sorry I missed you, sweet man. But I'm on my way and I love you. Oh, I do.

She hurried up the stairs and was informed through a partly opened door by a friend of the family with a completely closed face that all had gone to the cemetery and then gone home. Was Justin

Warmflash inside by any chance? Justin Warmflash, he informed her with a reproachful elevation of his voice, had neglected to attend his mother's funeral. They delayed the eulogy for as long as possible but he simply neglected to attend.

In a corner phone booth Lorrie put a call through to Viola Testi who assured her that Justin had left the hospital that morning although, in fact, he nearly didn't. The trouble was that after the sheriff had agreed to his release, the doctor refused. He simply would not take the responsibility for discharging a patient in that condition. Lorrie's father entered the picture at this point and suddenly the problem was solved. Beyond this Viola admitted that she had no idea where Justin was. "Shit, I hope nothin's wrong," she said.

Far off in his Village bedroom, Lorrie heard the phone drilling in vain against the silence. She listened intently for a long while and then calmly panicked. Her fingers flew through the shredded phone book until a fingernail punctured the word police. She dialed accurately and waited patiently. Then she shouted at the first voice she heard. *My fiancé! He's missing! He's probably dead!* The man grunted and switched her call to someone else. He received somewhat the same message, louder this time, and switched the call to a third man who was, as luck would have it, out. The next poor bastard had his ear blown off, handed the receiver away and was no more. Now a new deep Dublin voice questioned her at length and gutted her with the news that a man had been discovered dead in a second-class coach in Grand Central Station. No wallet was found. The body was being held for identification at Bellevue morgue.

A hot wind swept her down the street as she squeezed the coin she had meant to use for the next five minutes. A news-stand headline announced the sixth straight day of a pollution alert. And the sky sagged like a filthy circus tent. Perhaps it was only the air, then, burning her eyes. No, it was tears after all, she decided, as she climbed into a blurred yellow cab and sat deep in the back seat, shivering.

Oh, God, and what if her sweet man was dead? Caused by her arrogant rearrangement of the world. What if that unknown good guy on a hospital slab was truly him? She grew numb with icy premonition. Then there would be no purpose to life and no way to stop the torture of being left behind, stranded alone, without the only man she must not ever lose.

Becoming hysterical in the back of a taxi was silly. Plan ahead. That was the thing to do. She would write angry letters of explanation to all the local papers, add the duplicates to her box of carbons, mail off the originals and kill herself. Yes, that was the thing to do. It was all so simple, really. She would take a trip to Washington and use her Daddy's Esso card to buy a five-gallon can of gasoline. She could see the Capitol steps gleaming with an inner light as she climbed them with her extra weight. Near the top she would sit and hold herself tightly, gathering courage. Justin's name spoken softly might help. I'm frightened, she thought, shivering. Don't think about it, she thought aloud. She repeated his name several times and reminded herself that she had killed him.

A book of matches lightly resting in her palm. The shivering continues. Her teeth just won't hold still. Several people climb the glowing steps, glance her way, walk on. Justin. Justin. Above is a sick green sky. Automobiles below move in the distance. Everything is shivering.

Doused with five stinking gallons of slime (bad for the hair), she feels it seeping through her clothes, reaching her skin, heavy, cool, deadly. There is a great blazing fire and a girl in agony inside. The girl falls over, lost in the inferno, people running, unable to help, squinting from smoke, backing away. Oh, Justin, Justin. A girl in flames rolling down the pyramid. A helpless, tumbling human torch that leaves flecks of black, splashes of fire, a shoe. Her path down the steps the following day is easy to trace.

She entered the morgue aware of how foolish she looked. She must seem to them like someone so eager to become a widow that she had put on her funereal best even before she knew who was

dead. Trembling as if with fever, she watched them roll out the drawer and pull back the sheet.

"Well?" the attendant asked.

She opened her eyes. She had to. And death was there like a large gray piece of waxen fruit. The placid face, to her surprise, was that of someone else.

She was cheerful and afraid of being cheerful. A depression settled over her like the pale green tent of the sky and she grew pissed off at all who disappear without a phone call or even a postcard. Trying to contact his apartment again, her last dime was lost. She summed it all up with a goddamn shitty fuck and went home.

Only to find that she had been robbed. A pane of glass in the kitchen window was smashed and the various clamps and screws holding the frame shut had all been undone. A potted plant— her mother's gift—lay broken on the floor, its coffee-colored soil spilled. Feeling semi-raped, she marched into the bedroom to see what clothes and things were gone. In her prim and narrow bed, beneath the face of Che Guevara, lay Justin Warmflash, head bandaged, softly snoring.

His explanation was quite simple. He had been prodded awake in Grand Central Station by the rude hand of a loud conductor barking, "Last stop." Lorrie was nowhere in sight nor did she answer her phone. He got into a subway headed for South Ozone Park and found himself being prodded again. "Last stop, fella." To his groggy amazement, he was now in Coney Island. From the station platform he telephoned the funeral home and was told that it was all over, that he was even too late to attend the burial. Defeated, growing weaker, he headed for the nearest oasis, Clark Street and her apartment. But she still wasn't home. He went in desperation to the roof and down by the fire escape to her kitchen window. It was locked as was every window in the city. So he kicked it in with the calm of someone splattering champagne on the hull of a ship. Only when

he lay down in her bed did it dawn on him: he was a *parolee* and here he was *breaking and entering*. Should he run for it? he wondered. And the next thing he wondered was whose face that was grinning at him in bed.

She fed him food and aspirin and brought him the phone so he could call his father and apologize. He didn't feel up to breaking the news of the Warmflash Flying Circus and Road Company Gotterdammerung. His plea was illness. A visit was promised. He hung up with a sigh.

Lorrie ventured condolences. "I was like very sorry to hear about your mom."

"She died as much a victim of the war as if she had been killed in the States by a hemorrhage from inflation."

"Oh, wow."

"I think I'll go to sleep again."

"I should hope so."

In a few days he had improved enough for her to explain her plan: he to Canada, she in New York, meeting often, working for change. He resisted. She persisted. He grew adamant. She grew fervent. They discussed it, screaming. He would not leave the country, he announced, unless she came too. If her refusal meant jail for him, so be it. A hot dry wind swept through the room and she struggled for air even as she shouted.

"You're a fool. My God, they'll put you away for fifteen years."

"So be it."

"Oh, big man, big man." She rubbed the side of her face. "Big brave retarded type."

"We're leaving the country, Lorraine. Together."

"Sorry. I can't. So much to do. I really…"

"For me."

"No."

"Please."

"No."

"I love you."

"No."

"It's jail then."

"*NO!*"

She fled the room, slamming the door. He lay in bed, skull throbbing. Later she came back and said very calmly, "I need to get stoned."

"No."

"What do you mean, no?"

"You're not getting any."

"Why?"

"I threw it away."

"No."

"I threw it away."

"I don't believe you."

"I am not kidding."

She snatched up his jacket and produced the pocket watch, empty.

"Bastard. You can't stop me, not this way."

The door exploded again, wrecking his head. He lay in misery with no idea of what to do next. Having the walls lined with brave men didn't help. In time, the door opened.

"I'm leaving," she said.

With him or...? Fear stabbed the patient upright. "Leaving?"

"To do the laundry."

"Ah."

"And you should visit your father."

"Yes."

She flung a sack over her shoulder. Then, cool and precise: "I just want you to know that I'm not going with you. And I just want you to know that I'm sorry."

She walked like a zombie to the laundromat and stared inside at the line of portholes, each with its agony of dirty linen. Waiting on benches were a number of people, soiled with despair. She turned away, too heartsick to enter, for life seemed as miserable now with Justin alive as when she feared him dead.

She needed a joint badly, phoned several friends and found no one home. Nothing to do but to try and feel nothing. Perhaps suicide was safest. Certainly wisest. No long-term commitment. It had that, at least, to recommend it. Or maybe she should simply give up the fight. Quit and be done with the whole stinking mess. You made it, gentlemen, you clean it up. Benglesdorf is defecting to the other side, requesting political asylum in the suburbs, choosing, as so many women have before her, to mortgage herself into marriage, to anchor herself with motherhood, mesmerized by TV, doing a lifetime of battle with boredom and the laundry and all for a man who long, long ago she once had a passion for. Yes, nothing to do but to try and feel nothing. Perhaps a stroll then on the promenade with its view of the harbor might give, at least, a breath of peace.

At a busy crossing, waiting for the light to change, she was jolted from her morbid thoughts by a rush of U.S. soldiers shouting, "Search and destroy," as they sprinted up the street with rifles. Some Oriental peasant women were standing in their path. "Waste them, waste them," the captain shouted and startled bystanders heard a series of fierce, vast gunshot sounds and saw the shrieking women lurch, crumble, sprawl. Lorrie backed her laundry bag into a lamppost. Other peasants, old men and young boys, approached the soldiers to ask, "Why are you doing this?" More angry concussions and these peasants also fell. The soldiers piled them in a heap. "They're only gooks," they shouted. "Body count, body count."

Finally the army drifted away. There was stillness for a moment. Then the dead stood up. "What you have just seen," one said, "happens every day in Vietnam." As the mock guerrilla theatre came to an end, the performers dispersed, traffic rolled forward, pedestrians resumed their dreary shuffle. Having regained her composure, Lorrie recognized some of the faces from him clips Justin had shown her of a social-protest passion play that was given in pantomime in Washington Square Park.

Three laborers digging not far from this theatre in the crossroad climbed out of their trench as one of the actors, a man in a

coolie hat and burlap coat, passed near by. They pushed and called him a peace-freak. He pushed back, was punched, fell and jumped up, his hat still tied to his head. Lorrie gasped. A crowd followed the stumbling fight, blocking her view. She ran forward, her laundry bouncing and saw the man backing away, saying something, lurching sideways from a shove and backward from another as the crowd watched and no one came to his aid. Lorrie yelled for the fight to stop. They paid no attention. Again there was a blur of violence and she heard voices of reproach, voices of glee. During the next skirmish the laborers sent the man's hat rolling in the street and tore his burlap covering off his back. This produced, as if by magic, a blond youth with shoulder-length hair, dirty blue jeans, psychedelic shirt, leather vest, beads, rope belt, neckband, and peace button. Now his three enemies became even more furious.

Lorrie saw a policeman stepping from a liquor store. He seemed in no hurry to get involved.

"Over here," Lorrie yelled. "Quickly."

Gasps announced another flurry. She swung back to see blood on the actor's cheek. He kicked angrily and doubled over one of the hulking gladiators. A few classic John L. Sullivan jabs and a wild, windmill right made first one and then the other laborer retreat.

At last the policeman rushed to the rescue, a knight in shining badge and deep blue armor. Brandishing his stick with inflamed righteousness, he struck. There was a groan from the crowd as the young man stumbled in agony clutching his shoulder. He shouted an insult that offended the officer and spurred him on to renew the attack. Lorrie thought that here and now, without a sound, she would die of horror. Needles of fury sent her plunging through the crowd and out into the open. There she unleashed, with one mighty swing that hit the officer full in the head, the bulging laundry bag which split wide open and sent a gay assortment of colors and fabrics, towels and socks, triangular undies, copious bras, a snowstorm of hankies, even a warmflash of boxer shorts, all in a towering shower that landed over everyone and made everything ridiculous.

✣   ✣   ✣

Seated opposite each other in the police wagon, they rode across the city as the midday sun became blistering. He produced two joints from inside his psychedelic shirt.

"Look what I have."

"Throw it away before they find out."

"Like I'd rather smoke 'em 'cause my mom always said, Elmer, don't you ever waste anything now."

She grinned and took his burning gift. She drank it in as he did his and for a time both sat with their eyes closed rattling along in the summer heat.

Then her voices talked to her and they were tinged with desperation.

"I should have? I'm sorry. I didn't know."

"What's wrong?" he asked.

"Getting scolded."

"By whom, lass?"

"Tom Jefferson, for one."

"Hey, really?"

"Yup."

"Well, don't take no shit from him. I mean he kept slaves and all. You dig?"

"I dig."

"So what does he want?"

"He wants me to leave the country."

"Oh, and go where?"

"Canada for a start."

"Why's that?"

"Well, to stop the slaughter of the baby seals. Also helping army deserters. And would you believe, writing letters?"

"But why leave?"

"There's this sweet guy I know. He's out on bail. Helped me with ... well, with a science project, you might say. He'll probably get fifteen years."

"Wow. Bad trip."

"So he can't hang around."

"Dig."

She smiled. "I mean they practically *ordered* me to go with him."

"They?"

"My grade advisers."

"Who?"

"Jefferson. Washington. Madison."

"They really your friends, huh?"

"Yup."

"Crazy, man. Listen, there's a question I always wanted to ask those cats."

But the police wagon was coming to a halt. Elmer took the joint from Lorrie's hand and tossed it with his between the bars and into the road. Soon the lock snapped open. Peace, he said. Peace, she said. Then strong arms lifted her out into the burning sun.